A Deal With The Untethered

S.J. Stewart

S.J. Stewart

First published by S.J. Stewart 2026

First edition

ISBN: 978-1-990552-37-3

Cover by SJ Stewart

Formatting by SJ Stewart on Atticus

A NOTE TO MY FAMILY

LISTEN.

We're all adults here. I'm going to do this thing where I warn you this is a racey book, the kind that used to have naked people on the cover, abs bared and the whole shebang. You're going to tell me you're proud of me and my writing so of course, you're going to read this book.

COOL.

Cool, cool, cool, cool.

Read it. Enjoy it. Buy it and put it on the shelf and never read past this page. Do whatever makes you happy, but remember who I am as a person. Don't bring it up unless you fully intend for me to talk about it ... because I will.

YOU KNOW I WILL!

EVERY STEAMY DEATIL!

You've been warned.

Dark Monster Romances

THIS BOOK TAKES PLACE in the same world as the book *A Bite Full of Death*. Though it isn't a sequel, some of the characters from that book will appear in this one, and the chain of events in this book happens after *A Bite Full of Death* and the following short story, *Dex's Curse*.

If you are coming to this book after reading *A Bite Full of Death*, I want to let you know that the reason that book was heavy spice was because Poe was part succubus. Though this book is a monster romance as well, the spice in this book is solely for moving the plot and isn't as frequent as in the first book.

If you came for heavy smut, sorry, this book won't be what you're looking for. With that being said, there are open door, spicy scenes.

A Word To The Readers

HEY LOVELIES,

This book is a dark monster romance. It's a series where monsters are openly and unapologetically being monsters. Jumping into this story, you should be aware that there will be scenes with violence. Those violent scenes may contain blood, gore, and even death. The characters in this story will have villainous intentions that result in murder. There will be foul language. The characters in this book are all adults and behave as such. Outside of the scenes that may be somewhat "gross" or scary, there will also be scenes with sexual content. The sexual scenes in this book will not fade to black and may contain elements that may unsettle the readers. Because of that, this book is not one intended for younger readers.

I always write books with full transparency in mind. If you, as a reader, believe that I overlooked something that should be on this page that could warn potential readers of content that may trigger them, please feel free to reach out to me through my contact information in the back matter. It is never my intention to willfully omit any warnings.

xx

SJ

This one is for all the people who constantly feel torn. Like a part of them was stolen by the world they were forced to exist in, but they could still see it... just out of reach.

You're beautiful broken, my loves.

A DEAL WITH THE UNTETHERED

SJ STEWART

1

RUE

LIFE WAS HOT — at least it was when it left. It was a stream of heat that refused to leave peacefully, coating her hands with a stickiness that threatened to hold on, even though the vessel that housed it inched farther and farther away.

Rue's tears were hot, too. They burned her cheeks as her hands clasped over the slashes in Jinx's torso. Tried to seal them. The purple glow of her magic was bright on her hands as she willed all that she was into the spell she hoped would save them both.

On her knees in the cool sands of the Scarborough Bluffs with her hands coated in blood, she began to doubt if saving them was something she could do. Began to think maybe the curse that made them was more than just the obvious. It was also invisible shackles around her wrist, preventing her from doing something so big — something she could have effortlessly accomplished before.

Before her life went completely to shit.

Fucking coven bitches!

Fucking curse!

Fucking Jinx!

"You stupid thing," Rue hissed between her teeth, glassy eyes staring at Jinx with vehemence. "You stupid, *stupid* thing."

"Love is stupid," Jinx murmured, her words breathy like they always were. Like life wasn't slipping out of her and through Rue's fingers.

Their eyes locked, and the vulnerability Rue often tried to pretend she didn't house inside her rattled in her chest. Rue pulled her gaze away, swallowing the taste of bile that usually accompanied her vulnerability.

"*You're* stupid." For the first time in a long time, she was terrified to lose her.

Concentration knotted Rue's brow as she willed her magic forth. She watched as the etchings of a coven long forgotten danced up her forearms, like carvings highlighted in the very magic that would save them.

This was all so ridiculous.

Just another obstacle Rue would have never imagined being thrown into her path if it weren't for Jinx.

Her curse.

"A goblin... really?" Rue rolled her eyes as she chuckled, but it was a sad sight. Her nose ran onto the rim of her upper lip, the tears that sat in the creases of her nose desperate to join the snotty mess.

What would happen if she lost her?

That thought was paralyzing.

As much as she wanted to be rid of her vexing companion, she didn't want it to happen like this. She wasn't sure if it *could* happen like this.

A cough rattled Jinx's chest. It sounded wet. The clench of her abdomen only pushed more blood out through the claw marks in her flesh — tattered ribbons barely holding her together — into Rue's hands.

"I heard they had big dicks..." Jinx sucked in a ragged breath. "And we both know how desperately you need to get laid. I figured... go big or go... home."

Rue's laugh was a depressing sound. The saddest part of the entire night was that Jinx likely thought Rue would sleep with the goblin. Get her rocks off and become less surly. Like getting good pipe was all she needed to become less *Rue* and more *Jinx*.

It wasn't.

"Jinx..." Rue sniffled.

She waved her hand weakly. "I know, I know... he wasn't your type. Which is surprising because he was just as grumpy as you are."

Despite the grim situation, Rue laughed again.

Heavy-lidded eyes dropped to look at the glow of Rue's hands. "It's too much."

Fatigue had already set into Rue's flesh and made its way toward her bones. "It isn't," she argued, though she knew it was.

This spell was too much. Too much magic to battle a curse that constantly worked against them. A curse that wanted them to suffer.

Was there any suffering worse than death?

There was, Rue realized. It was sitting next to someone who held a piece of her while they died.

"Rue." The light knowing in Jinx's voice annoyed her just like everything about the wretched pain in her ass did. Forever whiny and dramatic.

"No," she hissed through her teeth, Rue's stubborn will more powerful than her magic. She wasn't about to let someone steal Jinx away, no matter how much she wanted to be rid of her. If she got rid of her, it would be because *she* got rid of the stupid ninny, not because someone else did. Not some trim, egotistical goblin with a god complex that came out in full force to try to hide the fact that his pickle was likely the cocktail variety.

Fucking asshat. If she got her hands on him — *when,* because she would make it her mission to make sure she did — she was going to tear that pickle off with her bare hands and make him eat it.

"Rue."

"Will you shut the fuck up and let me focus? You never have anything important to say. I doubt that's changed since you tried to seduce a goblin into a threesome." Maybe if she borrowed some of the magic she had already spent. Rue searched for a solution to their troubles. Her life was long. There was so much magic that was hers out in this world — this one and so many others.

"Tried?"

Anger surged through Rue, heating behind her ears. "You can't possibly think you succeeded. He's near dead, and you're bleeding out. Surely you can see a reaper around here somewhere waiting to collect you."

"No reaper for us," Jinx muttered.

No, she supposed there wouldn't be. They were as cursed as cursed could be, which meant their soul was damned. Contrary to popular belief, damned souls don't get carried away by reapers. Cursed souls couldn't be delivered to Death. No, they went back to those who cursed them.

Her coven.

"And I *did* succeed, but you have such a... bad temper. Growled louder than he did... scared him off."

Eyes widened as far as they physically could, Rue reminded herself to keep her hands where they were and continue the spell. "You can't be serious. He was going to eat you."

"Goblins don't eat witches."

"You're not a witch."

"Am too!" Jinx's voice was stronger than it should be with this much blood pooling under her. Of course it was, Jinx was designed to argue with her. Combative little bitch.

"Jinx..." she released a resigned sigh. "He was going to eat you."

"Maybe he was going to eat my pussy." Jinx chuckled at her joke until it brought on a coughing fit.

Rue snarled. "Really? You're dying. You do realize that, don't you?"

She waved off Rue's words in the irritating way only Jinx could. "You won't let me die."

As much as she hated to admit it, Jinx's confidence in her swelled the hollow of her chest. The purple of her magic coating her hands became more vibrant. The script travelled further up her arms, fading at her elbow.

Jinx was right. She wouldn't let her die.

No matter how much she wanted to. No, she would heal her first. Bring her back from the cusp of death so she could wrap her hands around her throat and squeeze until she passed out. Then, she'd wait until Jinx was conscious to do it all over again.

The thought made her grin around her gritted teeth.

Knowledge bestowed upon her by her grandmother blew through her mind. A strong breeze that didn't settle until the right thought was brought to her.

"I can undo all my magic and summon it back to me. Use all the magic I have in this world so that I can fix this." Her eyes rolled back as she searched for every last wisp of her magic in all of existence.

It would be more than enough. Enough to heal Jinx. Enough to fix everything she had done, so she could come up with a plan to rightfully rid herself of her irritating companion once and for all. Too bad it wouldn't be enough to undo this wretched curse altogether. Curses were funny like that.

Her lips parted, and she spoke a language she'd twisted over time, contorted from the cherished tongue of her coven to something that was as cursed as they made her. She felt the cool singe of her magic as it moved up to her shoulders. Her body jolted as the beach was lit with purple mist and smoke. It zipped toward them, some like brilliant fast rays of light, others butterflies that flitted beautifully, some like wildfire that burned across the lake. Magic was different depending on how it was used.

It merged to form a cyclone around them before it rose in the air.

This was it.

It was a majestic sight, one Rue never imagined she would see. It was powerful. All-consuming.

Cloudy white eyes stared up at the cyclone before it dropped into Rue's chest.

Her body jolted, but her hands held strong. She absorbed it all, took it all in, felt the way it filled every shadow in her mind, every crevice in her being, every darkened space in the void in her chest before it moved through her. The script spreading across her chest, glowing under the thin fabric of her tank top, was blinding. It moved down her stomach before it disappeared into the waistband of her black jean shorts and travelled down her legs to her booted feet. Teeth clenched, she put it all in the spell.

To save Jinx.

To save herself.

A flash of magic blew them apart. Rue was weightless. Wind whistled against her ears as she arched forward, looking at the beach between the frame of her hands and feet.

Cold water completely covered her, and she let herself sink. Rue's eyes fell closed as she imagined what her life would be like if things had been different. If it hadn't been for that crack-pot seer and a prophecy that painted a target in the centre of her brow. If her coven hadn't scorned her for the visions they had that branded her before she was even born. That pushed her mother to name her one and only daughter *Ruin* because that's what she was. Ruin. And she would ruin everything she touched.

Or so said the prophecy.

How different would her life be if she had been loved by her mother — by the whole of her coven — instead of just her grandmother? A woman who would happily see the prophecy come to pass, promised that if it did, she would hold Rue's hand through it all.

Her ride or die.

Such thoughts were stupid and a waste of time. Her mother hadn't loved her. Her coven had not only blamed her for all their shortcomings but cursed her in hopes that, in her current state, the prophecy of destruction would never come to pass. And her grandmother — well, she was gone.

Eyes open, she kicked her feet and swam.

Rue breached the surface and treaded water, looking out at the lake that seemed endless, the dark sky with stars hidden behind a film of light pollution, and the beach.

Everything was so still. Like this world hadn't felt the intensity of her magic or seen it light up the sky.

It was funny to think mortals could overlook something so world-changing. Had she directed all that magic at the city of Toronto instead of Jinx, she could have erased it. Swallowed it up. Devoured millions of beings.

Cough! Cough!

She shook those dark thoughts from her mind. She had no use for all those beings, no matter how easy it would be to devour them. Jinx... as annoying as she was... she had a use for.

And her coughs jolted Rue back to their sad reality. Her hands sliced through the water, feet kicking to carry her back to shore.

The sand under her hands was chilled as she crawled, exhausted. Summoning centuries worth of magic was no small feat, but she'd done it.

Jinx's hair was a mess of raven curls, twists, locs, and knots that hung down between her shoulders. Her brown skin was covered in a light dust of Rue's magic as she rolled onto her side and huffed in a deep breath. Her wide nostrils flared with each shaky breath, her full lips slightly parted.

As annoying as Rue often found her, there was an ache in her chest at seeing her look so... *mortal.*

Rue crawled beside her and lifted Jinx's hand. She held it to her chest as she searched Jinx's face. Her other hand dropped to Jinx's chest, skimmed over Jinx's full breasts and down to her soft stomach in search of any remnants of the goblin's slashing.

"You're supposed to buy me dinner first," Jinx teased.

"Oh, shut up!" Rue snapped.

She'd done it! She healed Jinx!

Thank the hollowed ground she would bury her coven under.

Relief filled Rue as she pushed damp braids back from her brow. Without hesitation, she pulled her fist back and punched Jinx with all her strength. Her fist collided with Jinx's right boob, and a startled yelp left her before she let it transform into a slow whine. Hand up, Jinx wrapped it over as much of her boob as she could before she turned on Rue.

"You punched me in the tit, you fucking psycho!"

Rue punched her again in the other one.

"Ow! Hey!"

"You almost died!" She punched her again. "*We* almost died!"

Jinx did her best to cover her boobs, but with them being 40D, she eventually crossed her arms over them and glared. "Will you stop? Do you really think the best thing to do right now is punch the woman who almost died in the boobs?"

She should count her lucky stars that all Rue was doing was punching her boobs. What she really wanted to do was wring her neck.

Rue bared her teeth. "It's your boobs or your face."

A pout dropped the corners of her mouth. "But..." Jinx groaned before she slowly dropped her arms. Her eyes squeezed shut, shoulders lifted as she prepared herself.

Another punch sent her onto her back in the sand.

At this point in her life, Rue thought she would spend a lot less time wrestling with Jinx on the ground. It felt like every night was the same. Jinx would get them into something Rue would have to get them out of, and, annoyed, Rue would throw hands.

Violence was often the answer between them. A little violence to keep Rue from killing her.

"Okay! Okay!" Jinx swatted Rue's hand away and pushed herself up to sit. "You can't hit me that much... I'm little."

"We're the same size," Rue argued. She eyed the boobs she'd just been punching and her own smaller chest. "In some ways, you're bigger than me."

"Yeah... well... I'm just a wee little thing. It's not nice."

"You're a *short* thing, but neither of us is little."

"Pfft." Jinx blew air through her lips. "Tits and ass don't count. Everyone knows that. And foopas... they don't count either."

Rue rolled her eyes so hard, she worried they'd get stuck. "So what *does* count?"

Lips pursed, Jinx thought it over. "Nothing. If I want to be a wee little thing, then I'm a wee little thing because I fucking said so."

"Fine. Whatever. You're a *wee little thing*." Rue was too tired to argue.

"Right," Jinx agreed. "So you can't hit me."

On her feet, Rue brushed off the back of her legs before she tried to pull the wet denim from the place where they'd bunched up between her thighs. An annoyed groan left her when she accomplished nothing, and she did her best not to plant her foot on Jinx's chest and kick her back into the sand to rid herself of some of her ire.

"If you're a *wee little thing* and we essentially have the same body, then that would mean I could hit you whenever I want because you're not a *wee little thing* compared to me." Rue cocked a brow and smirked.

Checkmate, bitch.

Jinx's mouth opened and closed before her brows dropped like confused blinds over her eyes. "Well..."

"Mhmm, *well,* yourself. Get up. Let's go. I don't want to be standing here when someone wanders over, wondering what the light show in the sky was. We're a bit out of the way for the Northern Lights." She turned on her heel and started back to the parking lot where she had left the car.

"Hey, wait up!" Jinx whined.

"I wouldn't have to wait up if you hurried."

A smile touched her lips as she imagined frustration moving through Jinx as she tried to keep pace. She hated when Rue '*marched off'. It* was an argument the pair of them often had, and right now, Rue was in a fighting mood.

Too bad that goblin disappeared.

Like a fucking baby. Just took off as soon as he started to lose. They just don't make immortal beings like they used to.

Oh well.

As relieved as she was that she healed Jinx, one thought chimed in her head.

With the risks Jinx kept taking, it wouldn't be long before she did something Rue wouldn't be able to undo. It wouldn't be long until she perished under the weight of her idiocy and dragged Rue along with her.

If she was going to remain alive long enough to get revenge on her coven, she had to tether them both back together.

She had to tether herself back to her soul.

2

JiNX

SHE LOVED THE NIGHT.

There was something about the endlessness of it. The shadows could hide absolutely anything inside their depths. She loved the sounds that took too long to identify, letting fear breed in the stretch of time before morning. It was like catnip to the chaos that beat in her chest. Out in the middle of nowhere, with the Greater Toronto Area something that would take them hours to get back to, that chaos beat so loud.

Gone were the high rises and endless lights. Out here, there was wheat, corn, and the dirt road.

The dark was enough for her to ignore the constant murmuring of Rue as she used her bare hands to dig in the dirt and bury their offering. Hands held out, Jinx danced around the dirt road, letting her light skirts twirl, creating a blend of greens as the different hues danced together. She hummed a song she wasn't sure she ever knew as she threw her head back and howled at the moon.

"Would you knock that shit off?" Rue barked.

Jinx giggled. "No."

Rue was such a wet blanket. Jinx wasn't sure if she'd seen her even close to happy... though, that was likely her fault. It wasn't that she *tried* to be combative and difficult. It was like there was something inside the core of her that was rotten and wouldn't allow her to do anything else. As though her very purpose was to complicate every aspect of Rue's life.

It likely was. She was Rue's curse after all. It wouldn't make sense to curse someone with a completely agreeable companion who had the answers to her problems.

What the hell kind of curse would that be?

"Not a very good one," Jinx said aloud, her voice a song.

"What?" Rue asked.

"I wouldn't be a very good curse," she answered, annoyed that she had to explain herself. Rue was a terrible listener. If she just listened, maybe they wouldn't argue half as much as they did.

"What are you going on about?"

"You never listen!" Jinx huffed.

Rue glared. Her box braids didn't quite reach her shoulders. They'd been longer once, but after the third fire, she decided it was best just to get rid of them and the hazard they created. Silly, really. Since Jinx's hair never caught fire. Rue really needed to be more careful. There was a white patch of hair right above her ear. As white as freshly fallen snow. The top of her right ear was missing, and a brown raised scar went across her cheek to her right nostril. Both things Rue would blame her for if anyone asked, but that was just Rue being Rue. Jinx couldn't be blamed for not having the skills to swing or throw a dagger. If anyone really thought about it, it was more Rue's fault for not teaching Jinx the basics in the first place. Rue looked severe. Villainous. It was a battle, but Jinx fought Rue enough to let her pull half her braids up into two Bantu knots. To make her look less... monstrous.

She'd be a cutie... if not for her constant scowl.

Jinx wondered how they were so similar and somehow so different.

Same height. Same deep, warm brown skin, yet they weren't identical. A part of her felt like they should be. Jinx was Rue's soul, after all. Shouldn't Rue look just like her soul?

It made no sense.

"Are you yelling at me about not hearing your thoughts again, you stupid thing?" Rue bared her teeth in an obvious growl before she turned and resumed whatever she was doing.

What were they doing again?

Oh, right! Summoning a demon. Fighting goblins and summoning demons, this was turning out to be quite the week.

Jinx giggled.

"Shut up!" Rue barked.

"You're so rude!"

"Maybe I would be less rude if you helped me with this instead of dancing around like some princess meant to be waited on hand and foot."

Jinx pouted. "I would make a wonderful princess."

Rue scoffed, muttering to herself.

She would, regardless of what her miserable other half said. Just look at her outfit with her corset and skirts. Not to mention her thick and beautiful hair — and she was stunning. High cheekbones, diamond-shaped face, big and beautiful eyes. She was most definitely princess material. Lips pressed thin, she crossed her arms and marched over to Rue.

"You know, maybe if you were more supportive, we wouldn't always be at each other's throats."

"Maybe I wouldn't constantly be at your throat if you didn't put me in situations where I have to save us at every turn. Propositioning goblins, trying to catch selkies, and there was that whole vampire thing..."

"Willamina was lovely," Jinx defended.

"She almost drank you dry," Rue argued. "If I hadn't kept almost losing consciousness, I never would have known what you were up to, and I wouldn't have gotten there in time to save you... again!"

"I don't need you to save me." Jinx pouted before she walked over and looked down at the dirt Rue had reburied. "How long is this going to take?" Hands on her hips, she looked around.

Rue shook her head as she waited. “Why? Do you have plans? Going to try to tame a dragon, princess?”

Head tilted, she thought about it. “Are there dragons in Toronto?”

The scoff that left Rue was one filled with derision. “If there were, I wouldn’t tell you.”

“Rude,” she gaped. “Just rude.” Jinx could *definitely* tame a dragon... if she wanted to.

“Yeah, yeah.”

Jinx danced over, draping her body over Rue’s back. “I would tame a dragon for you, *Rooty Pooty*.”

A tired inhale was her only reply.

She stayed where she was for a moment, enjoying the heat from Rue’s back without the burn of her ire before she stood, resuming her dancing.

The soil at their feet lit red from within before the ground cracked, and embers floated around them. Jinx enjoyed the burn of the unbearable heat as she jumped the space between the cracks with a giddy smile on her face.

“He’s coming! He’s coming!”

“How do you know the Crossroads demon isn’t a woman?” Rue asked.

Dizziness overcame her as her legs turned to noodles. The core of her belly pulsed as her heart thrummed. She felt intoxicated. Overcome with something akin to desire, but infinitely more dangerous. She held her breath, straddling the line between euphoria and damnation as red smoke shot out from one of the cracks to blow up her skirts. The cracks deepened, spreading all over the dirt road as chunks dipped low and others rose. The ground was unsteady at her feet. The world around her shifted between the mundane mortal realm and a darker place. The kind of place these mortals thought their sins would earn them passage to. The smoke thickened, the air around them stifling until everything was ripped away.

A giddy giggle left Jinx as her hands dropped from around her eyes, and she once again looked at the crossroads, only this time they weren't alone.

She gasped as her heart sped.

The Crossroads demon was... *scrumptious.* He was tall, dark and handsome. His flesh was rich brown, deep and warm at the same time. Curls as deep as shadows were pulled back from his face, fashioned in a small bun that let the rest of his curls curtain down his back. The sides of his head were buzzed, vine-like tattoos decorating his skull. Jinx wanted to follow those vines and see if the thorns were as sharp as they looked. Similar tattoos covered his forearms, exposed because his sleeves were rolled to the elbows. Gold rings on almost every finger. He was wiry. Long arms and legs hidden in dark clothing, much too formal for the humid summer weather. His slacks met the top of his scarlet brogues, the only pop of colour in his black outfit. His eyes were vicious things that threatened to cut her open as he stared. His lips were just as dangerous as they turned up at the corners in a Cheshire grin that hinted at all the mischief they could get into... together. His jaw was sharp, his nose broad, and his cheekbones high. Full lips were framed by his facial hair that was perfectly lined; it practically looked painted on.

Damn!

Jinx gulped.

"Well, fuck. Did they just cut you out of a magazine, or what?" Rue gruffed. "No wonder people sign away their lives."

Jinx took a shaky step forward.

Her heart was an erratic thing in her chest that refused to settle as her mouth gaped. Something in the depths of her felt like she was no longer hers. Wasn't even a part of the cranky Rue who stood with her arms crossed under her chest, hip cocked and distrust in her eyes. She wasn't the coven's. At that moment, she was his.

She swallowed hard at the thought, even though she knew it to be true. There was no disputing it. No joking it all away.

The demon's eyes met Rue's and searched her over. Jinx watched as she stepped up beside him, her eyes glued to the side of his face as he swallowed hard and his Adam's apple bobbed, looking sharp enough to slice through the night-brushed mahogany of his skin.

"You." His response was a single breathless word uttered between them.

Rue's brows dropped in that way that often made Jinx cower. "Me?"

The demon fell silent, watching her.

Jinx reached up a long finger and brushed it along his cheekbone.

As though she had cut through a magical moment, he flinched. His hand whipped up to encircle her wrist as he held it off his flesh, his attention suddenly on her. His eyes were evil things that peeled back her flesh and wrapped her heart in a grip more vicious than the one he had on her wrist. She blushed under the attention, craving more.

"Hello." Her voice was strange even to her own ears. Sweet and unsure but also broken under the weight of whatever magic this demon pushed onto her.

"Hi..." He loosened his grip.

Like a cat basking in the sun, she curled into him. Her boobs knocked into his chest, but they did nothing to move him from where he stood. A glorious statue that moved only when he deemed fit.

How wonderful! Elation filled her chest.

"Hello," Jinx repeated.

His chuckle was honey brushed over something she knew better than to taste but wanted to just the same. "You've said that already." His free hand lifted to press a knuckle under her chin, lifting her face to his. "What's the matter? Cat got your tongue?"

She wished *he* had her tongue. Anywhere. She wouldn't be picky about it.

Everything in her body wanted to belong to him.

What was this?

A quick slap separated them as Rue stepped between them. She swatted away the man who had been crafted by Fate herself for Jinx before Rue shoved a pouting Jinx behind her.

"Hey!" Jinx whined. What a ruiner. Would it kill her to just take a moment and admire the man? Damn.

Rue spared her no attention as she levelled the crossroads demon with a gaze. "I'd like to make a deal." The flat tone of her voice was all business. Luckily for Jinx, it was a tone she was used to ignoring.

She reached out from behind Rue, trying to grab the man who called to her like a siren. Her fingers flexed, annoyed that she had to press her whole body into Rue's back as she tried to walk through her to no avail.

She just needed to touch him a little bit. Just a little.

"Jinx," Rue hissed. "Will you fuck all the way off?"

"Mine!" Jinx groaned, flexing her fingers. When nothing was caught in her grasp, she stood up on her toes to look over Rue's shoulder.

The demon stood where he was, though the corner of his mouth curled into a smile Jinx would dare call devilish. He looked over Rue's shoulder, holding Jinx's gaze without effort before he forced his attention to Rue.

"Two," he muttered low.

"Two what?" Rue snapped.

She was always so annoyed. That was precisely why she couldn't get laid. No one would want to sleep with her if she kept snapping at people like that. If it wasn't for all the constant effort Jinx put in, Rue would die bitter and alone. Her poor kitty needed petting.

Jinx wasn't going to let her scare this one off. No. Not when he called to her the way he did.

She had to have him. If Rue was too stupid to feel whatever this was, Jinx would have it all herself. She would drink this down until she was completely befuddled.

Dancing out from behind her, Jinx skipped over to him. "And who might you be, handsome?" she sang.

An exasperated huff left Rue, but what was new? She was perpetually annoyed. "I don't think his name matters."

"It does."

"Why? We make a deal, sign our names on the dotted lines, and call this a day. It's not like we're meeting him for brunch tomorrow."

"Brunch would be lovely, wouldn't it, handsome?" Jinx batted her eyes at him.

"Seriously?" Rue groaned.

"Name, handsome man," Jinx demanded, ignoring her bitter companion.

"Killian," he said his name slowly, his eyes cast down at her with both caution and intrigue.

It made her skin pebble.

His name suited the vision he was. Dark and ominous. Dangerous enough to kill — and she had no doubt he would.

Jinx danced forward, her hand pressed against the side of his face, before he could do anything about it. His flesh was hot as hellfires, comforting something in the depths of her. Coaxed her. Soothed her.

"Do you feel it?" The whispered question left her lips before the thought planted roots in her mind. They needed to be freed just as she needed to touch him.

Killian's — *gods, what a name* — brow dropped as his eyes held hers captive. "Feel what?"

"That you belong to me." Wasn't it obvious? She could feel it in all the stitches holding together the fabric of her being, and he dared to ask? She would forgive him, of course. He didn't know any better right now.

But she would show him.

A grin stretched her mouth at the thought.

Jinx planned to show him all the ways he belonged to her.

3

KILLIAN

BEING SUMMONED TO A crossroads was like hearing a phone incessantly ringing. Sure, he could ignore it and continue on his way, but the intrigue placed at his core by the one who held his contract made sure he could only ignore it for so long before he went topside. And he was so close to the end — to his freedom — denying it was a foolish thing to do.

This crossroads was like so many others. An intersecting road surrounded by nothingness. Tall grass that had gone untended alongside the dirt road no one travelled anymore. It was like so many others, and yet, it wasn't.

This call was different.

It zapped him. Electrified every inch of his innards and dared him to ignore it.

He couldn't... and he didn't want to.

The moment he set eyes on the two women who stood at this crossroads, everything inside him felt placated. His desperation to complete these meaningless deals so he could be free of the crossroads once and for all and finally feel the cursed stretch of his own skin dripped away. All the demons housed by his flesh fell silent, and something at the core of him whined for them. Begged.

They were his.

Any doubts about that were wiped from his mind the moment she pressed her hand to his flesh and whispered the words.

He was so screwed.

Everything inside him turned into useless mush. He wanted to scoop her up and press her against anything so he could have her. Claim her. Mark her.

His mate.

Her hand was pulled from his face all too soon. Her hair jerked over her shoulders as she scowled, her hard eyes boring into the stern woman who looked as though she could cut the one who touched him down with that one look alone.

"Jinx, will you knock that shit off?" she hissed.

So that was her name. Jinx.

It made him smile.

"Must you always be so bitchy, Rue? They named you right, you *ruin* everything."

Rue — Ruin's — jaw flexed so hard at Jinx's words, he was sure he could hear her teeth grinding from where he stood. Her hand wrapped in the back of Jinx's hair, and she tugged her another step away from him.

He stepped forward, his hand wrapped around Jinx's wrist. His hand slipped away before it could take hold. "Wait."

Jinx squealed as a puff of smoke swirled above her head, and a large bat appeared. He was the size of an overgrown cat as he widened his wings and his small feet worked to grab at Rue's hair and pull her away from Jinx.

Rue squealed at the bat's attempt. "Bram! I swear I'll skin you alive, you little shit!"

The bat evaded the swipe of her arm. It became painfully clear this was something that happened often as Jinx twisted, escaping Rue's hold, only for Rue's arm to wrap around Jinx's waist. The bat dove to avoid being knocked from the air, flying around to reach a foot out to Jinx, who howled like she was being attacked by beasts and not her companion.

These women were... not what he was expecting. Not that his black heart dared to expect anything.

Killian stood frozen, unable to do anything but watch.

It was rare to be called up to a crossroads and not immediately hear the desperate pleas someone would make before a deal. Some needed to voice their sins, to unload their burdens before they signed away their soul. As though that would somehow make what they were doing feel less eternal.

The deal was the deal, no matter what sob story people brought with them to make it.

Boo fucking hoo.

Did that make him heartless? Maybe. But a sentence of being summoned to crossroads time and time again to fulfil the same wishes as penance for his own sins had darkened his heart. Numbed the parts of him that may have cared for these mortals lifetimes ago.

Riches. Fame. Prominence. Health.

It was always comfort, just painted in different strokes. They wanted the comfort of a life unburdened by finances. The comfort of being waited on hand and foot for their name alone. They wanted the comfort of blood that meant something to a society Killian understood, but found foolish all the same. They wanted the comfort of a life lived without ailments.

No matter how they painted it, that was what they always wanted.

He wondered now, looking at the women whose fight had brought them to the dirt, just what comforts they wanted.

A high-pitched yelp sounded as Rue pushed to her feet.

Jinx sat on the ground, her face dirty and hair in disarray as she cradled her breasts.

"Always the boobs!" Jinx whined.

Rue turned and looked at Killian. She had the look of someone so unlike the ones who made deals and the stench of something *other* beneath her skin. It was intoxicating. Dark smoke that reminded him of the twisted thing he once was. She was no mere mortal, and her deal was not one she would make as easily as most.

Killian shuddered, euphoria dancing down his spine.

She stalked toward him until her finger pressed into the centre of his chest. Black veins darkened the flesh around her eyes. Shadows fuelled by her anger slipped free from where she housed them.

"Tether us!" she commanded.

Killian's brows dropped, creating ominous shadows in his dark eyes. His eyes dropped to the thick scar across one of her cheeks. "What?"

Rue pointed behind her, and Killian looked at the woman who held the bat to her chest. She rubbed her cheek over and over against its head as she whispered, "She's so mean, isn't she, Bram?"

"A long time ago, my coven cursed me," she explained, her voice hard and her patience waning as each word felt like a stab to his chest.

Coven.

So these were witches.

Killian inhaled deeply, but their scent didn't strike him the way so many witches' did. It was chilled air coated in something slightly dark but also sweet. Something masquerading as mortal, if he didn't know any better. The things nightmares were made of.

Interesting.

"Cursed you?" Killian shoved his hands in his pockets to keep himself from tracing that scar that held all his attention. The feeling in his chest might be one strong enough to bring him to his knees, but he was no babe. He was old and wise, and he knew better than to merely throw himself at the feet of the woman — or women — he was almost sure were his mates. No, he would be the mysterious thing he always was and hear her out. Hoping he could learn more about them in the meantime.

"Yes!" Rue snapped. "With an endless headache."

She was willing to sell her soul to stop a headache. If she were a witch, surely she could fix something so derisory as a headache, and if not, she should be able to overcome it. To fall into the ache and make it hers.

She was no mere mortal whining about small inconveniences.

"You summoned a crossroads demon as a painkiller?"

"A pain in my head, my neck, and my ass."

"Hey!" Jinx whined, her eyes glimmering with unshed tears.

She looked so vulnerable. So unlike any witch he'd ever set eyes on. She sat with her dark skirt billowing around her in the dirt. Her brown shoulders were bare, the dark fabric held up by her heavy bust and her lush upper arms as her hair fell around her head in more frizz than curl — a few braids and locs mixed into the chaos. There were beads and other items woven through some of the strands as she clutched the bat to her, and her chin wrinkled.

The sight of her pulled at his heart.

"You love me!" she argued.

Rue ignored her.

"You do!"

If she did, she seemed determined not to say as much as Rue pinched the bridge of her nose and huffed out an exhausted sigh.

Killian still didn't follow. What did her love for the woman she just wrestled in the dirt have to do with a deal struck between them? What did it have to do with healing her of her afflictions?

"He loves me too!" Jinx proclaimed. "He won't do it."

The knot between his brows deepened further. Love. What a dramatic thing to say about someone she just met. Sure, he felt the swell in his chest and the shuddering of something he thought would forever remain dormant, but he would never go so far as to claim it was love. Love was something he never bothered himself with. He had no use for it.

Yet, the mating called to him, and he found it impossible to deny her words.

The dark thing the Crossroads King himself had caged banged against the bars in his mind, begging for freedom.

What a curious revelation. He had sat there, in the dark corners, content with the prison his very nature had earned him, and yet the mere sight of these women woke a fight in him he had long surrendered.

Interesting, indeed.

"A pain..." He tried to get them back on track.

"Yes." Rue stomped over and forcefully lifted Jinx by the arm. Her bat hissed but did nothing to stop her. "This one. The biggest pain in my ass imaginable. I want to make a deal. I want you to tether me back together with my soul."

4

RUE

THERE WAS A WHISPER of something in the emptiness that filled her. An annoying echo. A yearning that made something inside her whimper with wanting. A ripple she could feel but didn't understand because it moved through a part of her that no longer lived there. Shouts in the empty room where Jinx should be.

The annoying bitch.

No sooner had she declared her intent to be tethered to Jinx, her pesky soul burst into tears. There was something about the sound of Jinx crying that grated Rue's mind. It was fingernails painted beautifully with madness that dipped into the soft flesh of Rue's brain and tried to imprint the stain there. Every wracked sob that made her breathe that stupid sound made Rue want to pull out her hair.

It was just so annoying

And Jinx cried for *everything.*

At movies. When she fell. When she didn't understand something. She cried when the weather wasn't to her liking. When she couldn't find Bram. Just about everything reduced her to tears — except, of course, when she was dying on the beach. The only moment that called for her blubbering had none.

Stupid fucking thing.

Now Jinx just sat there and cried as the demon stood with a pensive look on his face that pissed Rue off almost as much as her soul did.

Just what did he have to think about? Making deals was his job. An easy one at that. She told him what she wanted, he wrote her name in his ledger, and after a decided amount of time, he would send whatever monsters he had at his command to come and collect her. Hellhounds. Wraiths. Nightmares. Things with vicious claws and sharp teeth. There really wasn't much to it. It was so simple, even mortals could figure this shit out. It wasn't like people became famous and successful overnight — at least not without help.

"No." His answer surprised her. She expected some manipulation. Some trickery. Maybe a negotiation of sorts. A flat-out refusal was something she hadn't prepared for.

Everything in her tensed. "What do you mean, no?"

Jinx sniffled but got to her feet. "He said no, Rue. You're not the boss of him. No. No. No!" She laughed, hugging Bram so tightly he squeaked under the pressure. "He said no," she sang.

Good. Maybe she'd pop him, and the little rodent would stop interfering in all their tussles.

"No," Rue repeated. It wasn't quite confusion. It was more of a disconnect. Rue heard the word and knew exactly what it meant, but she couldn't understand why. Her brain refused to accept the answer without knowing.

"No," he affirmed.

Well, fuck.

A deep breath filled Jinx's chest before she let it out, grabbed Bram by the wings, and started dancing around them. She was a blur of movement Rue phased out, her annoying companion unimportant as she stalked closer to the demon she summoned with venom in her eyes.

She felt that familiar sinking. Anger that blew out any light she tried to cover herself in and enveloped her in darkness, where she belonged. Rue tried to wiggle free, afraid of what would happen if she let herself disappear in the chilled dark.

"Come again?" she hissed.

The demon's gaze was glued to Jinx. They followed her like she was a flame and he was a moth, dead set on being burned to ash. Rue knew the heat of Jinx's flame all too well, and she was tired of constantly getting her wings singed.

Aggravation ignited her when she stood less than an arm's length before him, and he still didn't look at her.

Rue despised the way Jinx stole from her. She stole her attention, her patience, her energy — her magic. Even now, she stole her chance at making a deal. Patience was something she'd spent a long time ago. Now, finally having a solution to all her problems close enough she could practically touch it, there wasn't a speck of patience left to be found. Rue lifted onto her toes and grabbed the demon's face. Her pointed black nails dipped into his flesh, a single flex away from piercing his skin. Eyes raised, she looked at him.

She wasn't about to be ignored. Not when she stood so close to the end of her torment.

"I'm not about to walk away empty-handed."

His eyes widened. He took her in with something she couldn't identify in his gaze. His eyes dropped to her hand, tracing over her wrist as he swallowed hard and said nothing.

Rue found it hard to decide what was pissing her off more. His silence or Jinx's singing in the background. She was so *fucking* irritating.

When she couldn't take his silence anymore, she tightened her hold.

The feeling of flesh puncturing in her grasp caused a flutter to move through her chest. The scent of his blood was hot. Spicy. Mouth-watering. Powerful. The saliva in her mouth thinned as she looked up and watched his marmalade eyes flash black.

"I want to make a deal, demon," she repeated.

He stepped into her, humour in his eyes. "Killian."

"What?" Rue's brows dropped.

"My name." The darkness in his eyes cracked, leaving gossamer trails of fire through them. "It's Killian."

"Is that somehow important to the deal?" She wasn't there to make friends. She was there to unload the one attachment to another person she had; she wasn't about to leash herself to anyone else.

He closed his eyes, nostrils flared as he inhaled her. When he opened them, he looked like something had been unleashed. A beast he had kept hidden, lured from its hiding place by whatever he smelled. "There will be no deal."

Rue's hand dropped, and she wrapped it tightly around his neck. She may not be as strong as a demon, but she couldn't be killed. At least not if he attacked her body alone. She felt her power move through her as she stepped toward him, a mere whisper now, forcing him to take a step back.

"There will be." Her voice was hard. Somehow, she managed to keep the desperation from lacing her words.

Despite the power that radiated under his flesh, he kept his hands in his pockets. His jaw flexed as he looked at her, tongue whipping out to brush against his bottom lip, making the pale pink flesh glisten in the moonlight. "Is that right?"

His attractiveness irritated her as much as his refusal.

"Tell me why?" She needed to know.

Despite the ruckus sounding behind them as Jinx carried on singing and dancing, his attention remained glued to Rue. His face dropped, and he levelled her with a stare that made her knees feel like they wouldn't hold her up much longer. He was towering, yet he brought his face down to hers all too quickly.

He said nothing.

Rue was the one who held him in her grip, but she felt like it was *his* hand wrapped around *her* throat. It felt so tight. She was strangled by his stare alone.

"Because we're his," Jinx sang. "Both of us."

"What the fuck does that mean?" Rue rolled her eyes, regaining her strength as the thorn in her side that was Jinx sank deeper into her flesh, igniting her aggravation. "There is no *both of us*." There wasn't. They were both Rue.

"Yes, there is. Rue and Jinx. Jinx and Rue... and we're his." Jinx bumped into Rue's back, grinning over her shoulder. She wrapped her arms around Rue's shoulders as though she couldn't sense her about to explode. "Isn't that right, Killian?"

The sultry tone of her voice made Rue release him and step out from between them. "What the hell are you going on about now? It's always something with you, isn't it? You'd think with the whole *almost being killed by a goblin* thing, you would have smartened up."

"Almost being killed by a goblin?" Killian stepped forward, his eyes once again brimstone-lit voids.

His proximity did something. She felt that familiar flutter in her chest that tightened her throat and made her feel entirely too vulnerable.

Rue waved him off. She owed him no stories or explanations. Instead, she turned her attention to Jinx to try to figure out what the hell her soul was up to now. "I belong to no one. Most days, I don't even belong to myself."

"Mhmmm." Jinx giggled. That high-pitched annoying one that made Rue's left temple throb. "Mates. Don't you feel it?"

Her heart lurched in her chest, and bile rose in her throat. Of all the things Jinx could have said, that was likely the worst of them.

Rue staggered back, wanting to put as much space between the demon who stood with them at the crossroads and her as possible.

She couldn't have a mate. That was some old-world shit that usually had little to do with witches. Much like mortals, they'd been cursed to never feel the pull of a mate the way immortals did. Witches straddled the line in the middle. Neither mortal nor immortal. It meant they got some perks from the immortal world, but all of the weaknesses of the mortal one.

It was a shitty hand dealt by Fate herself — one made even worse by her coven.

Rue couldn't have a mate. Especially not while she was untethered from her soul. It would complicate things. A matehood came with perks. Powers. A sharing of sorts that would only anger her coven. Now, with most of her magic wrapped around Jinx to keep her safe, she was too weak. She wouldn't last long, and if her coven found out, they would be done for. They had to be tethered back together. Now.

"We're not mates." The shaky sound of her voice made her wince.

"We are!" Jinx was forever arguing. "We are! We are! Mated to the crossroads demon. Sexy Killian!"

Marching over to Jinx, Rue wrapped her hand over her mouth and pulled her back into her chest. "Would you shut up for a second and let me think?"

Jinx mumbled against her hand.

The crossroads demon they'd summoned, hoping to solve all their problems, just became the biggest problem Rue had. If this demon was her mate, what did that mean for Killian and Jinx? It looked like it meant he would be of no help to them. Whatever that stupid mate pull was doing to him, it was making him deny her the chance of a deal. The chance to finally be whole.

"We summoned you. You have to make a deal." Despite her words, she was uncertain.

"No."

That blasted word.

Helplessness was a stone in her chest as she realized she'd not only wasted her time summoning this demon, but she'd just made her life infinitely more complicated. She had to tether them back together, and she had just summoned someone who looked like he might decide to stand in her way.

“Fine.” She tightened her hold on Jinx until she turned into purple smoke, sent home and out of the way. Bram squeaked when Jinx disappeared, only to wrap his wings around himself and disappear in dark smoke of his own. He was always so quick to follow Jinx wherever she went. A familiar bound to her soul. Something else Jinx stole from her.

Killian stepped forward, his hand out as he reached for the space that was now empty before Rue. There was a question in his eyes, but he closed his hand into a fist and dropped it at his side.

“You don’t seem like someone who would give up so easily.” His chuckle was a dark sound that vibrated through him like a revving engine.

“Who says I’m giving up?”

Their eyes locked, and she felt the power radiate through the air between them. “I won’t grant your deal.” It was a threat of the worst kind. A promise that chipped away at the parts of her that were hopeful as she dug through the dirt and prayed to anyone who would listen that she would find respite.

The last thing she would do was fall to her knees before some man just because Fate thought he was something special. The last man who brought her to her knees had cost her everything.

Determination heated her blood as her eyes narrowed, taking him in. “Maybe not... but crossroads demons aren’t necessarily rare. I’m sure I can find one who will.”

They were at a crossroads all their own.

Mates. She rolled her eyes, scoffing. She needed a mate just about as much as she needed her soul walking around beside her. Not at all. And if Fate thought having him be the one to deny her deal would somehow make her give up, that bitch was out of her damned mind.

She would never give up.

Especially not now when her life hung in the balance.

He didn’t want to grant her a deal? Fine. She would find someone who would.

“Rue.” Her name on his lips was almost a plea.

Wrapped in her magic, she pulled herself home. She wasn’t going to waste any more of her time, especially now that she had a nagging pull in the centre of her chest that told her it might be running out.

5

JiNX

RUE WAS A POWERFUL witch. There was a time when she had been so strong, even in her mother's womb, that she made her coven fear what her birth would mean.

As far as Jinx could tell, all it meant for Rue was misery.

Miserable, Rue had stalked off to bed as soon as she arrived home. She ranted for a bit in the kitchen, mumbling to herself before she grabbed a book off a shelf and disappeared into her room.

It was good.

Great, actually.

Jinx wanted Rue to go to bed. She wanted her to lock her door to avoid being bothered. Not that Jinx would dare bother her there, she had learned her lesson when Rue had all but turned into a nightmare, eyes dark and terrifying. Even the memory of her then made Jinx shudder. She had been truly horrifying. It was like she sucked all the darkness from the room and existed in it as she calmly warned Jinx just what would happen to her if she trespassed again.

Calmly!

Such a temper.

Her heart lodged in her throat and threatened to live there as she scurried down the stairs, promising herself she would never *ever* go into Rue's room again.

Still, Rue locked the door.

Jinx waited until she heard the familiar sound of Rue's bedroom door locking before she walked down the hall.

Their house was simple. As much as Jinx wished it was more a reflection of them, Rue didn't want to collect anything. She said there was no point. She didn't want to set down roots anywhere, always waiting for the prophecy to come calling and for this sad life of theirs to be over.

So depressing.

Any time Jinx would sneak something in, Rue would toss it. It was infuriating, but not worth the boob punches, so she eventually gave up. She would save her energy for more important fights.

The walls, from floor to shoulder height, were framed and dark green; above was stark white and bare. There were no photos. Barely any decorations. A few plants that Rue had grown herself sat in woven baskets. They looked *ordinary*. It irked Jinx that everything about their home looked mundane when nothing about them was.

Jinx blew out air, vibrating her lips as she dragged her finger along the top of the framed walls.

This place was so boring.

Rue was boring.

There was little Jinx detested more than being bored.

Her hair blew over her shoulder as Bram appeared slightly above her. "We should go see him, shouldn't we, Bram?" Jinx whispered, careful not to be overheard by the big bore upstairs.

'Are you sure that's a good idea?'

"Of course it is!"

'She'll be angry,' Bram warned.

Jinx rolled her eyes at the warning. "And that's different from Rue every other day, how?"

'Jinx...' Bram flew over her shoulder, following her down the hall as he tried, and failed, to be the voice of reason. *'Are you sure about this?'*

"Yup!" She was more sure than she'd ever been; all she needed was a little magic.

At the end of the hall was a gold frame. It hung alone. No photo or artwork inside. All it did was frame the very boring wall, even more boring because that one was completely green without any type of framing.

"I don't know why she even bothers hiding it. It's not like anyone comes to visit. Not like anyone would stumble into there..."

Jinx rolled her eyes as she stepped through the empty frame. The sound of her toes hitting the metal spiral staircase droned on in the stone cave. The flap of Bram's wings was a constant noise echoing through the space as Jinx descended into Rue's sacred space in search of what she needed. The thick white candles lit as she walked past them, the warm glow swallowing up some of the cold and damp.

A trickle of fear moved through her. Hairs on the back of her neck raised as she thought about what would happen if Rue knew she was down there. The last time she was caught, Rue punched her right in the nose. It made her nose whistle... and it was impossible to watch her shows when her nose was whistling.

She wouldn't even heal it. Just let her whistle for three whole days!

Terrible.

Jinx swallowed hard.

It just couldn't be helped. It couldn't. Not now that she saw him. Nope. She had to do this... even if it meant her nose would whistle.

Familiar power pressed through her feet as soon as she reached the bottom of the stairs. The damp soils were packed with magic that leached out of Rue whenever she stood down there. Casting. Cursing. Calling.

Jinx liked the pulse of it.

A hum vibrated her throat as she dropped to a squat and pressed her palms to the earth. It was like a caress from Rue —

as rare as they were. She dug her nails into it, planting herself temporarily in the soil as the magic made the tips of her fingers buzz.

If only she could truly plant herself there.

Surround herself with rich soils in the place she knew Rue felt the most at ease. Where the menace melted from her face, revealing the sweetness she hid beneath. The soft smile she never shared with anyone, too afraid someone would use it against her.

Jinx sighed, her heart aching.

Poor Rue.

The memory of her whistling nose returned, and she scoffed, pushing up to her feet.

"Poor Rue, my butt." She rolled her eyes before she danced through the narrow passageway with its jutting rock walls and chilled earth. She should know better than to feel bad for Rue. She was a real piece of work.

With her hands lifted above her head, she shimmied and danced through the slim passageway until she reached the opening. It was lined with candles in a circle, and the symbol of their coven — or something similar to it that had been changed subtly over time — carved in the earth at its centre. The walls of the cave were lined with hovering jars, and more candles floated above. A stone altar stood in the middle, the book sat atop. It was an ominous thing. Sometimes, Jinx swore she could hear it whispering. Calling out.

Arms wrapped around herself, Jinx eyed it and shuddered. The sooner she got out of there, the better.

"Bram!" she whisper-yelled. "Find what I need."

'Got it," he answered. Despite his adorable eyes and that cute little nose, his voice was deep and serious.

They split up. Of course, they would have to. Some of the jars were set way too high for Jinx to see what was in them, and unfortunately for her, she may be Rue's soul, but the magic didn't always listen. She supposed it was because Rue never really listened to her soul. Why should her magic?

Stubborn, vexing things.

Rue and her magic.

Mostly Rue.

Bram's wings did nothing to the countless flames of the candles. The magic was more powerful than the wind they created. He was quiet aside from the flapping as he hovered before each jar, inspecting the contents before moving on to the next.

Jinx did the same. Bent at the waist, she looked at each jar in turn. She would need to find the petals. She remembered seeing them there the last time. She saw them right before Rue kicked her out. Made her sit upstairs until she was through with whatever she was up to.

So secretive.

A huff left her.

"Blue petals. Not just blue, but vibrant and beautiful. The same blue as the blown breath of... something." Jinx couldn't remember. Whatever it was that gave the valley where the flowers bloomed power. Not a witch, but something else. Something lighter. Rue had told her once, but there had been a song stuck in her head that was way more enjoyable than Rue's droning.

Blah, blah, blah. Always something boring to say in that boring, mean tone.

Jinx scooped up another jar and looked at the moving dirt inside. The dirt was dark grey like ash, and it wiggled like a worm, but there were no worms inside. She inspected it a moment longer, enthralled by the way it moved, before setting it back.

On to the next.

Green fire lit up the inside of the jar, brighter where her hands touched the glass.

Nope.

'Here!' Bram squeaked. The sound of his claws on glass was shrill as he pulled it from its place and dropped slightly before he steadied and carried it down.

"Oh, babycakes! Did you find it?" Jinx looked up, hopping on the balls of her feet as she watched her adorable little bat fly down from above. He hovered, the jar right within reach.

Jinx inspected the jar before she wrapped her hands around it and saw the black petals inside. A frown turned down her lips and knotted the space between her brows. She was sure the petals were blue; these couldn't be—

'Look.' Bram kicked the side of the jar, jostling the petals.

They lit blue before dimming back to black.

"This is them!" She ripped off the cork and pulled out a handful. If she had thought ahead, she would have brought something to put them in. Rue would notice the whole jar missing and would flip her lid. She was so fussy.

Shoving the petals in the front of her corset, she offered the jar back to Bram. "Put it back. Hurry! We have to go."

'Okay, okay!' Bram flew up, disappearing overhead as Jinx turned and made her way back through the passageway. Excitement coursed through her as her heart tried to escape the prison of her ribs.

Getting Rue to love her had proved more than impossible, but Killian... he was crafted to love her. And after all this time, there was nothing she wanted more than to be loved.

The night was so much cooler than the day. The humidity went to sleep, allowing the heat to change. Morph into something almost bearable.

She knew this wasn't something she could do in the house. Rue would smell the magic, and she would know. She always knew everything. So Jinx did the only reasonable thing — she snuck out.

Some things just had to be done.

Jinx turned her face up to the night sky and reached into the front of her corset. She held the petals tight in her fist, hoping with everything she was that this time the magic would listen. This time, it just had to work.

Rue was stubborn. If she decided they were going to be tethered back together, there was nothing Jinx could say to change her mind. But Jinx was stubborn too, and she wouldn't be erased before she could have him.

Killian.

He was hers just as much as he was Rue's. She could feel it in her chest. The way her heart moved. Weightless. Sitting too high. How each breath filled her but left her feeling empty. Wanting.

She wanted him.

Hand held out, she opened her fist and let the petals float around her. “Bring me to him.” They swirled around in a flurry before she felt herself move through time and space and toward her destiny.

6

KILLIAN

Fuck!

Sweat beaded on his brow as he looked into the blood-red flames. They weren't his. His flames weren't the kind he needed to craft something of the stubborn metals from the dark mountain. They didn't burn as hot as these. These fires were from dragons, at least that's what the peddler from the market told all who bought them. A peddler who knew better than to lie to someone like Killian.

He brought his hammer down on the heated metal, watching it spark with each strike. His workshop was his sanctuary. The floors were black stone, where the burn marks from rogue embers couldn't be seen. The tables, benches, and a lot of the other furniture were made of the same stone. His tools were arranged neatly on his worktable. Everything was exactly where he wanted it. Steam clouded the air around him, making him feel at home in the sweltering heat as he worked.

After seeing those women at the crossroads, he retreated to the only place that provided him even a semblance of peace — his forge.

What the hell was he doing?

An irritated groan left him as he threw the metal into a bucket of water, abandoning the task before he turned and leaned his hip back on his worktable. The smell of heat from the forge was a comfort behind him, still it did nothing to soothe his mind.

He lifted a hand to his bare chest and rubbed at the place that ached beneath his skin.

It couldn't be.

He was the last cursed soul he dared to ever imagine Fate would touch with her hands. He was sentenced to the crossroads, his soul held by the Crossroads King himself until Fate deemed his sentence spent. Knowing she had meddled in his life — a life he was sure she pronounced unworthy — heated him hotter than the forge at his back.

There was no way he was wrong. It couldn't be anything else.

But she was... untethered. Her soul had stood beside her, in the flesh. That was something he hadn't even known was possible. Something he hadn't felt as he looked at both of them and yearned for each in turn.

Why?

His brow dropped as he huffed another deep breath.

He held his hand out, observing a palm that looked completely ordinary. Lacklustre, even in this form. A sigh puffed his chest as he reminded himself not to want for the powers that had damned him.

"Just a little longer, Killian. Then you'll be free from this blasted task of the crossroads," he muttered. "Make the deals. Sign over souls. Don't overcomplicate things with thoughts of mates." He sighed again. Because damn if he didn't want to.

"Hello!" The word was sang toward him, making him tense as he straightened away from his workbench. "Is anyone home?"

"What the fuck?" he muttered as he marched out of his workshop, pulling the sliding barn door closed behind him to look at the woman who stood on the porch of his house.

"Hello!" She cupped the sides of her face as she bent at the waist and stared into one of his windows.

Killian was frozen as he watched her shove a strand of hair over her bare shoulder before she lifted her dark skirt and used it to wipe at his window. Her fat bat hovered in the air beside her.

"Well, where else would he be?" she spoke to her bat.

It squeaked its answer.

"Hmm... I guess." She stood, hands on her hips. "Well, what now then? If Rue finds out where we are, we are going to end up in her cauldron for sure. Her temper is hot as hell lately." Her cheeks puffed as she turned and looked right at him.

Eyes wide, she clapped as she jumped up and down, the brightest smile on her face. "You're here!"

"Yes..." he dragged the word out.

She was off the porch before he could make sense of it. A grunt was forced out of him as they collided, her arms wrapped around his neck.

"What are you—"

Her hand pressed against the side of his face as she smiled. "Sweet Lucifer, you're handsome. Would you look at this face, Bram? I guess demons would have to be handsome, though. How else could they get people to fall on their knees before them?" She batted her eyes at him. "Should I fall on my knees before you, Killian?"

His mouth opened, all the words locked somewhere in his throat, before he stuttered and closed it again.

What?

She grabbed his hands and placed them on her waist before she turned in his arms, pressing herself tightly against him, and looked at his house. "So this is where you live?"

What was happening?

Killian blinked hard, forcing himself to ignore the way his heart hammered like a vicious beast in his chest. He wasn't some feeble thing. He was a... well, right now he was a crossroads demon, a seasoned one at that. He could handle a witch.

He inhaled her, and the scent made his eyes flutter closed.

This was no mere witch.

Fuck.

She took a step, her hands closed over the top of his hands, holding them on her waist and forcing him to step with her. His steps were awkward and too wide as he tried to summon his faculties enough to avoid stepping on her skirt as she made her way back up the steps and toward his front door.

"Aren't you going to show me around?"

She sang everything. There was a joy to her he'd never experienced before. She celebrated without even realizing that was what she was doing. It was disconcerting. He didn't know how to react to her. She was too bright. He wasn't used to standing this close to the sun.

She pushed his door open without permission, leading them both into his house. Finally, she released her hold on his hands to step away from him and do a slow spin, taking everything in.

Killian closed his hands into fists, suddenly missing the warmth of her in his hold. His eyes widened at the thought before he cleared his throat and forced himself to look at her. "How did you get here?"

There. Words. He knew how to word. To speak. He closed his eyes to his rambling thoughts before he forced them open once more.

Lucifer, what was happening to him?

She paused with her skirts twirling around her ankles, showing him her bare feet. Her thick brows cocked as her smile broadened. She leaned with her hand cupped mischievously next to her mouth. "Magic," she whispered.

"Magic."

"Yes. Isn't it wonderful?" she beamed.

Again, he was at a loss for words.

Her bright eyes looked him over before she stood on her toes with her hands clasped behind her back. It pushed her chest on display, and Killian had to work hard to keep his eyes locked on hers. "Did you miss me?"

A phantom fist closed around his throat as his stomach bounced.

"You did, didn't you?" Her eyes dropped to his chest, looking over his bareness, only covered by his apron. "Mmm mmm mmm. I like this better than the suit."

His hands rubbed over his bare chest, suddenly lacking the confidence he had worn as well as his suits. Just how was this woman able to steal so effortlessly from him? She stole his words. His suave nature. His ability to make a deal.

A single step closed the space between them, and she placed her palm on his chest. The feeling of her hand sent a shiver through him and forced him to look down into the depths of her eyes. Unlike Rue, whose eyes were as dark as he suspected his soul was, Jinx's were light. They were darkness wafted over in a pale green that made them somehow vibrant and deep before they burned like fire around the pupils.

"Why are you here?" he asked the question he desperately needed the answer to.

Her eyes danced back and forth between his. "Isn't it obvious?"

Killian swallowed hard. This woman would damn him, he was sure of it.

"I was created with the sole purpose of bringing Rue misery. Of tormenting her with my presence... forcing her to feel my absence. There are parts of me that know how much she would hate being tethered to you, just as much as I would hate being tethered to her." She rose onto her toes. "Maybe that's why I'm here. Because I'm helpless against my very purpose..." Her eyes found his lips.

He stood rigid as her hands wrapped around the back of his head.

"Just as you're helpless against this pull... aren't you?"

Yes. "No," he lied.

She chuckled, and damn if it wasn't a sound he wanted to hear for the rest of his life. "Do you know how I know you're lying, Killian?"

"I'm not lying." He was.

Her brow cocked. "Because I'm a liar too..."

"What lies do you tell?"

"All of them."

She confused him. She was a bright light that he felt he needed to hide away from, knowing it could rid him of the shadows he desperately clung to. And yet, there was something sinister in her. Something lurking behind the light no one would ever see because no one could stare long enough without looking away. Without feeling the sting that bright light brought to their eyes.

"You're mine," she told him. "And hers too."

A sigh left him at hearing the words he knew out loud.

"Which is why you can't grant her wish... at least not yet." Her grip behind his neck tightened as she pulled him toward her. Their lips collided, and he felt the heat of her mouth against his.

Killian's heart battered against his ribs, desperate to escape its cage and meet the woman who had so freely claimed him. He should fight against this; being mated to witches could bring him nothing but trouble, but as the taste of her filled his mouth, sweet sunshine and honey, he lost himself yet again.

Her tongue dipped into his mouth, and his fires lit brightly inside him.

It had been so long since he allowed himself the space to fall into his urges. To let his wants leash and lead him. Now, with her mouth against his, he felt the restraint he so carefully kept in place snap.

Frantic need erased everything else as his hands wrapped around her waist, lifting her. He rubbed the soft flesh of her love handles as her legs wrapped around him, shoving her skirts up around her waist as he walked toward the steps.

This wasn't him. This wasn't the demon he became when he was sentenced to the crossroads. No, this was the thing he was before. The beast who craved the misery thoughtless chaos brought. Who yearned for the tears shed over poor decisions and the pain of harsh consequences. This was the Killian he craved to be, even though he knew it would damn him all over again.

He lowered her when his toes hit the steps, seating her as he knelt between her legs. The bare flesh of her thighs were warm, brown, and tantalizing as his chest heaved and his hands gently caressed her exposed skin.

She pulled the apron up over his head and gasped as her hand travelled teasing paths over his bare skin. "Jinx," she whispered as she loosened her hold on his neck to drop her hands to the button of his jeans. It was a scramble of fingers that couldn't work through their excitement to get it on the first try.

His were just as feral.

"What?" Killian groaned as his fingers finally pushed her panties to the side and found her hot centre.

"My name... use it."

It was a throaty command that hardened him in his pants. "Jinx."

"Again."

"Jinx." He pressed his fingers into her.

Her fingernails dug into his shoulders as she arched against the steps. "Killian," she moaned.

Fuck.

He was so screwed. He returned from the crossroads, telling himself he would never see them again. That he would put space between them so he could figure out what was going on in his head and his heart before he approached them... if he ever did. He would harden himself.

This wasn't in the way he meant.

He couldn't think with the grip of her around his fingers. With her breath in the air and that whine escaping through those perfectly parted lips.

Killian looked down at her dimpled thighs as he pushed them further apart.

Just a taste. A single taste.

He dipped his head and pressed his tongue flat between her folds.

"Yes!" Jinx cried.

Sweet Lucifer, if he didn't suddenly love the taste of sweet bitterness. Of hot sweat and recklessness. It assaulted all his taste buds, making his ears buzz and his stomach feel suddenly starved. He devoured her. His hungry mouth covered her in her entirety as his tongue thoroughly explored every inch of her. He pressed his fingers in, his tongue flicking against her sensitive bundle of nerves as she squirmed against him.

Jinx's chest heaved. Her breath quickened as her fingers gripped his head and her thighs tightened around his ears.

She was so responsive.

Every moan he pulled from her coated his flesh in flames and made his forehead throb as his horns threatened to make their appearance. The feeling of her coming undone burned something in his belly. Heated him unbearably. She cried out, coating his tongue in her taste before her huffed breathing jilted and steadied.

Killian sat back on his heels, his own breath lifting his chest as he watched her prop her elbows on the steps. The smile she gave him was both vulnerable and satisfied. Her tongue poked out, making his cock jerk in his pants as she dragged it along her bottom lip.

This wasn't what he was supposed to do. He was supposed to forget all about Jinx and Rue and carry on with his sentence at the crossroads until he earned his freedom. He was supposed to suppress everything he wanted to grant the wants of everyone else. He was supposed to —

Fuck if he knew now. Right now, all he was supposed to do was between her thick thighs.

"I knew it," she whispered.

She was right there, the heat of her body close enough to heat his own, and yet she felt too far away. Everything inside him begged him to reach out. To touch her. To claim her.

Mine.

"Knew what?" His voice was hoarse as he ran his tongue over his lips, savouring the taste of her that still lived there.

"That you were mine." That look. Her eyes were still bright, and yet... different. Like hellfire that whispered his damnation would come at her hands.

And he suddenly realized, with nothing more than a mere taste, that he would burn for her.

7

JiNX

IT WASN'T ENOUGH.

Every inch of her buzzed in a blissful way she had been denied her whole existence. Her body was both wound too tight and as loose as it could be as her chest heaved, her corset suddenly way too small. With fumbling fingers, she reached down and began working at the ties.

Killian's eyes followed her movements. Each laboured breath made smoke billow from his nostrils as the faintest of flames moved over his skin. She watched as they danced around his head before horns appeared from his brow. They were beautiful. Thick. Dark. Long. Twisted.

And this corset was suddenly her biggest affliction. Why did she wear this stupid thing again instead of the simple shirts Rue always wore? Oh yeah, because she was a princess. A pretty, *trapped* princess.

A groan escaped her as the strings got tangled and her escape became more difficult. She wanted to be bare before him. To feel the fires of his flesh against her skin. To see if they burned.

Her demon — because he was most definitely hers — leaned forward. His hands were huge, and she loved the way they made her feel small. She had never felt small before. Not that she didn't love the body she had been given, in a similar shape to the one Rue wore proudly, but there was something so wonderful about feeling dwarfed by those hands. He gripped her corset, the smallest of pulls turning the strings to nothing but frayed fabric as it opened, allowing her the first full breath.

He stared at her, his hands moving up the thin cotton of her dark shirt. His fingers grabbed hold of the ties at her neckline.

Rip it!

The thought was loud in her mind.

She wanted to see the viciousness in him. Wanted to see if he was the monster they both so desperately needed. The dark thing that could free them both.

Killian obliged her, his hands fisted in the neckline before he tore the shirt down the middle.

The worn fabric fell open, baring Jinx to him.

Hungry eyes took her in. They moved over her heavy breasts as they fell to the sides without her corset and shirt to keep them where she wanted them. Her brown nipples were already pebbled. Her stomach was soft and half hidden by the high waistband of her skirt.

Their eyes locked as he held the waistband and slowly pulled her skirt down. She lifted her hips as the elastic pulled, almost forbidding its removal over her wide hips. She usually took it off over her head, but she wasn't about to stop this. Not now.

The fabric groaned before threads cried, and he tugged it off.

Jinx smiled.

He was perfect. The perfect thing for her. For *them*.

She held her hand out to him.

His eyes traced her body like it was something he knew better than to take, but he was just as helpless as she was. She let her thighs fall open.

The bob of his throat as his eyes dropped to take her in thrilled her. She wanted to curse Rue for always being so difficult where sex was concerned. Jinx had barely begun, and she was already filled with so much. So much joy. So much pleasure. She knew this was different, though, and there was no one Jinx could have found for Rue that would have made her feel even a fraction of the way she did now.

Because he was theirs. Damn, if that thought didn't make her giddy.

How lucky they were, even cursed.

She wished Rue were there. That she could feel this. That she could see for herself. Maybe if she did, she wouldn't be so difficult. She would see. It was so clear... how could she not?

"You're going to damn me, aren't you?" Killian's words were a harsh whisper.

Jinx nodded. "I hope so."

She did. She wanted to brand him. Wanted to mark him like sin. Damn him for any retribution that could be found anywhere else but with her. With them.

Killian chuckled low. The button she had struggled with on his jeans was suddenly open, the thickness of him jutting up over his belly button. He wrapped his hands under her thighs, tugging her closer to him. She felt her butt hang off the step, but he held her up as he dipped his hips and pressed the swollen head of his dick against her opening. He slid the length of him up through her folds, coating himself in her slickness before he pressed the head once more at her core.

"You're so ready for me. Let's hope I can control myself." He thrusted.

Jinx cried out.

Her toes curled as her head fell back against the step. Stars lit behind her eyes as her chest burned. Chanting played in her ears, but it was a chanting she had learned how to ignore a long time ago. She ignored it now as her breath caught in her chest, and Killian slid slowly out of her. She felt every inch of him. Every vein that covered him, the movement a tease that made her moan in a low voice that was a stranger to her ears.

"I've sins enough, I should have been damned a long time ago," Killian said as he leaned into her, the heat of his chest pressed against hers. His hot breath blew against her cheek as his lips ghosted a kiss against her flesh. "But there has been no one brave enough to do it."

Was it brave to surrender to him the way she felt she was? To completely lose herself?

Rue had always called her foolish, but was she brave?

Now wasn't the time to seek out those answers.

Her mind was filled with nothing but thoughts of Killian and how best to make him hers, even if just for a little while. She knew it wouldn't last. Knew before long, he would feel the same pull in his chest he felt toward her for Rue. Knew it would make him want to give her the very thing Jinx hoped with everything she was — especially now, as he moved inside her — he would deny.

"Look at me," Killian demanded.

Her eyes snapped up, meeting the intensity in his.

His pace quickened. It was erratic and rough, every thrust sending her back into the steps behind her, eliciting a pain that made the moment all the more brutal. She welcomed it, loving the way it made her feel human. Real. Like the flesh wrapped around her wasn't just a spell.

"What is this?" his words were barely more than expelled breath. Words she wouldn't hear if his lips weren't so close to hers. He was feral in his thrusts. Like he had been on reins up until he sank into her, and finally, they snapped, and he was free. That first taste of freedom made her erratic. The kind of erratic that made her insides clench and beg to be used.

Fuck! Disobeying Rue had never felt so damned good.

What was this? His question played over in her head. Did he not know?

He was a demon that was likely older than Rue. He knew what sins looked like... what souls looked like. Didn't he know what the marks that painted them looked like, too?

Pleasure inflated her. Her toes curled as her fingers dug deeper into his shoulders. Every thrust threatened to undo her as she leaned forward and took his lips. The heat of his tongue filling her mouth snapped the thin thread of her control. Everything in her tightened as brightness exploded behind her eyes. She called out, ecstasy making the sound harsh, feral, and wonderful.

What was this?

It was everything.

She exploded, everything fading but the ceaseless chanting keeping time with her breath and the fullness of him still moving inside her.

8

RUE

WHAT THE FUCK?

Pleasure assaulted her.

Her flesh felt too hot as she kicked off her blankets and tossed and turned, still under a sheet of sleep. Sweat mottled her brow as her breath quickened, her thighs pressed together as something deep in her core begged for relief. The pit of her stomach was knotted over and over as her lips parted and she breathed a moan into the darkness of her room.

Visions of his lips moving over her flesh played in quick bursts in her mind. His lips wrapped around her nipples, tugging at something that made her hold her breath. She knew they weren't hers. It was like watching the scene through someone else's eyes.

Bliss suffocated her.

Rue threw her feet to the floor, desperate to escape a heat she didn't understand. She paced, hands fisted in the braids by her temples as her chest heaved, eyes bleary.

This wasn't real.

She tried to breathe through it, but she couldn't. This was unlike any pleasure she'd ever felt before. It filled every inch of her body like cement, turning her into something that couldn't move through it. Couldn't escape it. She was encased in it. Stuck.

Rue gasped.

Tears pushed their way out of the corner of her eyes as the language of her coven echoed through her room. The voices of those who cursed her danced dangerously with the sounds of pleasure. Colliding like vicious thunder. Green smoke fashioned into ropes wrapped around her over and over. Binding her. Cracks moved through the magic, darkening the light of the spell with each moan breathed into her ear. Each wet sound of flesh against flesh.

Rue's arms were ripped out at her sides, her knees forced into the floor as she struggled to catch her breath. To breathe around this onslaught of passion while being punished by a curse so deeply rooted, she could never fully enjoy it.

It was too much.

Pleasure filled her to bursting. Almost pain, but sweet enough to trick her into thinking it wasn't. She pulled against the ghosts of her restraints, desperation clawing at her as she tried to soothe the heated flesh between her legs. To press and prod at it until she released herself from this build-up of tension. She just needed something. Anything to make this stop. To end whatever this was.

Relief poured into her as she freed herself enough to sink her hand between her thighs. Fingers pressed into her as she bit into her bottom lip. The pleasure was short-lived.

Pain ricocheted through her as she felt a lashing at her back that stole her breath, the chanting so loud she couldn't even hear her panted breath through it.

A gasp filled her ears as she suddenly felt too full. It was more than her fingers inside her as her body jerked and heat pressed over her. She felt the fires of every temptation she denied burn through the ropes. She heard the snap of a whip at her back as her bottom lip was sucked into her teeth. The moan that left her was pained as much as it was one of ecstasy.

'Ruin Crowe,' an ominous voice repeated her name, taking vicious whips at her with each uttered word. It was like her sentence was being doled out, and she finally had to face it.

'Ruin Crowe.'

'Ruin Crowe.'

'Ruin Crowe.'

'Bind her.'

'Trap her.'

'Curse her.'

'For the coven.'

'For the coven.'

'We curse you, Ruin Crowe.'

"Mine..." The deep voice erased the voices of the coven that damned her.

Her eyes fluttered as her toes curled and her back arched.

"Fuck!" Rue screamed, and everything inside her fractured. Her fingers were vicious, her thumb pressed against her clit. Waves wracked her body, sending shudders through her that were almost impossible to breathe through. Her head whipped back, a moan inflating her throat as her toes curled against the floor. Her orgasm was brutal heat and vengeful suffocation. It was being held down and forbidden to try to escape.

It kept hold of her.

Each breath was too sharp.

It wasn't enough.

The phantom ropes at her arms snapped, the runes and script lit from beneath her skin. Magic coated her fingers and up her arms. She collapsed forward, her brow pressed into the wood.

She pressed hard against the bundle of nerves she knew would only further damn her. *Fuck,* she was right as her fingers moved with forceful thrusts. Her pussy clenched, opening and closing as it tried to hold onto her fingers.

More! her mind begged.

This desperation was uncontrollable. Sweat made the fabric of her shirt cling to her back as she rasped out a ragged breath, thrusting her fingers into herself.

'Killian,' a familiar voice gasped.

Jinx.

Her eyes snapped open, and her fingers paused their ministrations as realization hit her. This was not *her* orgasm. Well, it was because her fingers made sure it was, but it wasn't *just* hers.

This was theirs.

Bitterness filled her as the depths of her stomach coiled like a spring pressed tight, and she gritted her teeth. They weren't done, and that meant neither was she. A huff of frustrated breath filled her as fingers resumed their pace. Tears clouded her eyes as she felt the intensity wrack through her body and that spring released.

A full breath filled her as she felt her body relax.

Her pleasure was short-lived as she sat back on her heels, her hands resting on her bare thighs. She stared up at the ceiling, watching a fog of green magic highlighted by the runes that carved out her curse lift into the air. Rue watched as the remnants of magic dissipated to nothing, alongside her pleasure.

Rue didn't need to question what had happened; she already knew. Jinx had taken it upon herself to go to Killian, and he had fallen to his knees before her. Given all she went there for.

Jinx just damned them both.

'We curse you, Ruin Crowe.' The whispered voice made a shiver dance down her spine.

A sigh inflated her chest, but she didn't set it free. She was too afraid of what else would be set loose when she did. Anger. Frustration. Disappointment. Grief. It was a bitter cocktail she was often forced to swallow, and she was growing tired of feeling the buzz it left in her. The haze of discontent.

Bitter cold pressed against the flesh around her eyes as darkness rimmed her vision.

A shaky hand pressed against her chest, rubbing at the numbness there.

She couldn't undo it. All she could do now was what she had been forced to do since her untethering.

Rue would have to clean up the mess.

Forcing herself up, she walked on shaking legs to her bathroom. She didn't bother turning on the light as she let the cold water run and splashed her face with it. The silhouette of her reflection in the mirror stared at her as the voices of her coven continued their droning. This time it was more pointed.

They knew.

Her throat tightened as she grabbed her toothbrush and started brushing her teeth. With each aggressive drag of the bristles, the burn of her eyes mounted until she was forced to blink and set her tears free. They took slow trails down her cheeks, the balloon of her emotions in her throat still gagging her.

She sighed and instantly regretted it. The dam was broken, and everything came pouring out.

Why me?

Her hands braced on the sides of the sink as she hung her head. The mint toothpaste added an odd scent and flavour to her misery as a sob escaped her.

As usual, Jinx had done exactly what she wanted, damn the consequences. Why would she care about the consequences? She was never the one who had to pay them. Rue forced her eyes up as she shut off the tap. Her eyes had adjusted to the dark, forcing her to see her reflection.

Her eyes sank into pools of pitch. Black veins travelled out toward her cheek and up past her brows.

She looked pitiful.

The drone of the voices of women she had long tried to forget but was forced to remember continued. They grew louder and louder until a buzzing in her ears replaced them. Her fist slammed hard against the mirror. The sound of the glass shattering broke through the buzz, replacing it with her heartbeat.

She gasped, chest heaving as she pulled her fist away.

Shards of glass stuck in her skin. Splinters of mirror. She turned the tap on again, running her hand under the stream as she watched the water run dark. It looked black in the dim light of her bathroom. Everything from the claw-foot tub to the glass shower looked ominous. It was fitting because her situation had suddenly gotten infinitely more baleful.

Her coven had always been out for her blood, but they had never been strong enough to take it. The most they could do was curse her. Separate her from Jinx and hope that, in time, she would be so irritated with her blight that she forgot to seek vengeance. All that had changed on the beach when she surrendered all the magic she had ever wielded to keep Jinx alive and safe until a deal could be struck.

A deal she had been denied.

"What have you done, Jinx?" she whispered. She turned off the tap, blindly yanking pieces of glass from her skin. If it hurt, she couldn't feel it. Her mind was too loud for pain to whisper its existence.

Jinx had proclaimed Killian was theirs. Even without her soul, she felt it too — as much as she tried to deny it. Now, with the binding of her soul to that of her mate's, another part of the prophecy had come to pass, and her coven had been alerted.

They would come for her, and this time, because of the curse they set in place to bind her and the powers she'd sacrificed to protect Jinx, she would be almost defenceless.

Her magic — nothing more than a ghost of her power now — swirled around her as she wiped her tears away with bloody hands, leaving morbid streaks on her face. She would try another demon. Try to make another deal.

Her life depended on it.

Steady hands buried her offering before Rue stood, clapping to rid them of the dirt that clung to her skin. The upside of Jinx running off to be with Killian was that both were out of her way. The downside was that she was once again eternally screwed, but it was pointless to keep track of frivolous things like that anymore. What was the point if she'd been damned since her first breath anyway?

It was crying over spilled milk and all that.

A calm settled over her without her counterpart there dancing around, or the endless squeak of Bram keeping pace with her steps. It was nice to tackle a problem without the chaos of Jinx at her back.

She pinched her eyes closed as another wave of blinding pleasure moved through her.

Unfortunately, she wasn't completely rid of them. She could still feel the tight hold of their pleasure wrapped around her.

Fucking animals. Just how many times were they going to go at it? Her knees were practically shaking.

The ground rumbled at her feet before dramatic cracks cut open the dirt. It felt oddly settling to know all demons were this theatrical, and it wasn't just the one likely lying somewhere next to Jinx. *In* her, if what she felt was any indication.

Rue shook the thought away as fresh anger bloomed in her belly.

She'd deal with them later.

Black smoke parted, and a woman stepped through the heat. She was as domineering as Killian had been, clad in black and sharp lines. Her slacks sat on her waist, her waiflike shape somehow bold. The shoulders of her black shirt were sharp and boxy, but her arms were bare and black sigils and marks covered all of her pale skin. Her red hair was the colour of freshly drawn blood, and it was pulled back, the length of her ponytail stiff down her back.

Alright, alright, she got it. Demons. Whew!

Rue rolled her eyes, her arms crossed over her chest. "I'd like to make a deal."

"Is that right?" Her steps were slow, but her long legs effortlessly closed the space between them. Her hand reached out, caressing her cheek as her black eyes looked her over. The demon's features were severe. Everything looked entirely too sharp. A pointed chin, a thin nose, wide lips and cheekbones so defined they made her cheeks look gaunt. Mischief was carved into her face as she looked Rue over. Dipping her head, she inhaled her. "It seems like you've already made a deal. You reek of our smoke and fires."

"The last demon wasn't up to my standards," Rue replied, her voice flat. "Hopefully you won't be as disappointing."

Her head fell back with a bark of laughter. "Disappointing? Interesting." The tips of her fingers pressed into Rue's shoulder, and she dragged them across her skin as she walked behind her. "Just what is it you want?"

There was no point getting excited. She knew better at this point. "I want you to tether me back to my soul."

Her slow circling came to an end as the demon stood toe to toe with her. The harsh slash of her thick brows dropped over her eyes, somehow darkening the depths of their obsidian. "Your soul. You don't have it?" Without waiting for the answer, she pressed a palm to the centre of Rue's chest.

The sudden contact made her tense. Her feet widened, adjusting her stance as the demon's eyes set on her hand, as though she could see past Rue's flesh to the hollows inside.

"Then we have a problem."

It was Rue's turn to frown. "What? Why?"

The demon stepped back, her eyes staring at Rue's chest with a quizzical look on her face. "Fascinating. In all my years, I've never seen the likes of it before."

The wrath that was neatly housed inside Rue started hammering against her chest the longer the demon left her question unanswered. "Why do we have a problem?"

Arms crossed, the demon mirrored her stance. "Because we make deals not with bodies but with souls. Every deal we make marks a soul. Tags them so we can carry out the terms of the deal when the time comes. To make a deal with someone without a soul is impossible. There is no part of you I can make a deal with. Nothing I can take when all is said and done."

Frustration tightened Rue's throat as she tried to stifle the tears that threatened to make an appearance. This had been her last chance to try to fix this.

"No matter who you summon, no Crossroads demon can make this deal."

But one could... it would just have to be a deal marked in Jinx. A deal *she* made.

What were the chances she could convince the Crossroads demon, who had already slept with her soul, to make a deal that could make Jinx disappear forever? Probably about as good as getting her pain-in-the-ass soul to ask him for the deal Rue couldn't.

Well, fuck.

9

RUE

HER ELBOW RESTED ON the window as she gripped the wheel of her little black Fiat. The night had long slipped away as she drove north out of the city to a place she had barely escaped. Every moment in the car alone let her thoughts scream at her.

A part of her should worry about leaving Jinx behind when she knew she'd be gone so long. If the call of mates was as strong as she always heard, Jinx would be safe. Killian would keep her out of all the trouble Rue usually had to. At least, that was her hope. If not, she would die in her car before she got there.

That didn't seem so bad.

At this point, death was almost welcomed. At least dead, she would get a break.

Her eyes dropped to the clock above her navigation.

6:41 am.

Nine hours into the drive, and she had just passed Hearst. It wouldn't be long now until she was where she needed to be.

Until she was in the thickness of the north her coven called home.

Time in the car passed both too slowly and too quickly. Broken up by nothing but her thoughts. One of the positives about leaving Jinx behind was that she didn't have to deal with her endless chatter. It also meant there would be no way for Jinx to find her unless Rue herself called for her. The soul wasn't bound to a body the same way the body was to the soul. Rue was cursed to feel all her soul did. Every sliver of pain Jinx felt was hers to hold onto, and yet Jinx was always blissfully unaware of everything Rue. She wasn't plagued by her thoughts, her anxieties, her fears. All her pain was hers and hers alone, which meant whatever was about to happen would be solely Rue's problem.

Good. She missed having troubles that were just hers.

Her inner compass honed in on the feeling that brought bile up the back of her throat. She wondered what it must feel like for other members of her coven. Witches who weren't damned by the very ones who were supposed to protect them. What did they feel when they got this close to home, and their heart started its anxious pull?

Trees lined both sides of the highway, but she turned off. Most wouldn't dare; there was a ditch on both sides, but she knew the spot where there was a road unseen. She could feel it in her bones.

The tires were silent as she drove straight toward a row of trees. There was a chill that moved over her. Pressure. It felt like walking under a waterfall when she was still dry, and the frigid water touched every single part of her. She ignored it, teeth clenched as the urge to chatter went through them.

The mirage of the trees shimmered around her car as she drove through.

Unease boiled in the pits of her stomach, making it churn as she parked. The woods got thicker, and there was only one way to go any further. On foot.

As soon as the soles of her boots hit the soil, it felt like a ghost moved through her. A shiver danced up her spine, and she had to grab the sleeves of her plaid sherpa, pulling it over her hands. This was her coven's work. The unease was supposed to send mortals who had made it this far turning and running from these woods.

Each step made her think of what her coven could have been. To witches like her gran or her mother. Ones who were welcomed and celebrated. Not ones who were cursed before they were even born. Ruin Crowe, who carried the dark shadows of reapers on her back.

She could still see the village she once called home in her mind's eye as she made her way through the woods toward it. The cobblestone streets and shiny storefronts. The townhouses and courtyards. It would have been quaint to some, paradise to others. To Rue, it was a prison.

"I never thought I would see the day."

The voice halted her steps. It was one she hadn't heard before, but the abhorrence in it she knew well. It dripped venom. Condemned her with every uttered word.

This witch would have been hers in another life. A sister to the craft.

Rue should have been more afraid knowing her magic was currently being kept in Jinx. Anything she had left would be a dull shadow. Worthless if this witch held any true power.

But that didn't matter. This witch could cut her down. Shred every inch of her flesh, and it would do nothing to call forth the reapers to claim her. She couldn't be killed... not while separated from Jinx. Hopefully, she could make this witch angry enough to retie the binds between her and her soul.

"Ruin Crowe, back in the Lumena woods. It's as though you have a death wish."

Her steps were silent as they carried her from behind Rue. She kept to the trees, a blur of dark movement until she stood before her. Her eyes were dark things that were loud as they stared. They told Rue just what she would do to her if given the chance. And she would give her every chance she wanted... she had to if she wanted this to work.

"Was your curse not enough? Back for more, little plague?" Her smile was as dark as her eyes. Her chestnut hair was pulled back from her brow, her olive skin darker in the night. Her nose was turned up at the tip in a way that felt familiar, but Rue couldn't place. It was borrowed, but from whom, she didn't know.

"I've been told I'm a glutton for punishment," Rue muttered, eyes honed on the witch before her.

"Or maybe now that Fate has intervened, you think you finally have the power needed for your vengeance." Muscles jerked in her jaw. This witch wasn't happy to know she'd been mated. She could join the club. Still, she forced a wicked smile, leaning in. "We curse you, Ruin Crowe," she hissed.

"Maybe." Rue stood still, unafraid of the way the air felt too heavy, and the witch's smile tightened, making her cheeks look unbearably tight.

She leaned in, inhaling the air around Rue. "Just what kind of beast could have claimed you, I wonder. Just what threads has Fate woven for a damned thing like you? A pestilence that has rotted the very coven she came from?"

Rue scowled. "I've rotted nothing. Any hardships you suffer are ones you brought on yourself, banning the only powers that could have protected you and allowed you to thrive." It was her turn to inhale the air. "Pitiful, really. I can barely smell the magic on you. Are you a witch or a mortal peddling spells and crystals?"

"Hardships..." Fortuna bared her teeth. "We could say the same of you. How you love to drown in misery... almost as though it's of your own making."

"Or the makings of a curse."

"A curse." Fortuna's brow cocked, a chuckle vibrating her throat. "Right."

"A curse that seems to damn us both. How dull the Lumena coven seems now. Cowering in the woods, living in a village all but abandoned. Weak. Sad."

Fortuna lunged.

Metal glinted, and pain jolted through Rue as her hands shot up, wrapping around the hand at her stomach. Wetness slicked their fingers, hot and sticky. The witch leaned in, her hot breath sour on Rue's face. "The Vossen witches have always been the powerful hands of the Lumena coven. To believe otherwise is to live in the mind of a fool."

Vossen?

The surprise left Rue's face as the heat of her blood soaked into her shirt. "Ah. You're the wretched spawn of Ferula. Tell me, just how is the priestess? Still scouring the mortal cities in hopes of abandoned witches and powers? Hoping for another teat she can suck on that will fill her coven the way the Crowe women did?"

"You dare speak of my mother that way?" She twisted the knife in Rue's belly.

Being stabbed was such a mortal affliction. She had expected the burn of magic. The swell of her veins as she fought against power surging into her, suffocating her from the inside. Instead, she was stabbed.

How very boring.

Ordinary.

Rue rolled her eyes at the thought. She would need to do more to get what she wanted. She just hoped this witch with her measly knife would have the power needed to give it to her.

"If your mother is Ferula Vossen, the priestess who damned the Lumena coven, then yes. I imagine I will dare to say a lot more."

The blade was pulled out. Relief was short-lived as it shot forward again, sticking her flesh right beside the first wound.

How her coven had fallen. What was next? Bullets?

Even though Death wouldn't claim her, she couldn't escape the dizziness that came from losing blood. She adjusted her feet, widening her stance as her head swayed slightly.

"My mother may be on her deathbed, but she did more for this coven than the Crowes could ever dare dream. All you and yours have done is bring misfortune. And when my mother finally passes, and this coven becomes mine, I will use the powers of the Vossen and the Lumena to finally be rid of you."

Rue frowned, a rasped sigh leaving her. "Ugh. You mean to say I have to wait until that old hag is dead?"

How annoying.

She'd come all this way. Ventured into a territory that should have been the death of her, hoping she could anger someone enough to finally get tethered back to her soul after being denied yet again, and once more, she'd failed.

Just what the hell did she have to do to be rid of this curse and the annoying bitch that came with it?

Another stab to her gut pinched at her skin.

Rue laughed, but the sound was darker than the woods around them. "Don't tell me you're stupid as well as powerless, witch."

"It's Fortuna," she hissed through her teeth.

Her laugh this time was one of derision. "Fortuna? Seriously?" The superstitions of Ferula, the old bitch, were bound to be the end of a once prestigious coven. That she would name her daughter Fortuna was almost as laughable as Rue's mother naming her Ruin.

"And I'm not stupid." She stabbed her again.

She may not be stupid, but she was a bit overzealous with a blade. "Stab as much as you like, you and I both know that as much as that curse has damned me, it means there is nothing you can do here to be rid of me."

Fortuna's eyes widened as realization struck her. Her eyes narrowed, searching the woods. "Your soul..."

"Is not here at the moment." Rue's laugh turned into a wet cough, filling her mouth with metallic bitterness. "I'm just the casing, though it seems that even empty, I have more power than you do. You could, however, try to change that. Scrounge up whatever is left of this pitiful coven and put me back together... even if only to put me in my place."

Come on. Take the bait.

Fortuna scowled. She twisted the blade as she looked down the end of her nose at Rue. She had a cold authority in her eyes that she didn't earn, but Rue would forgive her the pretense if she could accomplish what she wanted. This bitch could wear whatever mask she wanted, so long as she wore it while she threw Jinx back inside Rue, where she belonged.

Rue held her breath, swallowing the wince that needed to be set free as Fortuna continued to turn the blade. "You'll learn your lesson when I'm ready to teach it."

Disappointment was a bitter taste on her tongue. "What? You don't have it in you to teach it now?" She should have known. Whatever feeble powers the Lumena managed to keep were likely the only thing keeping Ferula alive.

"I will destroy you!" Nothing but empty words. "Drain you of every drop of your magic until you beg me to let you live."

What a waste of her fucking time.

Her blood warmed as she set her hand on Fortuna's chest. A burst of her magic lit the space between them purple before Fortuna was sent flying back into the darkness of the woods.

She disappeared into the shadows, and relief filled Rue as the blade was ripped free. Her hand slid over her belly, barely covering the wounds. She didn't have the strength to heal now, and she couldn't risk borrowing magic from Jinx to do it. Not when she had no idea where she was or what she was up to.

A groan swelled in her throat, but Rue swallowed it down, her eyes glued on the darkness where she knew Fortuna lurked. "You want to be rid of me? Tether me back to my soul and see if you can. Otherwise, I'll just keep coming. And next time I won't just stop at the woods."

The threat was left like a thick fog in the air as Rue turned on her heel and started back to her car. Her feet dragged, fatigue bone deep. Her mouth was a vile concoction of metallic bitterness and disappointment. She spit, trying to rid herself of the taste as she broke out of the trees and got to her car.

They would come for her now, and with Jinx safely hidden inside her magic, there would be nothing they could do so long as they kept the curse as it was. Her mind turned over, calculating.

A demon may deny her the deal she wanted, but she wasn't going to give up. She was going to get tethered back to her soul even if it killed her.

Settled in the driver's seat, she felt the heat of her blood pool in her lap as she started the car and left the woods. If her first meeting with Fortuna was any indication of what the witches in her coven would do to her now that she had found her mate and essentially strengthened her power and her soul, killing her might be exactly what they ended up doing. The weak little witch just needed some time to get her ducks in a row.

Death or this life?

Fuck. Hard call.

A part of her wanted to tell herself she would live just to spite her mother and her coven, but she knew this life was lacking, and she was tired of being nothing more than a shadow of herself. Tired of only feeling the ghosts of what she should.

Tired of Jinx.

Was she tired of Jinx? That thought was a constant knocking at the back of her mind. Some days, when the chaos died down, there was a quiet companionship that almost felt right. A warmth that fed into the hole in her chest, filling her as close as she would ever come to contentment.

It was her loneliness, she reminded herself, that made her want to cling to her curse when she knew Jinx did nothing but torture her.

Her head slumped against the window, but she kept her eyes on the road. Eyes glassed over, she cursed under her breath, annoyed with herself.

She wouldn't cry. Crying accomplished nothing.

There was an ache in her chest that was hard to ignore. An ache knowing Jinx was out there somewhere with the man who was supposed to be hers. That he would love Jinx and that losing her might mar whatever they were fated to have.

Pop!

A puff of black smoke filled the air, and her hand was yanked.

Her car swerved into the middle of the road, tires squealing before she turned the wheel and got back in her lane. She slammed her foot on the brakes, thankful there was no one behind her on the two-lane highway.

Bram squeaked.

"Bram!" Anger boiled her blood as she tried to untangle the fat rat's wing from her hair. "What the fuck?"

He continued his infernal squawking until Rue finally ripped him from her head, ignoring the way her scalp screamed and tossed the bat into the passenger seat. Her chest heaved, the turmoil she felt before instantly replaced with a hot rage only Jinx and the familiar that was hers but wasn't could light in her.

Bram pushed himself back against the door, eyes wide and pointed ears somehow slightly dropped as he folded his wings and looked at her over the top. A braid was still attached to his claw.

Hands wrapped around the wheel, Rue screamed as she threw her weight around in her seat.

As though going against Fortuna and being faced with the mess of her life wasn't enough, she had to deal with this stupid winged rat popping up.

Rue didn't know how much time passed before she finally settled, releasing the wheel and slumping back in her seat. Her throat burned from her screaming as she stared at the roof of her car, emotionally spent.

"I thought familiars were supposed to be helpful," she muttered, sparing the bat a single glance out of her peripheral.

Bram was as he'd been since she tossed him over there.

"Go!" She waved a hand at him. "Shoo! Go back to Jinx, wherever the hell she is." Rue knew just where that hoe would be, but she knew better than to think about it too much. She was in too much pain for whatever pleasure they felt to seep through. "Get out of here."

He stayed where he was, cowering.

"Fine!" Rue yelled before she threw the car in drive and pulled back onto the highway. "Sit there for all I fucking care. You never listened to me before, why the hell should you start now?"

She avoided looking at the bat as she made her way south and back to the city. It was just another relationship that would be ruined when she got what she wanted anyway. Ruined. Because just like her name, that was all she was ever meant to do.

10

KILLIAN

NOTHING BUT THE SOUND of their laboured breath filled the air as they lay in his foyer. The black wood at his back was chilled, and he was thankful for the way it attempted to soothe the fires that threatened to become all he was. He felt the weight of his horns — simple, thick black curves — on his brow, and the tail on his lower back pressed against the floor. His horns felt heavier as a crossroads demon, the tail something he hadn't gotten accustomed to after a century in this form.

Time became something with no meaning. His flesh burned when he wasn't touching Jinx, and every second he spent not seated inside her made him feel like he was slipping into madness. He had lost count of how many times they had taken turns riding each other. Their bodies slicked with sweat, though he still felt like he could go for hours more.

When will it be enough?

Will it ever?

Jinx pushed herself up. Her eyes were wide as purple smoke billowed around her. It stitched her torn clothes, fitting them back to her body as though their time together was nothing more than a dream, as she jumped to her feet.

"Bram!"

Killian jumped to his feet, too, scrambling to find his jeans. When he couldn't see where they'd been thrown, he resigned himself to standing there with his hands cupping himself.

The bat appeared, flapping overhead. It squawked in an irritating way that sounded like a chastisement.

"How mad is she?" Jinx asked.

The bat — Bram — squeaked his reply.

Killian had lost his mind. He'd denied a deal and slept with a witch who was chatting up a bat as though that was a completely normal thing to do. Still, he couldn't keep the panic from inflating his chest as he held his hand out in an attempt to calm her.

One of his mates.

"What's wrong?"

She whirled, eyes on him. The panic melted from her face for a moment, replaced with that mischievous smile that was quickly becoming his weakness. "Wrong? I guess nothing. I mean... if you think about it, she's pretty much *always* mad at me. So really... this is just another Tuesday."

Killian's brows dropped. "It's Friday."

Surprise comically widened her eyes. "We've been having sex for *three* days?"

"No..." He couldn't stifle the chuckle that rose in his chest. "Yesterday was Thursday. It was just the one night." He cleared his throat. She was so chaotic.

Lips pursed, she nodded slowly. "Hmm... are you sure?"

"Pretty sure." He was once again useless before her. He could do nothing but stand there and answer her questions, frozen to reason.

Jinx shrugged before she reached out and grabbed one of the bat's small feet. "Friday. Good to know." She pressed two fingers to her brow, giving him a lazy salute. "I'll be seeing you."

"What?"

The bat flapped its wings, surrounding them in a cloud of smoke and magic, and they were gone.

Killian took a staggered step toward where she had been. He stood in the nothingness as though that would somehow make her appear while his heart hammered in his chest. Longing.

"What the fuck?" He whirled, looking around.

It was as though she had never been there.

The stairs were empty, showing no sign of a night he could already feel changing him. The foyer floor was just as bare.

As much as he enjoyed his solitude, he had never felt more lonely standing in his house alone. With the smell of sunshine and honey in the air, making him salivate.

Killian lifted his fingers, dipping them into his mouth. The ghost of her was still on them, and it teased at his taste buds, nowhere near as flavourful as she had been.

She was gone.

Just like that.

The witch's soul.

This was quite the predicament. To be mated was something he never dreamed of, and if he were being perfectly honest with himself, it was something he would have laughed at had it been promised to him before them. Before the hurricane that blew through his life that was Jinx, leaving nothing but devastation behind. And Rue... his dark cloud.

Settling on a step, he dropped his face into his hands.

Rue was anything but his, and that frustrated him.

She had sought him out at the place where desperation lived. The crossroads where people went when all other hope was lost. If she went to those lengths to be rid of Jinx — to tether them back together — denying her wouldn't earn him any favours.

The chances of him getting in her good graces now were slim. Worse than that, standing in her way and preventing her from getting the only thing she'd ever asked him for would likely build a wall between them that he would never be able to knock down or climb over.

And yet...

He brushed his fingers along his bottom lip, teasing himself with Jinx's scent. His eyes rolled back in his head, saliva thickening in his throat.

He'd have to do just that.

A sigh that felt like it came from the deepest depths of him lifted to inflate his chest with captured frustration. It was the heaviest breath he had ever taken, practically caving in his ribs. Elbows propped on the steps behind him, Killian folded his ankles and leaned against the stairs. He looked down at himself, still slicked with Jinx.

He blew out his breath like smoke, but it did nothing to rid him of any pressure.

Of all the hells he delivered to people, he never dared imagine he'd be responsible for his own. Because that's what falling for Jinx would do. It would damn him to a hell where only a piece of his mate could love him.

A growl rumbled through his chest.

It seemed Fate had found a way to screw him again, only this time she decided to really make it hurt.

11

JINX

SHE WAS IN BIG trouble.

The first ripple of Rue's emotions was enough to startle her awake. The second came with enough magic to fully dress her, which meant she was in for a boob punch the likes of which she had never felt before.

Luckily for her, Bram appeared to take her home. Wait... was that lucky?

The tension in the air when she arrived told her it likely wasn't.

"Rue? My precious, precious girl whom I adore more than life itself." Her voice was sweet syrup meant to catch, but she knew it would do nothing against Rue's ire.

Why did Rue have to be so terrifying?

She was a beast. A wretched thing that could tear her apart with a mere look. That could devour her without even opening her mouth. Her heart — or whatever the hell lived in her chest — beat so hard against her ribs, she was sure one of them cracked as she rounded the corner and looked at Rue.

Rue stood in the kitchen. Her heavy boobs were in the black lace bra Jinx was always trying to steal as she pulled a thread through a hole in her abdomen. The stitched flesh bunched, signs of a job poorly done by shaking hands. Bloody rags and towels covered the counter, next to an open bottle of tequila, as Rue focused on her task, even though there was no way she didn't know Jinx was there. Slippery fingers did their best to keep hold of the needle as she weaved it through thick ribbons of her flesh.

Bram hovered in the air behind Rue. Jinx couldn't tell if she was actually tolerating Bram or if she was just so focused on sewing herself up that she didn't notice him.

Fat chance. Rue noticed everything.

Okay, this was no big deal. So Rue was mad. When the hell wasn't she? All she had to do was reason with her a little bit. Explain to her that if she had to fade away, or be absorbed or whatever the hell was bound to happen to her eventually, she should at least get a few free rides off Killian. That was only fair, right? And fair was fair!

"So, the thing is, if we... I mean, *you*... finally get around to undoing the curse, or whatever, then I will just be gone. And as your soul, he's mine too. Right? No. I mean, he is! So, I just thought—"

"Did you have fun?" Rue muttered.

The sound of her voice made Jinx jump. Her hand flew up, covering her mouth as a yelp escaped her. "Christ, you scared me."

The sound of scissors cutting the thread was deafening in the room. "Do you have any idea what you've done?"

The cold tone of Rue's voice was unlike any Jinx had ever heard. She'd heard Rue speak to her with annoyance, with anger, with sharp hatred, and sometimes, when Jinx was really *really* lucky, she had heard her speak to her with quiet acceptance, but this was something else entirely. It was detached and frigid. It made a shudder move through Jinx as she forced herself to step further into the room. Her hands fidgeted in front of her as she bit down on her bottom lip, thinking.

Change of plans. The only thing she could do was deny everything.

Deny. Deny. Deny.

Lies were her friend.

"Me?" She pointed a finger at her chest. "What could I have done?"

"Do you know why I hate you so much, Jinx?" The eyes that finally looked at her were dark abscesses that bled terror onto her face. They weren't haunting; they were a dark promise to bring about a harm Jinx had never dared to imagine could be delivered.

She swallowed hard as fear stole any reply.

"Because you get to live your life exactly as you want. Free from any burdens or consequences, and me... I get to swallow down the bitter taste of it all. So while you set eyes on the Crossroads demon and decided you had to have him, it was me that got the sharp end of a blade for it." Her hands planted on the kitchen island, and she looked at Jinx, freezing her where she stood.

Jinx was sometimes a nuisance. A thorn in Rue's side. But even when they were at their worst, Rue couldn't despise her because she was hers. There was always something there, deep down in the depths of her eyes, that told Jinx she was safe. Whatever that was had disappeared, been lost somewhere. Bled out on the kitchen floor as she stitched herself up.

A lump formed in Jinx's throat. Her mouth opened, but she couldn't deny everything the way she wanted to, and she couldn't lie to save herself from whatever this was.

Rue's nod was slow. "My curse is one to keep me from becoming an issue with the Lumena coven, so naturally, should something happen that alters my powers, they would have made sure they would know of it. Set little failsafes to let them know when I grow stronger. You've slept with Killian. My... *mate*," she spat the word out as though it was something sour she didn't want to taste for too long. She huffed out an angry breath, but it lacked the strength it usually had. "Sending ripples through whatever toxic waters this curse is meant to drown me in. I should be angry with you, but in a way, you've done me a huge favour."

Jinx sputtered over her words. Her smile was anxious and forced as she cleared her throat. "Me? I did?"

That had to mean she couldn't be mad. A favour was good.

"It seems this curse has run its course. Either the demon will grant my deal and tether us back together so that he doesn't lose us both, or the coven will... even if just to kill me." The rattle of the scissors as Rue tossed them against the granite counter was startling in the silence. Her hard eyes sliced into the already tender parts of Jinx, and she felt the familiar burn build in her eyes as an unforgiving grip wrapped around her throat. "So thanks, I guess. This time, your fuck up will finally serve a purpose."

She didn't like this. Didn't like the way every word spat at her felt like a goodbye.

Jinx jumped as Rue swatted the air above her, sending Bram flying before she stalked from the kitchen, disappearing down the hall.

The slam of her door made Jinx jump again.

Tears swelled in her eyes as she stood there, lost.

"Well, I..."

A sob strangled her, but she forced it down, turning on her heel to stare at the doorway that was now empty.

"Well... he's mine too!" she shouted, knowing Rue wasn't there to answer.

Rude!

She couldn't just be mad because Jinx had gone and gotten a taste of what was hers. Especially not while Rue was constantly threatening to be rid of her. If that meanie succeeded and she was put back in the casing of Rue's flesh, she deserved to at least get her rocks off once. To ride the dick that was meant to be hers until stars shone behind her eyes and she got a glimpse at paradise.

The corner of her mouth curved up at the memory.

Hell, he sure was paradise. Demons did it better; no one could tell her any different. She knew now. Knew just why people tried to scare others away from demons. Because they wanted all that good pipe for themselves.

Bram fluttered up from the floor and slumped onto the counter. *'You shouldn't poke at her so much. The two of you are supposed to be harmonious. Always being at odds isn't beneficial to either of you.'* He tried to fly, slumping back down and deciding better of it.

"Ah! Bram. Baby cakes!" Jinx ran over, pulling the bat into her chest. "Did that mean old Rue hurt you?"

Bram, the beloved beastie he was, pressed his cheek into hers. Affectionate little thing. *'I'm meant to be her aide, even if all I can do is be an outlet for her anger.'*

"That doesn't seem fair." It felt like Bram got the other end of her short stick.

'Life is not fair for her, why should it be fair for her familiar?'

Her eyes dropped to the rags, bandages, and other first aid supplies scattered over the counter. She shouldn't care about what Rue had been up to. She was probably plotting to be rid of her, so serve her right... whatever happened.

Lips pursed, she pulled the bat away, looking into his beady black eyes. Rue often thought Bram was Jinx's alone, but he was drawn to them both in equal measure. The only reason he stuck to Jinx's side was because she didn't slap him away whenever he got close. If something happened to Rue, he would know.

Guilt wormed its way through her belly, making it shift uncomfortably despite her best efforts.

"Was it bad?"

'It wasn't good. Ferula, the priestess of Lumena, is at Death's door, and her heir is determined to finish the job her mother didn't.'

"The coven?" Her brows dropped. "Why would she go there?"

'Your mating with Killian has set off waves that can't be ignored. The coven knew, and Rue paid the price of their knowing,' Bram replied.

She rolled her eyes. "She doesn't always have to be a martyr."

'You didn't have to make her one,' her not-so-little bat lightly chastised. *'Would it kill you to try not to agitate her?'*

Why was no one on her side? He was supposed to agree with her because being with Killian made her happy. She deserved to be happy. No matter what it costs her.

But it hadn't cost her anything; it had cost Rue.

"Ugh, this is frustrating!"

'Now, imagine how frustrating it must seem for the person who got stabbed.'

Her brows wagged. "Oh, I got stabbed."

He huffed a tired squeak. *'With a knife, Jinx.'*

She hated it when Bram did this. When he made her feel guilty for Rue's moods. She avoided his gaze, sinking onto the stool and crossing her arms with a huff.

Rue going back to Lumena was a big deal... she would admit that at least. It seemed like, for as long as Jinx existed, Rue had been hiding from them. Plotting, but keeping her distance. To just go back meant... Jinx wasn't sure what it meant. Not really.

"So... she wasn't just being dramatic?" It felt like everything Rue did served no other purpose than to complain. Of course, Jinx would think this was no different. Rue didn't want Jinx to have Killian because Killian didn't do what she wanted. It was Rue's nature to lash out. To spread her misery like seeds that would bloom into wretched blossoms of sorrow and grief later.

Such a downer.

Seems that wasn't all it was.

'No. If anything, I would say she underreacted.'

"Well... shoot."

Still... Jinx would do it all again if she could.

Her worrying was short-lived, and that was wonderful, because it really didn't suit her.

Shoving the rags to the end of the island, she kicked open the trash and pushed it all in. She couldn't bother herself with whatever was going on. Whatever battles came, they were Rue's to fight. Such was her curse. And Jinx, well, she was there for all the fun.

Damn the consequences.

12

JINX

HOURS PASSED, AND RUE hadn't emerged from her room. Jinx had even cooked, hoping the smell of her cou cou and macaroni pie would be enough to bring Rue wandering down the hall. She would usually scowl her way through a meal, eating her fill, but couldn't deny herself food.

Jinx ended up eating alone, filling the silence with weighted sighs.

So she slept with Killian and brought the wrath of the coven to their doorstep. Big freaking whoop. Jinx rolled her eyes for the millionth time.

She took her time cleaning, even moved some furniture around, but boredom gave her way too much time to think. She hated how loud her thoughts were when she didn't constantly interrupt them. Before she knew it, she was upstairs.

Night was a time when she was restless. She didn't need as much sleep as Rue, and though she wasn't worried, something in the pit of her stomach made her uneasy.

"I'm not worried," she whispered as she paced the hall outside Rue's bedroom. "It's not my problem. What's the point of being one of the strongest witches there is if you're going to fret about every little thing? If you ask me, Rue is cursed because she's so damn miserable. Yeah..."

She pressed her brow against the door. The smell of blood and rosemary wafted through the door, and Jinx inhaled it. Rue's smell always did something to her. It burrowed deep in her chest and made her feel...

Just *feel.*

It ripped away the carefree nature she wore like skin and made her something darker. Something that felt like it better belonged to Rue. When that scent hit her like a punch to the chest, it was like they were whipped together. Jinx overlapped with Rue, settling almost where she belonged.

She hated how comforting it was. Hated how much she longed for the discomfort of almost being a part of Rue.

Creak!

The loose floorboard in the hallway downstairs whined. She'd know the sound anywhere because it was one that usually sent Rue into a rage... well, when she wasn't in one already. Jinx was always careful to avoid that board when she was up late. Rue came down swinging without even waiting for Jinx to tell her why she was up. After the hundredth or so boob punch, it was better to just be cautious.

Her hands instinctively wrapped around her boobs as she stood at the top of the stairs and stared down into the darkness.

"Hello?"

Was Rue angry enough to use her magic to avoid her? Maybe she went down for some food. She made good cou cou. Even the evilest of witches wouldn't be able to deny that scent.

Jinx took the steps two at a time, giddiness filling her. If Rue was down there, she could apologize and get her to stop looking at her with that stare that cut her open and made her feel weird. Then, when all was well and good — or as good as things could get with Rue — she could sneak off to Killian's and do this song and dance all over again.

Better to ask for forgiveness than sorries or... something. She didn't really remember how the saying went.

"What a fucking rip-off. I go through all the trouble of breaking into a witch's house, the least I could get for my efforts is a bit of pain." A mysterious woman stood in the living room. Her lips vibrated together as she rolled her eyes. "I mean... honestly."

She smelt of death and roses. Of damned grave soil and something in full bloom. Jinx lifted her face, inhaling the air. This woman wasn't a witch; she was something else. Something volatile.

How exciting!

The woman took another slow look around. "How boring."

That was exactly the opposite of how Jinx felt. This was a far cry from boring.

"Very boring indeed," the woman complained.

She was dark and beautiful. Her hair was an array of tightly coiled dark curls around her head. It made Jinx want to walk farther. She wanted to see just what this little trespasser looked like. They had never had someone wander into their home before.

The woman held her hands out at her sides and brushed what very few decor items Jinx managed to sneak in off the table as she passed.

"Hello?" She had to say something. Every crash was a siren that would bring Rue barrelling in, and she wasn't sure if she wanted her counterpart to interrupt the fun before it began.

A squeak came from the kitchen.

"Bram? Is that you?"

How did he get down there? He didn't like it when Rue and Jinx were at odds. The cute little beast. It made her momentarily forget about the beautiful stranger as she strutted forward.

"You know I detest when you throw these little fits, my adorable little—" her words faded as her eyes widened and she stared at the woman in her midst.

She stood with ruin at her feet. Broken glass crunched under her knee-high leather boots as she met Jinx's wide gaze and pushed yet another one of Rue's whiskey glasses off the drink cart.

"You're not Bram." She knew that, and yet she had nothing else to stay. Something about the woman called to her. A dark chaos that billowed off her like expensive perfume.

Yes. She was going to be very fun.

The woman pulled a knife from the holster attached to her thigh and flipped it in the air, catching it by the blade. "Nope."

Jinx looked around the room behind her interesting intruder. "Have you seen him?"

Brow cocked, she shook her head slowly. "No."

"Hmm... are you sure? He's usually around here somewhere."

"Hold that thought." The woman pulled her phone out of her back pocket, tapping at the screen.

What was she doing?

Girlfight by *Brooke Valentine* started playing as a slow grin pulled at the woman's lips.

A knot creased the flesh between Jinx's brows before her shoulders lifted in the barest of shrugs, and she started shimmying to the beat. Her fisted hands shook in front of her chest as her hips made the layers of her skirts sway. She hadn't really been in the mood to dance, but this song was a hard one to stay still to.

If only Rue were this fun. Random dance parties in the middle of the night would make her cursed life worth living.

The woman swayed her own hips, eyes narrowed. Every move seemed angry, like she was trying to dance away all her burdens.

Couldn't she do that in her own home? The floor plan in here did not scream Dance Party.

"Stop it!" the woman hissed.

Hands above her head, Jinx jumped in place. "Stop what?"

"Stop dancing!"

Aw man, this one was bossy, too. How disappointing. "But... you're dancing."

"Yeah... it's my thing."

Jinx's brows dropped. Dancing couldn't *just* be this woman's thing. Maybe it was her thing too. Did she have a thing? Well... now she did. "Well, this is my house so..."

"So what?"

"So, I'm going to dance. Plus, you don't know me. Maybe dancing is *my* thing!"

How rude. Coming into their house and telling her not to dance. Who did she think she was?

Jinx leaned forward and shimmied her heavy bust at the dancing woman. She was going to show her dancing could be her thing, too! Jinx turned and started shaking her ass.

If this were a battle, she was going to win!

She whirled when she felt the force of Rue's magic. It made the hairs on her arms stand on end, and a shiver ran up the back of her neck. A knife stuck in the air between them, the tip pointed right before her brows, sending puffs of purple smoke between them.

'Jinx!' Bram screeched. His wings created a breeze in the air strong enough to blow at the woman's curls as his adorable little feet wrapped around the handle of the knife. He pulled it from its lodged spot, crossed through the threshold of Rue's magic and dropped it into Jinx's hands.

"That wasn't very nice," Jinx sulked. She looked down at the blade in her hand like it was something that merely hurt her feelings instead of something meant to kill her. With Rue's magic surging through her veins, all it *could* do was hurt her feelings. But that didn't mean it didn't sting.

Why was everyone being so mean?

Bram flew behind her. His feet sank into the doorframe above Jinx's head as he kept a watchful eye on the woman Jinx now knew meant to do her harm.

"I should hope not, I'm here to kill you!" the woman hissed.

"Me? Why?" She pouted, saddened by her admission. No good time came for free.

"Dex." The name buzzed in the space between them. The venom in this woman's eyes told her she was supposed to know who that was, but for the life of her, it meant nothing. Rue was better with names. Maybe if she weren't in her room sulking, she would know why this beautiful woman was suddenly trying to kill her.

Rue really did ruin everything.

"Who?"

The woman lunged.

A yelp escaped Jinx as she shrank back, her hands opening before her. Bram screeched, his claws sinking into the flesh of her shoulders, trying to pull her away. All she could do was swat at the woman, trying to whack her. She wasn't sure if Rue's magic could protect her from everything or just the things that could be fatal.

Her irritation bloomed. "Get her, Bram!"

She didn't like this. She would much prefer dancing instead of potentially fighting for her life.

The woman hissed at her, teeth bared like a wild thing. Her canines were longer than they should be, and suddenly Jinx feared being bitten. Would this woman break into her house and bite her? She didn't smell like a vampire, so what the hell was her *dance battle losing* deal?

'I'm trying!' Bram squeaked. The sound was distressed as the woman wrapped her hands around his little leg.

Anger boiled Jinx's blood. No one touched Bram! Well... aside from Rue. "Hey! Bram! Don't you hurt him, you... you..." she struggled over her words.

Bram disappeared in a puff of smoke before he appeared behind Jinx. He squeaked, watching the mysterious woman with newfound caution. *'Be careful, Jinx. This one is powerful.'*

"What?" She gasped. "Truly?"

Bram flew a little further away from the intruder. *'We should let Rue handle this.'*

It was hard to miss the look on this woman's face. It was a look people often directed at her. One where they judged her and tried to figure her out. Pfft, she didn't need this woman to figure her out. This mean woman attacked cute little bats and didn't let people dance. She was officially on Jinx's shit list.

She wasn't about to call for Rue, not while she was in the middle of being pissy.

"What do you want?" Jinx crossed my arms, thankful for the magical barrier that separated her from this maniac.

"I'm here for the witch that cursed Dex. You."

Curse? Despite being the soul of one of the most powerful witches in this world, there was no way for her to curse anyone. Even though right now she wished she could. "Not me."

Anger made the muscles in the woman's jaw flex. "What do you mean, *not you*?"

"Well, I guess I am in a way, but not really. That was way before my time... well, kind of. I mean, I was there, but not there as I am now. You know?" It was a tricky thing to explain.

"Aren't you the witch?" And clearly, she'd done a bad job because the woman had no idea what Jinx meant.

"The witch," Jinx scoffed and rolled her eyes. "That sounds so dreadful, doesn't it? A bit rude too. That's like me asking you if you're the halfbreed." Jinx could smell it on her. The clouds of power clashed, creating a chaotic storm inside this woman.

"I am," she retorted.

This woman was a tad prickly, but Jinx was used to being pricked. "I'm Jinx."

"I don't care. You're going to restore the curse you placed on Dex, or I'm going to devour your soul."

A long sigh left Jinx as she dropped her head slightly. "Well, that does put us in a bit of a pinch."

She took a threatening step toward Jinx. "The only one here going to be in a pinch is you, witch."

Jinx sighed again. "I'm not *that* witch exactly." Man, this woman really didn't listen.

"Liar! If you didn't curse Dex, who did?"

"That would be me." Rue appeared in the doorway behind the woman. Jinx's mouth gaped. She hadn't cooled since she'd seen her last. Her eyes dripped menace, and she looked ready to wreak all kinds of havoc. Her only hope was that Rue would point it at this woman instead of her. She didn't wait. The woman's feet came off the ground as magic flew at her and sent her through the far wall.

Well, not so much through. More into. She was lodged in the wall as she spat dust and debris from her lips.

Jinx's eyes moved back and forth between the two women. Yikes on bikes, it was hard not to feel small with all the power thickening the air. The woman swiped a thumb over her bottom lip, her eyes honed on Rue as she stalked in.

"Be careful, Rue," Jinx whispered, Bram hovering at her shoulder.

Rue's hands rotated in the air before her, purple smoke dancing between them that lit up her eyes. "Don't worry about me, Jinx."

It was hard not to worry a little. Especially knowing almost all Rue's power was wrapped around her like a protective blanket. If something happened to Rue, what would she do? Anxiety clawed at her. "But I—"

"Just stay out of the way," Rue interrupted.

Jinx huffed like a petulant child as the woman lunged at Rue.

The intruder laughed. The sound was maniacal. She wrapped her legs around Rue's waist, Rue's back pressed against her stomach as her arms roped around Rue's throat.

"Put back the curse," the intruder hissed against Rue's cheek.

Magic shot from Rue's hands.

Jinx's heart was lodged in her throat. Of all the foes she'd forced Rue to go up against, none seemed as strong as this one. She sweat power. Her pores opened and filled the air with something she could barely breathe through. It fogged her mind, blurring her senses. She felt drunk off it.

"What curse?" Rue hissed through her teeth.

"Dex's curse."

Who the fuck was Dex? Jinx shook her hands anxiously at her sides, wishing with everything she was that she knew.

"The zombie?" Disbelief made Rue's voice sound high, even as the woman's arm tightened and cut off her airways. "I can't."

Zombie? ZOMBIE!

How could she forget? Dex was the Duke who set everything with the coven in motion. The greedy man who used Rue's magic in a way that cost her everything and paid the price for it. Although if it had been up to Jinx, she wouldn't have turned him into an eternal undead monster. She probably would have done something a bit meaner. Something where he couldn't just carry on.

So he had to eat flesh now and then... or a lot. Big freaking whoop. How much trouble could that really cause him? Probably not as much as Rue being untethered from her soul, but that kind of worked in Jinx's favour.

"You will!" she warned.

"Or else what?"

"Rue!" Something didn't feel right.

The woman's fangs lengthened. "I've never been one to ask twice, witch."

"And yet you will. I can smell him on you. The scent of death is wrapped around you so tightly, I can smell nothing else."

Humour stretched the woman's smile. She looked unhinged. "That smell of death is completely my own."

She bit her! Jinx's mouth gaped. The woman fucking bit Rue. Like... with her teeth. Just chomped her neck like a rabid beast.

Rue gasped. Her hands reached up, still coated in magic as they scrambled for purchase, trying to grab hold of the woman and wrench her off. All she could do was grab onto her arm.

The woman's brow furrowed, confusion lighting her features.

"Let go! Bad half-breed!" Jinx had to do something. This woman was latched onto Rue's neck. Panic surged through Jinx as she ran at her, wrapped her hands in the back of her hair and pulled.

The intruder landed hard on her side, confusion clear on her face as she moved her tongue around her mouth and tried to make sense of it. "What the fuck?"

Rue's hand clasped her neck, her footing wavering. Her eyes were still alight with magic as she scowled down at her. "Tough luck, devourer."

"Listen," Jinx tried her best to keep her voice firm. "You've broken into our house, left a big hole in our wall, and bit Rue. I think that's more than enough for today. Why don't we all just take a breath and sit on all this for a night or two and reconvene in a few days?" Jinx hummed thoughtfully, ignoring the way they growled at one another. "Maybe a week? How long do you think it would take to fix up this wall?"

The woman scowled, grabbing Jinx's leg.

Jinx hit the floor hard, all the air whooshing violently from her lungs. She wheezed, thoughts of death dancing in her head like stars. She had to be dying. This was death. Jinx scrambled, struggling to suck air into her lungs, her foot kicking out as she dug her nails into the floor.

Oh fuck. This crazy woman was going to bite her. With her big teeth.

"Rue!" Jinx rasped.

"Let go!" Rue leapt forward.

"You have your own curse, don't you, witch? One of your own making." Knowing deepened the woman's eyes. There was something there Jinx didn't understand. She never bothered with things that deep. With thoughts that transformed people as she looked at them.

Rue's eyes widened as her magic flickered in her hands. "Get away from her."

"Put back the curse!" she warned.

Jinx tried to kick her grasp free. It was no use; she had already sunk her claws into her. "Let go! Rue! Bram!" Somebody needed to do *something*!

Bram returned, his feet wrapped around Jinx's shoulders as he tried to pull her away.

Her fangs lengthened.

This woman was terrifying. She was a hunter. A monster. Villainous. Her mouth opened as she pulled Jinx closer, her neck just within reach.

"No!" Rue's magic exploded in the room.

13

RUE

THE SMELL OF DEATH called to her. It was tantalizing. Something she craved even though she knew she would never be able to taste it. She wasn't someone Death could claim anymore. Not someone a reaper could deliver... that didn't mean she didn't know the smell.

A reaper was in her house.

Her anger still burned in her chest, but she surrendered some of it to figure out what new hell Jinx had thrown them into. What else could her curse possibly do to her at this point?

The thought had only stoked the flames of her ire when she heard Jinx talking to the woman. The reaper who wasn't a reaper. She was that and something else. Something... tempting.

Succubus.

The thought paused her steps. Froze her on the other side of the doorway. This was a creature of the most vile concoction. The allure of a succubus with the waiting hands of a reaper. No... magic didn't blend the way many thought it would. It was unpredictable. Wild. Vindictive. The beast who spoke to Jinx in the other room would be a wretched blend of both.

Half-breeds usually were.

It was a curse all its own.

Dex was a name she didn't think she would hear again. It had been lifetimes since she saw him last. Duke DuTuerie. The greedy man who thought he could have magic for free. A mortal soul who thought his ambition was enough to save him from the cost of magic. The man who thought he had been victorious when he pricked that pin through her chest and stole her blood. The blood of a witch. Blood he believed he needed to turn all his family owned into his and his alone.

He harnessed her blood and used it as a weapon.

Marking her.

The final black mark that brought forth her curse.

He had used her blood to kill his brother and his brother's wife. All so that he alone could be the heir to whatever silly life they thought was worth the damning of Rue's soul.

'The blood of the unborn Crowe witch will bring death, spread it through the mortals like plague, and so shall be the beginning of the end of the Lumena Coven.'

The hands of that greedy duke had sealed her prophecy.

Dex DuTuerie.

Rue grinned to herself as she brushed debris off her drink cart before she pulled the moonstone topper from the top of an amber bottle in an obscure shape and poured herself a drink. This wasn't mortal spirits. This was something strong enough to shake her foundations and blur memories that had been branded into her mind. As much a punishment as her curse.

"Rue..." Jinx's voice was shaky behind her. "What's happening? Who was that?"

If she were going to guess, it was the lover of the man she cursed all that time ago. A man who, thanks to Jinx and her lack of forethought, was now human.

Thoughts of the woman who bit her returned. She had been right. She felt the aftereffects of reaper magic under her flesh even now. It sought a soul that wasn't there but not to deliver — to devour.

A humourless chuckle left her.

Someone as powerful as her knew the feel of magic under her skin. She felt the pull of succubus magic as it tried to lull her into complacency. A venom that should have relaxed her and filled her with endless lust, but only rose her hackles.

Interesting.

A reaper who devoured souls instead of delivering them. A succubus who took more pleasure than she gave. What an anomaly.

A human lover would be a dead lover. The removal of the curse that turned Dex DeTuerie into a zombie — a man destined to live a soulless eternity needing the taste of flesh as desperately as he once needed all the things that fuelled his greed — would mean the woman who left their house in such disarray could no longer have him.

Fuck, Rue knew what that felt like.

Rue rested the glass on her bottom lip, eyes glued to the missing chip on the opposite side as she poured it down her throat. She liked the way it burned. It ignited her belly before it sent shivers through her. Hopefully, it was worth what she paid for it. She wanted to feel nothing for a little while. Nothing was better than all this.

"You're hurt," Jinx whispered.

Bram hovered somewhere overhead, the flap of his wings shifting her baby hairs.

"Should you... set a ward?"

"Nothing can keep death from entering," Rue huffed the words out before she picked up the bottle and poured herself another glass.

"Death?"

"She's a reaper... half of one anyway," Rue answered.

"A reaper?" Jinx slumped onto the couch, a faraway look in her eyes. "And Dex? What do you think happened to him?"

Drip. Drip. Drip.

Rue looked down, watching her blood splatter against the brushed gold cart as it dripped from the wound on her neck. She'd already put all the first aid stuff away, and hauling it all out seemed like such a task. Not for the first time, she wished Jinx were gone. That she was once again inside the casing of her flesh so she could just heal her wounds and be done with all this.

Done with the Lumena Coven.

Done with homicidal hybrids.

Done with mates.

How she would curl into the arms of loneliness if it meant she could be done with everything else. She tossed the second drink back.

"Rue? Do you think when you saved me on the beach, we did something to him? We must have, right? I mean... why else would she come here?"

Bram perched on a shelf close to where Rue stood, his beady eyes watching her. What the hell he was doing by her instead of hovering next to her soul on the couch was beyond her. Usually, the familiar didn't give her the time of day.

"Rue."

She slammed the glass down, ignoring the slice of broken shards in her palm. What was one more? She'd been stabbed by the heir of the Lumena Coven. Fortuna... what a ridiculous fucking name for those power leeches. She'd been bitten by a still unnamed hybrid. The throbs of lust still pulsed under her skin, light, but they made some of these wounds more bearable. After all that, her palm was nothing.

"Rue. Are you even listening to me?"

"Will you shut up?" Rue snapped. "I just want one fucking day where I don't have to hear you nagging at me. Souls are supposed to be these wise things. Surely you can cross some of the *T*s and dot some fucking *I*s on your own." She shook the shards from her palm before she grabbed a cloth, angrily whipping it out, and pressed it to her neck.

"Stop yelling at me! I'm the one who got attacked!" Jinx whimpered, her bottom lip quivering. "She just came in here and told me I couldn't dance and then tried to knife me." She sniffled, tears pooling on her lids.

Rue's eyes rolled so hard that it made her wince when something pulled in her wounded neck.

"I should go see Killian," Jinx pouted. "At least he would care that this happened to me. He would go all demon with fiery horns and flames! All sexy and all that..."

"He's a crossroads demon. They're not very high on the hierarchy, but by all means, go and see if he can protect you from whatever fresh hell you decide to bring to his day-to-day, Jinx." Rue didn't have the energy to placate Jinx. She didn't have the will anymore. Saving her. Preparing herself for all the chaos she brought. Wanting nothing more than to tether them back together so she could be free — so she could be herself once more — only to have Jinx thwart the process at every opportunity.

All of that was about to end.

If she wasn't killed by Ferula's death imbuing her wretched daughter with the power of the Lumena, then the hybrid would kill her.

Death may be her only escape now.

Maybe it was time for just that.

An immortal life wasn't all it was cracked up to be. Even if she was tethered back to Jinx, she had no idea what having her soul would mean now. She could no longer go back to the woman she was before Dex. Before they were both cursed. She would be the same miserable witch this curse had made her — the only difference would be she would suddenly have one less person constantly nipping at her. Perhaps now, her soul wouldn't even fit right anymore. Jinx had grown to be too big. That would be just her luck.

"Maybe I will!" Jinx threatened, only it felt like something Rue would wish for instead of feel threatened by.

Rue fell into a chair, bleeding all over the furniture. "Go."

"You never used to be this way. Back before..."

"You never knew me before."

"Didn't I? I always knew you, Rue. I was—"

"Just go." Her voice lacked the venom it usually did when she snapped at Jinx.

"I..." she whimpered.

The look of Jinx like this, vulnerable with her emotions on display, always rubbed Rue the wrong way. Jinx felt everything all the time, without restrictions. She didn't even have the decency to go and be all dramatic in her room. She had to sit there, staring at Rue while she cried. Forcing her to watch. To participate.

"I don't know how." Jinx waved her hands. "To go to him or whatever."

Completely sapped, Rue couldn't even summon the energy she needed to be annoyed. Her hand lifted, blood darkening the space between her fingers and around her nailbeds. The purple that surrounded her hand was the only comfort she knew. It pushed everything to the back of her mind, warming her chest as she flicked a hand, and Jinx disappeared.

Thank whatever gods still watched the sorry story of her life, that she still had enough magic to accomplish the little things.

Bram squeaked. He flew over to where Jinx had been before he settled into her spot. His silence irritated her. Bram used to have so much to say to her... once upon a time.

"What? You're not going to follow her?" A pity party was coming on; she felt the way it made her bones feel heavy and her chest hollow. An exhale deflated her before she felt warmth pool on her stomach. A hand swiped, coming away red, and she sighed. Rue flicked her fingers, sending droplets of blood everywhere. "Usually, you two are attached at the hip."

He squeaked again, and she sighed, slumping lower as her vision wavered at the edges. Squeaks were all he gave her these days, saving all his conversation for Jinx because he was hers. Just like Killian was hers. Her life — it stopped being Rue's a long time ago.

Eyes closed and full of self-loathing, she surrendered to the dark.

14

KILLIAN

His brow creased as he flipped another page. He'd spent hours pacing his library searching for answers.

Rue spoke of a curse as though it were an anchor wrapped around her waist, slowly pulling her down into the depths of her despair, but no matter how many books he read, he couldn't find one that fit.

A soul could be removed. Stripped out of its casing to punish someone, but he'd never thought about where it went. So often it just... disappeared. Held hostage somewhere, maybe, he really didn't know. But to have a soul made real. Sentient. Completely separate. He'd never heard of a curse that even came close.

And yet... Rue was desperate to undo a curse she claimed did just that.

How much power did the Lumena witches hold to accomplish something that no one else had ever done or written about? Surely, power like that was documented somewhere.

"Sweet Lucifer!" He jumped as Jinx appeared in front of him in a puff of smoke. Coffee splashed from his mug as he was forced to step back to avoid crushing her. She was squatting on the large Persian rug in the middle of his library, her arms wrapped around her legs as she rocked and looked up at him. The book about curses he'd been studying toppled to the floor, narrowly missing her. Black smeared down her cheeks, and snot pooled on her upper lip as her head fell back and she let out a wail.

Her forearm dragged under her nose as her lips pouted. She was a mess.

"Jinx." In a squat, he ran gentle circles over her back. "What happened? What's wrong?"

"Shealwaysblamesmeforeverythinganditsnotmyfaultbe-causeshewastheone..." her words all blurred together as she wailed.

"What?" He tried to decipher the words pouring out of her. "Who always blames you for everything?

"Rue!" she shrieked.

Killian pulled her in, holding her tightly against his chest before he lifted her into his arms. Coffee mug abandoned on the floor, he carried her to the couch and settled with her on his lap. Her whole body shook, making his heart ache as that familiar pull was tugged with every sob. He tightened his hold, doing what he could to hold her together.

"It's not my fault, you know. She was the one who was all miserable just because she was stabbed or whatever. I had nothing to do with that. She decided to go confront the priestess all on her own!" Jinx complained.

Everything in him tensed. Fear was a sledgehammer that took vicious swings at his stomach, and he could do nothing but force himself to breathe around the blows. "What?" He held Jinx at arm's length, trying to garner her attention. "What happened to Rue?"

Jinx grabbed his arm, wiping her nose on his sleeve. "She was stabbed by the priestess of Lumena, I think. Or maybe she wasn't the priestess? I forget now. Oh... and bit."

"The priestess *bit* her?"

"No. That was the hybrid." Jinx gave him a weird look. "Aren't you listening to me?"

He was trying but quickly learning it was almost impossible to understand Jinx at the best of times, and this was clearly not one of the best of times. "I am," he assured her.

"You're not." She wrapped her hands around his face, pulling him toward her. Her watery eyes bore into his, commanding his focus. "Rue went to confront the priestess of the Lumena coven, who cursed us with our untethering, hoping she could make them mad enough or something to tether us back together. Only she stabbed Rue. Bloody mess, the whole thing. All these cloths everywhere... she didn't even clean them up. And she was so mean to me after. Like it was *my* fault... but I didn't stab her. It's been forever since I stabbed her... so that wasn't really fair."

His heart hammered. "Rue was stabbed."

"Mhmm. And then she just iced me out. She gets mad at me all the time, but she never just ices me out like that... but she said it was my fault. Because if we didn't have sex, then the coven wouldn't know she found her mate, and they wouldn't be after her... well, us, I guess. But like... how was I supposed to know? She never tells me anything! And she's mad because if I didn't try to make her have sex with a goblin, then she wouldn't have had to call back all her magic to keep me from dying... us... because if I die, then she dies. And if she didn't call back all her magic, then Dex would still be cursed, and that crazy woman wouldn't have told me I couldn't dance before trying to stab me and biting Rue. And she even hit Bram! Could you imagine? The fucking nerve on that one!"

"What?" A confusion the likes of which he had never felt before strangled him. A throbbing started at his temple as the vicious thoughts he tried to hide away threatened to be heard.

"Yeah!" She nodded, fresh tears falling. "Like a big chunk. Right out of her neck like some beast or something."

Killian ran his hands over the shaved sides of his head. He scraped his nails through the short hair, marvelling at the feeling against his scalp. It calmed the storm brewing inside him, however so slightly. He felt a pull to this woman in his lap, but even as enthralled with her as he was, it was hard to deny that a lot of this sounded like her fault.

"Jinx... where is Rue?"

"Home." She sniffled again. "She just kind of... waved me off. I've never seen her like that before. So..."

"So what?" He was desperate to know.

"Mean!"

Hard to say he wouldn't be mean in her position. He was torn between wanting to do everything he could to comfort the woman he held onto now and going to see the one who was left in pieces alone.

"You're a demon! Can't you heal her?" Jinx looked at him with wide eyes, her grief dampened slightly by her building excitement at the idea.

His head shake was slow. "No. Unfortunately, I can only heal myself."

She pouted. "Really? You know, before Rue had to pull back her magic, she could heal so quickly. I'd blink, and whatever happened would be gone. Cuts, scrapes... even that time my bone was sticking out of my leg!"

"Bone?" Sweet Lucifer, what the hell did these women get up to?

This was a lot of information to sort through, especially when Jinx was the one giving it. With a deep breath, he resumed rubbing soothing shapes on Jinx's back as his mind worked.

The Lumena Coven was infamous. Sure, he didn't hear about them as often anymore, but there was a time when one couldn't mention witches without the Lumena Coven. They were to witchcraft what Lucifer was to the Dark Realm. They went hand in hand. That these witches were part of that coven stalled him.

But, she'd also said the priestess was out for blood. Rue's.

Why?

His eyes dropped to Jinx's face, tracing the lines and the wrinkles in her chin as her lip trembled. She wouldn't be a reliable source.

He had to speak with Rue. That thought made knots tighten in his belly. She hadn't seemed overly happy with him the last time they met. If sleeping with Jinx had set off a series of unfortunate events for her, he doubted she would be any happier to see him now.

Fuck.

He had royally screwed up this being a mate thing.

Somehow, he had only mated with half. Mated with his mate's soul while her body detested him.

Fuck. Fuck. Fuck.

On his feet, he clutched Jinx to his chest.

"What are you doing?" she asked.

"We have to go see Rue." His fires surrounded them, taking him to the other piece of his mate.

His heart pounded anxiously as he clutched Jinx to his chest, looking at the wreckage of their living room. There was a hole in the wall large enough for him to fit inside. Glass was scattered over the floor, and a lamp flickered behind a deep green couch, making the scene look infinitely more ominous.

Despite her protesting, Killian set Jinx on her feet. She pouted, arms crossed over her chest as she stomped a foot.

Bram was perched on the top of a high-backed chair in the same shade of the couch that, as he walked further into the room, he noticed was shifted from where it was supposed to be. One side off the carpet.

"What the fuck happened here?"

"I already told you." Jinx was impatient. She didn't like repeating herself.

His eyes were glued to Rue, who was slumped in the chair Bram perched on. There were dark hollows under her eyes, her flesh sallow. Blood splattered her jawline and dripped onto the floor under the chair. His feet moved without his permission. The desperation in his chest was a balloon that kept inflating until nothing else could exist in the cage of his ribs. He dropped to his knees, hands skimming over her as he sought out every wound.

"Jinx, do you have supplies?"

She scoffed, rolling her eyes. "She's fine. She can't die!"

His lips pursed. It bothered him that Jinx didn't care. How could a soul lack empathy? "Jinx. Supplies. Now."

Jinx huffed. "Fine."

She was a petulant thing, and as he stared at the state of Rue, it suddenly became apparent why she could detest her counterpart so much. He found himself unhappy with how she was behaving.

"Quickly," he said more firmly.

"I said fine!" she snapped. "Ugh!"

Banging sounded behind him as Jinx managed to open and slam every cupboard in the kitchen before she slowly trodded over, thrusting the tackle box at him. He opened it, hitting her with a disapproving glare before he searched through the supplies.

Rue was so still.

Jinx said she couldn't die, but the hue of her skin made him fear she was wrong. Shaky hands hovered by her face before he gently tilted her head. He brushed the handful of white braids back from her face, uncovering her neck. The wound was vicious. Flaps of skin barely held on, baring the sinew and muscle beneath. Blood steadily streamed from the wound, pooling in the neckline of her dark shirt.

"Fuck," he hissed.

"Yikes," Jinx whispered, leaning over his shoulder. "Still not the worst wound I've seen."

"You can't be serious?" His anger burned bright. He didn't know who the hell did this, but he was going to make them pay. He was going to drag them down into the darkest parts of the Dark Realm and make them beg for the chance for penance.

Unable to properly see all her wounds, Killian resigned himself to lifting her from the chair. If she woke in his arms, she was going to show him the point of her anger; he didn't doubt that, but that was something he would risk to try to piece her back together. The feel of her in his arms was so right it tightened his throat, and his eyes blurred. He felt like he was created to hold this woman, and being able to do it now, while the metallic scent of blood wafted off her like an overly used perfume, fractured parts of him into pieces.

It broke him.

"Where is her room?" he forced out.

Jinx's eyes widened. "Well… it's upstairs, but she doesn't let anyone go in there. Not even me."

"Show me."

Her bottom lip pulled into her teeth as she tugged at the fabric of her sleeve. "I can show you, but if she wakes up, you have to tell her it was all your idea." Her hands cupped her breasts. "She hits hard."

"Fine." It was an easy thing for him to agree to. He would gladly take whatever strikes Rue threw at him if he could only patch her up. "Show me."

Jinx turned on her heel, prancing before him. She led the way, Bram following behind them, his squeaks filling the silence. "I know! But he doesn't listen, so what am I to do? He won't just leave her down there."

Bram squeaked some more.

"Well... that's going to be his problem. Look at him, though, I'm sure he can handle her. Not that she deserves it..."

"Can Rue also speak to the bat?"

"Bram?" Jinx looked over her shoulder with a grin as she paused before a door. Her hand tightened on the knob, and he could sense her hesitation. She wanted to stop to answer, not because she wanted to give him clarity, but because it would prolong their journey and keep them from entering a room she had all been banished from.

Her lips pursed as she turned, pressing her back against the door with a slow nod.

She lifted her shoulders, and sadness deepened her eyes for a split second before it was gone. There was more to Jinx. Something hidden there she didn't let anyone see. "He was her familiar, and they were close once, but once we were untethered..."

She let out a slow breath. "Familiars are tethered to a witch's soul. It annoys her that he's always with me when he used to have so much to say to her. They just... don't speak to each other. Not anymore."

Jinx opened the door, stepping into the room. She wandered in, far enough that the distance swallowed up their conversation.

It was an attic space. The room had a steepled ceiling that came together in the middle. The wood ceilings and upper walls were painted black, and the bottom half of the walls were the same deep green as downstairs. What wasn't black or green was gold. A simple gold metal bed frame sat in the middle of the room, an isosceles triangle window with a thick wooden frame set in the wall behind it, with a bench beneath it covered in deep green pillows. They were scattered papers bestrewn in the places between. Old trunks lined the walls. Gold candlesticks set on the floor, breaking up the endless piles of old, weathered books.

As they crossed the room, the candles lit. Dim light poured through the room as Killian stepped around piles to set her on the bed. Jinx wandered, touching everything in sight as the bat perched on the head of the bed. Black beady eyes watched him lay her down, gently arranging her hair on the pillow.

Bram flew from the room, the gust from his wings making some of the candles flicker.

"It's been forever since I've been in here," Jinx admitted as Killian settled on the edge of the bed. "She says she doesn't let me in here because it's the one place that's hers. '*You're a thief, and this is one thing you can't steal from me'*." She rolled her eyes.

"Does it hurt you when she says things like that?" Killian asked.

Jinx paused with her fingers pressed to a black vase. "It should. I know it's true. So many things are latched to a soul, but because people usually have their souls inside them, they don't realize it. They don't have to see just how much you can lose if you lose it. If you're separated from it." She tapped her nail against the glass, refusing to turn and look at him. "She knows... and I'm sure it makes it seem like I'm a thief."

"That doesn't answer my question."

"No. It doesn't, does it?" She turned, a firm smile on her face. She looked different. Crossing the threshold into Rue's room had done something. Peeled away a part of the mask Jinx wore and forced her to be the raw emotions that screamed underneath, begging for attention. The ones that pleaded to be heard.

"Jinx, if this is going to work, I think we should be honest with each other."

Her lips pursed as she gripped the table behind her, nails digging anxiously into the wood. "Honest." She chuckled lightly. "What's that?"

He stared at her, trying to see the parts of her she kept hidden. These two women were so much more than they seemed, but they kept who they truly were carefully guarded. Even from each other. “Which of you keeps the heart?” he asked the question lightly, watching her face for a reaction.

Jinx’s nostrils flared slightly. “Isn’t it obvious? Rue clearly doesn’t have one.” The smile she donned then was tight and painful. It was parts of her trying to put on the mask when the room wouldn’t let her. The thick air held her suspended just as she was, making her sit with herself.

“It’s obvious to me that both of you seem to have something in you that’s broken. Two halves to the same broken heart with jagged edges you use to swipe at each other.”

“Hmm.” She tilted her head, letting her long curls, braids, and locs fall forward over her shoulder. She picked one up, toying with the curled end and adjusting a yellow jewel attached there. “Sometimes it feels like that. Sometimes it feels like there is a hate that explodes in the space between us just because someone decided it should be there. A hate that consumes us. One that makes us two broken pieces. But then, where does that leave you?”

“I imagine it leaves me standing in the middle.”

She reached forward, flexing her nails toward him. “We’ll take slices out of you, Killian.” Her playful tone did nothing to add levity to their conversation.

His eyes bore into hers. “You already have.”

Jinx straightened. Her body was tense as she clasped her hands behind her back and started to slowly walk away. She made her way toward the door, bare toes swiping at papers as she went.

“Jinx,” he called when she got to the doorway.

“Hmm.” She looked back over her shoulders, and as she stood in the threshold, some of her troubles melted away, and that bright smile returned.

“My heart is the kind that is black and drips tar. You’re wondering where I fit between your two broken halves.” He smiled lightly. “I fit between them as the glue that will sloppily hold you both together.”

A braid found its way into her hands again, her slender fingers fidgeting. “Sometimes being half of something is better than being a part of something whole, but constantly bleeding. Something that collects misery because it doesn’t know how to hold anything else.” She lifted her shoulders lightly, stepping completely out of the room. “But what do I know?” Grinning, she turned and skipped away.

Killian stared after her. It was hard for him to know just what happened. Was it magic, stale and unused like flecks of dust that floated through this room, forcing Jinx to be more Rue? More serious? More the soul that once fit inside her? Or was this just Jinx, as unpredictable as she’d been since he met her?

Bram appeared with the tackle box in hand. He placed it on the bed before he resumed his post.

Their eyes locked, and he felt an urgency whisper through the air. A demand he knew better than not to follow.

“Alright.”

Killian gave up trying to figure it out. These women would give him nothing they didn’t want to, and Jinx didn’t want to give him an answer. Any answer she gave felt like an offered riddle she was daring him to solve. And he would. Eventually. But right now, he needed to tend to Rue. He would clean her wounds, patching her up the best he could.

That was all he could do for now.

Until she woke up.

Then, he would get all the information he would need to help Rue and Jinx with all their problems.

Because whether they liked it or not, he was their mate, and he wasn’t going anywhere.

15

KILLIAN

ALL THE DARK EMOTIONS he felt like storm clouds up in Rue's room were gone as he made himself useful. He tidied the living room, taking Jinx's word for where things went. She waved away his offer to patch the wall, claiming Rue would handle it.

He didn't want to leave her such a big task, but Jinx assured him that even with just a pinch of her magic, she could fix it. It made him wonder at the ferocity of the scowling witch he'd yet had the chance to truly get to know.

"Ta-da!" Jinx kicked the door closed behind her as she strutted into the room. Her shoes went flying as she whipped her feet out, sending them in different directions before she skipped into the living room with a stack of pizza boxes.

The aroma was intoxicating. Pizza was one of the few things humans got right.

"And they say Rue is the only one who can do magic," she quipped before she put the boxes on the counter.

Killian's brows shot up as he walked into the kitchen, opening cupboards to find dishes. "Isn't magic tied to the soul?"

Jinx flipped open the box, shoving a slice into her mouth. She bit off a hefty chunk, eyes cast up to the ceiling as she thought about it. "It very well should be. I would be *amazing* at magic. Casting spells. Conjuring whatever my little heart desired..." She picked up the pepperoni that fell onto the kitchen island, shoving it back into her mouth.

His eyes widened at the very thought of Jinx wielding magic. Maybe Fate had gotten it right by not giving her access to magic as powerful as Rue's. "You can't do any magic at all?"

She shrugged. "I have no access to her magic, yet I understand her familiar. None of it really makes sense where Rue is concerned. I heard the Crowes were one of the most powerful families of witches to ever exist. If that's true, maybe something went wrong with the curse. You know, it kind of makes you wonder how Rue was able to be cursed in the first place... weird, right?" She grabbed another slice of pizza, biting into it. "There's a book!"

He was baffled at how quickly she slipped back into the woman she was before Rue's room. Killian looked at the slice of pizza pointed at him. "What?"

"A book! Old." She used the pizza to mimic the shape before her. "It's got a crow on the front, so I think maybe it's a family book. It has my favourite story in it. The one with the powerful witch who rules over all witches, but Rue doesn't tell me that story unless I really annoy her. Thick as all heck. Maybe the answers are in there. Oh… but she would kill us if we touched it." She folded the pizza and shoved the whole slice into her mouth before grabbing another.

"A grimoire?" Most witches had one. A book of spells passed down through the generations. Within those pages, they also marked their history.

She shrugged again. "Sure. I guess."

Jinx didn't know much. She existed alongside a witch and had never bothered to find anything out about Rue or witches, likely not even their coven.

How… unnerving.

A war waged inside him. He was equal parts upset with Jinx for approaching everything that had to do with Rue with such nonchalance, as much as he found her personality endearing and understanding. This was a lot to juggle; he understood not doing it if she didn't have to.

A frown turned down his lips.

What ungodly concoction did Fate use to weave their strings of fate together, connecting them as mates that would make him think such flighty behaviour was adorable, was beyond him.

A huff of exasperated breath left him.

He didn't like this. Didn't like feeling so torn. This wasn't who he was.

Killian was usually a hard beast. One who wasn't swayed by emotion — hell, he wasn't swayed by much else, either. His sole purpose was to make deals. To fill his ledgers so, eventually, he could be free from his posting and his powers could be restored.

Being a crossroads demon was penance. A sentence doled out to those with enough black marks that Lucifer herself noticed. He'd done more than enough to earn his punishment, but now he felt broken down by it in a way he hadn't before. Now, with his powers bound, all he could do was wrap measly supplies around his mate and watch her suffer.

Fate, you cruel bitch.

Killian likely wasn't the only one in existence who had it out for the elusive being who marked everyone's paths. Binding him to a woman — a witch — untethered from her soul had to be a special kind of cruelty. Meeting them untethered... falling for them separately...

Fuck.

He shook his head. He hadn't had the chance to bond with Rue. To connect with her on any level that made her see him as anything but another stone in her shoe she was forced to endure. She had no interest in him. Not after he did the very thing he swore he would never do.

Denied a deal.

He'd lost all his senses.

"I'll ask her to see it when she wakes." The last thing he wanted was something else to drive a wedge between him and Rue. He needed to play it safe with her if he expected to get anywhere.

Jinx scoffed. "Good luck with that, sexy man. There is no way in this or any world she'll let you see it. She doesn't even let me see it... and I'm her soul."

The door slammed open. Music boomed in from the front door as something fell, crashing. "Hey, bitches! I'm back!"

Jinx's eyes widened as she scurried around the kitchen island, hiding behind Killian. "Oh no! The dance police is back."

"Dance police?" Killian needed a manual to understand her. Everything she said felt so far removed from the situation.

"Is that *It's Going Down* by *Yung Joc*?" Jinx tilted her head, listening.

"Fuck if I know," Killian hissed, gently holding her behind him when she tried to step out to get a better listen. "Who's this?"

"That's the half-breed that bit Rue."

The scent of death hit him first. It was strong enough to make his knees buckle. His knuckles lightened as he held onto the counter, his eyes rolling back in his head as the second scent hit him.

Lust.

Pleasure.

Euphoric bliss that made his blood pulse and his mouth water. He knew that scent. He'd often paid a sin or two to get it at the right apothecaries. A scent like that, as heady as it was, could only come from two beings. An incubus or a succubus.

The woman stood in combat boots and distressed black denim shorts. She had a belt around her waist with a large silver skull and crossbones buckle. Her curls were wild and floated above her shoulders, bangs curtaining her eyes as they lit bright, and she snarled, baring teeth and fangs.

Power hit him like a punch to the face.

"What is it you want, monster?" Killian asked. He didn't know what she was, so he didn't know what to call her.

"Poe," she corrected easily. "Poe Wiley. You're right, though, I'm a monster, and you've pissed me off enough to show you just how monstrous I can be!"

Jinx pointed a finger at her chest as she peered out from behind him. "Me? Okay! I admit it! Dancing isn't my thing! I don't know why I lied. I just don't like people telling me what to do. I can dance if I want... but I won't. There! Don't kill me."

What the hell were they on about?

"Alright, Poe. What is it you want?" Killian tried to feel her out. No one did all this for nothing, and he prided himself on being someone who could make a deal. He could fix this.

She pointed an accusing finger at Jinx as she marched into the house like it was hers. "I already told your little witch here! I want them to put back Dex's curse."

"Why? Not many people put up this much of a fuss once a curse is removed."

"You've ruined him by removing it! Without the curse, he's nothing but a mere mortal and this..." Her chest heaved, and her chin stuck out. "Put. It. Back!"

"She's so bossy," Jinx muttered from her hiding place.

Anger flashed over Poe's face before she lunged. She was fast. A blur of movement barely registered before she was up on the counter, a boot planted atop one of the open pizza boxes, as she wrapped her hands in the front of his shirt and leaned in. Their noses bumped together as her eyes flashed the deepest scarlet he had ever seen.

"It seems you've found yourself at the wrong place at the wrong time, demon. No..." She inhaled him. "You're so much more, aren't you? Everyone here is so much more than they're supposed to be. A witch that isn't a witch, a demon who isn't a demon... a soul that's more than a soul."

He couldn't think. Darkness pushed its way into him, throwing all his thoughts into shadows. His blood pulsed in a soothing rhythm that made him relax in her hold as Jinx screamed and tried to knock Poe's hands loose.

Jinx went flying, her back slamming into the wall. Her flesh shimmered the lightest purple. Brushed over with Rue's magic even now.

He should go to her. That thought was there as quickly as it was gone.

Poe leaned in. "Don't worry. This won't hurt... quite the opposite. It'll be the best thing you've ever felt right up until you feel nothing at all." She opened her mouth, fangs glinting in the light.

She was going to bite him. He should be more worried about it, but all he knew now was darkness and the whisper of bliss. He was a cat chasing that mouse of pleasure through the dark. Nothing else mattered.

Killian's mind whispered that he should brace himself, but he didn't as his eyes closed in a slow blink. He wanted to close them. To fall into the chasm of bliss she surrounded him in, but he also wanted to look at her. He wanted to trace the scarlet of her eyes and see the way they brightened when she tasted him.

He wanted her approval. Wanted her to taste him and tell him he was good. Delicious. The best. He craved her praise as she consumed him.

With that scent around her, he was sure she would somehow manage to give him all he ever wanted.

16

RUE

DEATH.

The scent of it whipped her eyes open as she shot up — *in bed*? Confusion moved over her, knowing full well Jinx would never take the time to put her in bed, even in the state she was in. Her feet hit the floor, and she moved with the swiftness of someone desperate when fear pulsed through her veins. It wasn't hers, but it was nauseating.

Her feet hit the landing, and her eyes whipped to the kitchen.

Jinx was on the floor, that irritating wailing coming from her as thick tears rolled down her cheeks, and her hands reached out like a baby searching for comfort.

Killian stood on his toes, his shirt fisted in the hand of the woman who would likely bring about Rue's end. She'd prefer her over Fortuna and her wretched coven being the ones to finally deliver her to Death. Death could come swiftly at the hands of a succubus who seemed like she had lost the better parts of her sanity a long time ago.

His eyes were closed, and the attractive idiot looked completely enthralled as her mouth opened and she readied herself to take a bite out of him.

"Fucking hell. Do I have to do everything?"

Annoyance overtook all the pain that pulsed through her as she ran forward and shoved her arm between the woman's lips. Her fangs sank into Rue's flesh. She felt the familiar tearing. The agony ripped at her, pulling at her muscles and foretelling of the pain she would be forced to feel without being able to heal.

Rue's hand planted on Killian's chest, and she shoved him back.

His waist hit the counter, jolting him. Confusion moved through him as his eyes snapped open and he shook his head. Rue wasn't sure if he'd be able to fully find clarity. The lust in the air was potent, and maybe she'd be able to feel it if she wasn't filled with rage.

That was all she needed, another chunk torn from her where she couldn't even be buzzed with bliss. Fate had dealt her a shit hand.

"Rue!" Jinx cried, her voice a shrill blend of excitement and horror. "She's back! The monster is back!"

Jinx crawled over to Killian, wrapping her arms around his waist as she continued to wail. Killian groaned, his hand pressed to his brow as he tried to come back to his senses.

"I already told you, it's Poe," the woman stated as she lifted Rue, tossing her on the island. She straddled her, her knees pressed so tightly into her sides that it made her wound scream.

Did the name of the woman who was making a habit of biting chunks from her matter? Nope. Rue wrapped her hands in the fabric of Poe's shirt as she tried to keep her from biting her again.

Poking at the woman who seemed hell-bent on killing her didn't seem like a good idea, but she'd lost so much blood, good ideas weren't something she could conjure up. "Are you sure you're not the one I cursed? Seems like you have a taste for flesh," Rue quipped.

Poe's eyes darkened to red. "Don't you dare make fun of me, it's not my thing."

"Oh... well, excuse me if I don't prioritize my insults to your kinks."

Eyes wide, Poe pressed a hand to her collarbone. A slow smile stretched over her face that hinted something unpredictable was about to take over the hybrid, who seemed like she often needed a leash to reel her in. A leash Rue had no idea how to get hold of. "Kinks?"

She dropped down, running her tongue slowly up Rue's neck. Heat assaulted her. It struck a match in the depths of her belly, stirring something that made her toes curl against her will.

"Kinks is something you've long denied yourself. Isn't that right, dark shadow?" Her hot breath blew against the flesh of Rue's neck, making her shudder before Poe closed her lips on her skin and suckled ever so gently.

The gentleness of it made Rue's eyes squeeze closed. This was a woman who scratched and bit; she didn't offer softness. And yet, softness was exactly what she was giving. It made her feel unsteady. Like her feet sank in sands she couldn't get her footing in.

"No. You crave something far simpler than depravity, don't you? Belonging. A love that's just yours." Her nose dragged up Rue's neck. "I could give you somewhere to belong, a love you can put in your pocket and covet." Her chuckle felt like it seeped into Rue's flesh, living inside her skin. "Would you like that?"

Her eyes rolled back in her head as she fought against the potency of Poe's magic. She was an enigma. All the powers of a succubus amped up by the blissful call of death. It was dangerous. Comforting in a way Rue denied but wanted all the same.

Lips dragged against her cheek before they pressed ever so gently against her own. "You're not broken," she whispered, capturing her lips.

Heat poured into her, but it was the words that made tears pool in her eyes. That was the thing about death: it had a way of seeing into your very soul. Poe saw her, and to be seen so thoroughly made her ache.

Poe deepened the kiss, awakening something Rue thought would never rouse. "Just what would become of you, I wonder, if you learned to love yourself instead of expecting love from others? What wondrous, monstrous thing would you become?"

Each soft kiss whispered her undoing. Poe's hand slid down her belly. Lower...

No. She didn't have time for this. This was all magic. The lure of a succubus and nothing more.

Memories of the Duke she had cursed so long ago played through her head. Her on her knees, her coven staring down at her with hate and joy in their eyes.

Rue shimmied her knees up to Poe's stomach and shoved.

Poe lost her grip, falling off the island. Her booted soles poked into view, a barstool toppling. "How very boring," she muttered from wherever she landed. "We didn't even get to the good part."

Rue's brow furrowed as music rang through the air. Where it came from, she had no idea.

An angry snarl sounded as Poe got to her feet. Her hands braced on the island as scarlet eyes bore into Rue. "Restore the curse," she demanded, any hint of lust completely gone.

Rue shoved off the opposite side of the island. She needed to put some distance between them. Being bitten wasn't something she was enjoying. "Sorry, it's not on my to-do list."

Poe's fist slammed against the island. "You have no idea who you're messing with, witch."

"Rue," she corrected. Inhaling, she cocked a brow. "And I've got a good idea. Half-breed. Part succubus, part reaper." She sucked air in through her teeth, lips pursed. "What a shit deal. Let me guess, undoing my curse has ruined your little romp with the zombie now that you can't fuck him without killing him. If you even try, you'll devour the soul I put back."

Her eyes widened, the scarlet retreating slightly, but the dark hue was just as ominous.

"The duke has found himself a hybrid..." Rue shook her head, laughing.

"Duke?" Poe leaned over the counter, her pose threatening.

Killian groaned again. Jinx's head was under his arm as she held his wrist, trying to steer him away from the kitchen. Sure, why have the demon help? It wasn't like she'd used most of her magic to save the soul that was constantly her curse or anything like that.

Poe swiped over the counter, her black nails pointed and dangerous.

Rue flinched back.

"Careful now," Rue warned, her voice gravelly. "You kill me, and you kill any chance of having your zombie back. It's not a curse just anyone can pull off."

Poe's face hardened, teeth bared, and jaw clenched so hard, Rue was surprised her teeth didn't splinter and crack. A chime echoed through the room, and Rue's eyes dropped to a Bluetooth speaker hanging from a clip on Poe's belt. *Party Up* by *DMX* started, and her features hardened. The power around her intensified as the tips of her nails dug into the granite.

As far as Rue knew, there weren't any beings whose powers were amplified by music and yet, somehow, she was.

"I will be your worst nightmare," Poe promised.

A slow exhale left Rue, flaring her nostrils. "You know nothing of my nightmares."

Truth be told, she didn't have nightmares. Not anymore. There was nothing that could torment her as drastically as her life, so usually, her nights were filled with nothingness. There was too much darkness in her to call to sweet dreams, too much bitterness to hope for something different, and her life was enough to scare nightmares away.

This beast before her could do nothing but bring her the relief of death, and that was a far cry from a nightmare for Rue.

"We can..." Killian's words slurred. "We can make a deal."

Poe's brow quirked. Her face lifted, and she inhaled the air. "No... I don't think we can. What I need is nothing something a crossroads demon can fulfil."

She wasn't wrong. The kind of change that needed to be made to Dex's soul was something only magic with the depths the likes of hers could accomplish. A deal was too simple. To remove his soul completely would be to make him mindless. To make him into what this world believed to be a zombie with a deal alone would not give her back the man she knew. Who was everything he was before... minus a soul. He was undead. A zombie who ate flesh, but his humanity was intact. It had to be so that his deeds haunted him. Twisted his mind into the dark thing she believed he likely became.

It was a punishment, after all.

No, a crossroads demon couldn't accomplish it. This was beyond a simple deal.

"I..." He pinched his eyes closed, head thrown back as he tried with everything he was to pull himself out of the fog of lust he was lost in. "I can do it."

Poe laughed.

"Hey!" Jinx snarled, baring her teeth, though she lacked the menace Poe emitted effortlessly. "Don't you laugh at him!"She was merely a soul standing among monsters.

Rue narrowed her eyes and wasn't surprised to see Poe doing the same. Rue wasn't the only one irritated by her soul.

"I'll laugh at who I please. I take my joy where I can get it... especially now that you've thrown me into a pit of despair!" Poe practically wailed.

Wow! Dramatic much?

Jinx scoffed.

The sound hit Poe like a slap to the face. Everything in her tensed as her eyes quickly whipped over to Jinx.

"Could you not antagonize her right now?" Killian forced out, his words still hazy and too slow.

Finally, someone with sense.

"It seems we have a problem." Rue's hand slipped slightly across the granite, slicked with blood from her new bite. "You see, the amount of magic it takes to lay a curse the likes of which I put on the duke all that time ago is... extensive. And right now..." A wince moved through her, dropping her brows and creasing the skin between them. "All my magic is kind of tied up."

"Tied up?" Poe leaned in further, her knee braced on the counter like she was preparing to hop over it.

Rue's nod was slow. If she had her soul where it should be, maybe she would have hesitated before saying what she was about to say, but she was too tired to protect people she wasn't sure she cared about. "Yup. I was going to try to fix that by making a deal with a crossroads demon, but he popped up and slept with her, further fucking up my life... so here we are."

Jinx's mouth gaped. "Rue!"

She didn't have the energy to argue.

Poe's brow cocked as she looked Rue over. "What sort of deal were you trying to make? Trying to tie you back to your soul?" She pointed an accusing finger at Jinx.

Rue grabbed the dishcloth from the handle of the stove behind her and wrapped it around her arm before she leaned back on the counter. "Something like that."

Poe inhaled the air again, and not for the first time, Rue wondered just what a reaper smelled when she did that. "And he's refusing..." she paused, a knowing Rue didn't fully understand in her eyes. "Because of the mate ties?"

Killian cleared his throat.

"You know... I could toy with him a little. Even if he's not able to give you what you want, surely you'd like to see him on his knees." Poe turned, ripping all her attention away from Rue and casting it fully on Killian.

No relief came from being away from her hungry gaze. Instead, Rue's anxiety returned, knowing Jinx cowered behind the man who had the reaper's attention now. Well... mostly reaper.

Potent passions wafted in the air again.

Rue waved her hand in front of her face, trying to keep it from filling her nose.

Killian's eyes glazed over, and Rue watched as his body went slightly lax. He leaned toward Poe, the muscles working through his jaw like he was fighting a losing battle.

"Get on your knees," Poe cooed.

Rue's brows dropped. Having Killian on his knees wasn't what she wanted. She wanted a deal. She wanted to be tethered back to her soul so she could finally have a semblance of a life not filled to the brim with misery and longing.

"I..."

Jinx snapped her fingers in front of his face. "Killian?"

"I..."

Poe grabbed his face, squeezing it in her hands.

"Come now, don't be difficult." Poe's eyes darkened as she leaned in. Her hips swayed seductively, her hand reaching out to snatch Jinx's wrist and pull her away.

Jinx stumbled, no match for Poe's strength. She fell to a pile on the floor behind Poe, her hand around her aching wrist as she whined. "Rue! Do something!"

She was going to do something. Wait. She wanted to see how all this would play out.

Poe's touch was featherlight as she ran the back of her hand along Killian's jaw. His eyes dropped, the colour dull and clouded as he looked down at the woman before him. He leaned into her touch, flames dancing up from his brow to reveal the horns he'd kept hidden.

Rue's heart quickened, her bottom lip held between her teeth as something tightened in the pit of her belly and heat spread behind her ears. Watching Poe's hands explore him did something to her she was too afraid to admit.

"On your knees." She looked back over her shoulders, eyes glinting with dark mischief. "Before your mate."

Killian's steps were the kind someone took when their mind was muddled, and intoxication had wrapped around their bones. His eyes were glazed over as he rounded the island, taking steps toward her.

Rue held her breath. She'd expected him to stop before the mess of Jinx on the floor, but he stepped past her. Toward Rue. Her eyes widened, throat tight.

His hands trailed lightly against her arms, making a shudder move through her. Their eyes locked, and she felt her knees buckle under the weight of his gaze. He looked at her like a treasure he'd finally set his hands on after a lifetime of searching. He lowered, slowly getting on his knees before her.

She swayed, his hands still wrapped around her wrists as he pressed his face into her abdomen. Inhaling her. He rubbed his forehead against her, the moment far too intimate.

Poe ignored Jinx's wailing, resting her elbows on the island and her chin in her hand as she watched.

Rue swallowed hard, pulling her gaze away from the top of Killian's head. His curls piled there looked so defined. Coils that would wrap perfectly around her fingers. She felt the press of each ring against her wrists as he held onto her tight enough that she felt she couldn't escape him, but loosely enough to let her know that was completely her choice.

This wasn't real.

Still, she stumbled over that thought. She wanted it to be real. That realization was a punch to the gut as she looked at Poe like a pitiful thing. How did this monster know her so well?

"You..." Rue's voice was a tense rasp. "This is a waste of time. You don't have to do this. We're supposed to be tethering me back to my soul, not doing whatever the hell this is."

"A waste of time?" Poe's brow quirked as she looked up, lips pursed in thought. "I don't think it is."

"Rue!" Jinx cried.

"Hush." Poe didn't even spare her a glance to accompany her chastisement. "The grown-ups are talking."

Her sobs turned into hiccups.

"Tell her," Poe urged. "Tell her what you think of her, *demon*."

She said the word like it was a lie she wanted discovered.

Killian slowly lifted his head. His chin rested on her, like he couldn't bear to have his face not pressed into her. "I ache for her."

Rue held her breath.

"Since I saw her and first smelled the misery coursing beneath her skin, I've craved to know just what that tasted like.

Craved to know how it would feed the hungry parts of me that miss the way it fills me." He pressed his lips to Rue's stomach, the kiss slow enough to pull the butterflies out from where they hid. "I crave to know what she will taste like when I devour that misery and replace it with the obsession I've had to live with since the very first moment I saw her."

What? "Don't toy with us," Rue forced the words out past the tightness in her throat.

"How deep the truths are when we believe we have nothing to lose and everything to gain." Poe grinned. "When lust makes us take wicked risks, turning bedrooms into confessionals."

She shook her head. He didn't feel anything for her. He couldn't. The soul he was bonded to sat blubbering on the floor, and she was nothing but the empty shell it escaped. He couldn't—

Another slow kiss to her belly stole all her thoughts. Her eyes pinched closed. All she needed to do was escape this scene. Remember that he wasn't hers. Not really.

Like the hard slap of reality, Jinx let loose another irritating wail. "Stop casting your spells on him!"

Right. This was just succubus magic. Nothing more.

Eyes opened, she watched annoyance transform Poe's features as she stalked toward Jinx. Dropped down into a crouch, her hand cupped under Jinx's chin, and she lifted her face. Her hold was tight enough to prevent Jinx from shaking her hand free, nails digging half moons into her cheeks. "How very irritating you've become... just because you think it's all you should be."

"I'm not!" she cried.

"Do you even remember how to be anything else?" Poe clicked her tongue in disapproval. Her nails dug in, making Jinx wince. She held onto her, debating for a single moment before Poe pulled her forward and pressed a light kiss to her lips. "Surely, you do."

Jinx's crying stopped. Her eyes widened, and her mouth gaped. "I don't! I'm not... I am exactly who I'm supposed to be."

Annoyance contorted Poe's features before she shoved Jinx back.

She fell, rolling onto her side as whimpers made her body shake.

Rue stepped out of Killian's hold, sucking a desperate breath into her lungs. She wouldn't fall for Poe's magic. Killian fell onto his hands and knees, forcing Rue to step farther away so she wouldn't have to look at him and remember the words he'd uttered against her stomach.

Arms crossed under her chest, Poe cocked a hip and directed her attention back to Rue. "Well, this is getting me nowhere."

"Now you know how I feel," Rue groaned.

Jinx got to her knees, falling back to her hands when her skirt caught under her feet. "You can't just keep coming in here and doing whatever the hell you want. Rue will—"

"Do nothing. You've made sure I can't." Rue's tone was sour. Her eyes lifted, locking onto the woman who she knew wouldn't give up. It was time for them to have a chat. "Look... you want your curse, I know how you can get it."

Poe hit a button on the speaker. The music stopped abruptly, leaving nothing but Jinx's whimpering as the soundtrack to their conversation. "Go on."

"Have you heard of the Lumena coven?"

"Nope." Poe lifted a shoulder, shoving the trampled pizza off the counter and flipping the lid of a crushed box. She pulled out a flattened slice, biting into it. Leaned back on the counter, she looked at Rue, almost bored.

What? Surprise made Rue's heart jump. "Are you serious?"

"A coven is a coven. Who the hell cares what little groups you all gather into for your little seances? It makes absolutely no difference to me. A witch is a witch, is a witch, and up until a few days ago, that was really all I cared to know about witches. I don't have much need for magic, and truth be told, you taste a bit sour. Some taste downright rotten..." She bit into the pizza, chewing slowly.

"Taste?" Jinx's eyes widened. "You *eat* them?"

"Not all of them." Poe grinned a devilish grin, putting her fangs on display.

Jinx scurried to her feet, hurrying to Killian's side. She pulled him slowly to his feet before she stepped slightly behind him. What she thought he would do while he was still under a sheet of lust was beyond Rue.

She tried not to look at him, afraid of what seeing that look on his face would do to her when she was trying to regain her faculties. Rue cleared her throat, remembering the task at hand.

This probably wasn't a great idea. This monster before her had made no promises. She hadn't pretended to be anything but bloodthirsty, and giving Poe any additional information could be hammering the final nail in her coffin.

Desperate times call for desperate measures and all that.

And Rue had passed desperate a long time ago; now she felt like she was walking in a purgatory, merely waiting. Wherever she was delivered to would be fine by her, so long as she didn't have to stay there anymore. In this cursed place in between.

"There is a priestess on her deathbed. Ferula Vossen. Once she dies, her powers and the magic of the coven will be passed on to her daughter, Fortuna."

Poe curled her hand in front of her face, inspecting her nails. "And I should care about this? Why?"

Time to bait the hybrid. "Because they're the ones that untethered me from my soul, and they're the ones you'll have to kill if you want to get Dex back to the way he was when you met."

Her eyes widened, her interest piqued. "Kill two witches? Witches that... *cursed* you?"

"Fortuna will probably let you kill Ferula... she's just waiting for the power of the Lumena coven to be hers, but Fortuna... the coven will probably stand in your way there."

"Witches?" Poe scoffed.

"Some of the most powerful witches there are," Jinx told her. She had defiance in her voice. She wanted to argue with Poe, to try to convince her it was something that couldn't be done. Whether that was because she was angry with her or because she didn't want her to succeed was anyone's guess. Nothing Jinx did or said often made much sense.

It made Rue question the condition of her soul if Jinx was the embodiment of it.

"What fun," she grinned. Poe turned on her heel. Her eyes narrowed at Rue and then Jinx in turn, before she moved back to the island. She braced her hands on it, leaning over. There was a threat in her eyes, her smile too wide, and her eyes too dark. "How do I know you're not setting me up?"

Rue lifted her shoulders. "Well, you know where to find us if we are."

Poe threw her head back and laughed. It was a bark of a sound at first before it transformed into a lyrical rasp.

Fuck, Poe was something. The succubus side of her seemed to be front and centre, if she could be enticing even while looking so unhinged.

Her laughter finally died down, dark eyes boring into Rue as though she was weighing her very soul. She didn't need to stare at her to do that; she merely had to look at the blithering mess hiding behind the dazed and useless demon. Still, she smiled. It was a petrifying thing. An innocence that lured someone into a mouth filled with sharp and hungry teeth. "You know what... I like you, Rue."

"Great." Rue couldn't care less. Being liked was a burden.

She hummed to herself, a familiar tune Rue couldn't place. "It will make it all the more sad if I have to kill you."

Lips pursed, Rue nodded slowly. "I'm sure it will."

"Lumena coven... Ferula and Fortuna..." Poe hopped over the counter, the movement so quick, Rue didn't know it happened until she was pinned to the counter at her back. Poe had her thigh pushed up between her legs, her hot breath on Rue's lips as she stared down at her, her arms planted on the granite, boxing her in. The heat of her nose brushed along Rue's cheek.

"What are you doing?" There was no fear in her question. Fear was something she couldn't find anymore.

"As much power as you claimed you've used, I can still smell it on you. I'll need a taste of it to find your coven."

"A taste?" She'd already taken chunks out of Rue; just how much more of a taste did she need? She could have sucked her soul out of her mouth already if she had one inside her. This *taste* felt like nothing more than an excuse for Poe to flex her power and remind Rue just who she was messing with.

And damn, she had to respect that.

"Mhmm... a taste..." Her bottom lip brushed against Rue's. "Show me how pretty your magic is." Poe fisted the braids at the back of Rue's head, and she jerked her face up before she stole her lips.

Heat filled Rue's mouth as Poe's tongue dived in.

Surprise made her tense before she remembered Poe's words. She wanted some of her magic. Just a taste.

Poe's thigh glided between her legs, and she was reminded of the torture of feeling Killian and Jinx together. Of feeling the bliss that could have been hers had she not been cursed. Had she not been untethered. Her eyes glassed over as she let some of her magic seep from where she kept it.

The kiss was slow. It was the kind of kiss that could undo someone if it wasn't being given to her by a psychopath who had tried to kill her. It teased at the parts of her that longed for the life she once had, and as Poe suckled at her magic, some of the succubus's poured in.

It was like bursting from the surface after she'd been drowning all these years. Her magic hit Rue's lungs like the first gasp of breath she'd been desperate for but denied all this time. The curse that was finally at its end — one way or another.

She surrendered to it. Letting it fill her as much as she could.

Rue's breath quickened. Her heart beat a frantic rhythm against her ribs as her eyes rolled back.

Poe pulled away on a sigh.

Battling against the pleasure that suddenly pulsed through her veins, Rue opened her eyes in time to watch Poe drag her tongue slowly along her bottom lip. It was far too red, and it drew all her attention. Her thumb cleaned the flesh under her bottom lip, her black nail too long and looking sharp enough to pierce.

"You're filled with need, dark little beast," she whispered.

Rue said nothing. Her throat was too dry to speak. All she could do was cling to the edge of the counter and stare.

"How lonely your heart must be when all the ties to it have been so harshly cut. It's on an island all on its own... crying out. Begging."

Rue's teeth bit down on her bottom lip, and she pulled her eyes away. She couldn't look at Poe now, not when she spoke words that cut her open. "Right..." she cleared her throat. "So... you've tasted my magic."

Her chuckle lacked the manic energy that had danced in the sound before. “I’ve tasted so much more than just your magic.”

What more was there to taste? Besides her magic, there wasn’t much left of Rue.

“But maybe that’s a conversation for another time.” Poe chuckled again. “Alright... I’m off to hunt a witch or two.” She stalked off, dragging a slow hand against Killian’s jaw as she passed, leaving the door wide open as she disappeared into the night.

17

KILLIAN

His mind was somewhere he couldn't reach as he watched the woman who introduced herself as Poe hop over the counter and box Rue in. Everything in him wanted to fight. He felt his blood heat to a boil. Wanted to wrap his hand around her pretty little throat and make her regret ever setting foot in the house where the women who would be his lived. Darkening their doorstep with her treachery.

He could do nothing but live in the haze. Frustrated.

This beast was a strong one. Stronger than the ties of Fate herself, because even those couldn't push away the haze she covered him in and free him from where he stood. Worthless to both of them.

And Poe *kissed* her.

Killian hadn't even gotten the chance to kiss Rue. Rue was always just out of reach, and that only got worse with every encounter he had with Jinx. Still, Poe claimed her lips like they were hers.

Anger moved through him with every passing second. It burned through the passion she filled him with, turning it to ash that sat all too heavy in the pit of his stomach.

Time moved slowly from the moment Poe strutted away from Rue like she had the world in her hands and disappeared into the night. The air remained thick with the scent of death and a haze of lust, a clock ticking somewhere inside their house, counting off the seconds.

Jinx was the first to move. Eyes wide and face covered in tears. "She's so rude," she whimpered. "I thought there was no one who was meaner than Rue, but boy, was I wrong."

Rue's eyes hardened. Her lips pressed thin as she opened the fridge, grabbed a water, and slammed it. She spared them a single glance before she disappeared down the hall, a slam of a door fully snapping him out of whatever succubus stupor he'd been put in.

Killian's hand lifted, rubbing over the flesh of his chest.

This was not good.

He had never believed himself to be the kind of monster who would stand idly by while someone touched what was his. While someone *tasted* them. In the span of a few minutes, he'd done both. Helpless against the succubus's magic.

Fuck, it was potent.

The words he'd spoken to Rue on his knees played over in his head. He *did* ache for her, but confessing that under a thick fog of lust likely didn't do him any favours. A frustrated hand rubbed at the back of his head as his chin dipped against his chest. "Fuck."

Jinx wrapped her arms around him, her face pressing into his back as she breathed him in. It was an unsettling feeling, so completely relieved by her embrace, enthralled by the love he knew was deep-rooted in his soul, and also feeling at odds with her. The accusation that Jinx was a thief bore into him. Everything she was belonged to Rue, and the part of him destined to be hers, was angry for her loss. Even wrapped up in the arms he wanted to call home, he was angry.

"She'll be in there for a few hours at least," Jinx whispered into his back. "She'll need to plot everything out. To make sure she knows what can go right by inviting that meanie in and telling her everything. What can go wrong..." She released a slow sigh. "The Crowe women were not just strong in their magic... their minds... they worked in a way no other witch even dared to dream they could. Never relying on just magic. They could likely change the world with their thoughts alone."

Killian turned in her arms to stare down at her. She sounded, once again, like the Jinx who spoke to him in Rue's room. She sounded insightful. Unlike the woman who seemed to sprint head-on, emotions leading the way. "You sound like you admire her."

"Only as much as I could admire myself."

His head tilted as he considered her. “Is she you?”

Her lips pursed, eyes avoiding his as she stared up at the ceiling. “Maybe once. Not anymore.”

Confusion was a blade they effortlessly thrust into his chest. “How do you know?”

“Because the world has coloured me, transforming me into something different. Is your soul the same as it was when you were young? As even a few years ago? Or did it change, even slightly protected by the casing of your skin?”

He stared into her eyes, expecting to see Rue looking back at him. She sounded more like Rue, harsh and cold.

That light smile spread slowly across her face as she lifted onto her toes and pressed her lips to his. “If we were the same, you would have already found your way into her bed, wouldn’t you?”

Her tone was teasing, but it caused an ache in the pit of his stomach. “Maybe I will.”

Jinx’s nose curled. “Fat chance. She’s too mean. Her misery is a rare kind.”

It was the misery he smelled first, a misery that smelled so much like home.

“Oh? And why’s that?” he asked.

“It doesn’t want company.”

Leaving Jinx and Rue alone felt wrong. His insides were wrapped too tightly as he stood in the middle of a country road, watching as the four roads met in the middle.

Desperate times...

His teeth tore into his wrist, and he splashed his blood on the dirt and waited.

The world fell into complete silence. There was no whisper of the winds, no chirping of insects hiding in the tall grass, no animals calling into the night. Nothingness surrounded him before the dirt cracked, lines lit bright with hellfires.

Time slowed, then it stopped altogether.

"Killian."

He didn't turn; he knew who he would see if he did. "Eshu."

Eshu's voice was deep comfort. Earthquakes that shook the ground at his feet, accompanied by a warm breeze that enveloped him through the chaos. Held him tightly inside a single breath. Ebony skin made the white of his luminous eyes look all the more bright as he walked around Killian, staring at him. His brawny chest was bare, taut skin stretched over wide expanses of muscle. The scarlet fabric wrapped around his waist was adorned with skulls on one side, their contents rattling. The fabric fell to hang behind his knees, parted at the front where his muscular legs were painted in the same colour, white and gold dots and lines decorating them. His bare feet floated above the dirt, a staff in one hand and a flame in the other. It billowed, red, then orange, before it changed to a white so vibrant it rivalled his eyes. A necklace of bones hung around his neck. There was a slice of red across his harsh cheekbones as he stared.

"Eshu, my warden. Holder of my contract... and my soul." Fear abandoned him as he addressed the one being who could set him free. He needed his freedom now more than ever. It was the only way he could be of help to the women he was quickly falling in love with.

"Just what, I wonder, has brought this fallen beast calling?" He paced around Killian, his presence sucking the very air from his lungs. "Ah... it seems Fate has touched a hand even to one with a soul as black as yours."

Killian bristled. "I need out of my service."

"If monsters could merely decide when they were through with their penance, it wouldn't be a punishment, now would it?"

Muscles worked over his jaw as he waited until Eshu made another lap around him, stopping before him. He hovered slightly, the space below his feet billowing with black smoke. "My sentence is nearing its end."

"And yet... near the end isn't the end, is it?" His pitch brows, topped with white dots, rose.

Killian's pride burned away to nothing. Ash that could join the smoke Eshu floated on as his hands rubbed at the front of his thighs, and he dropped to his knees. His hands pressed into the dirt, head bowed as he did the unthinkable — prepared himself to beg.

"I'm not denying my sins. My viciousness at the hands of my... *needs* was immeasurable at the best of times. This penance is one I've earned, and though this work is tedious, I have carried it out knowing this is deserved."

"And?" Eshu implored.

"And I will gladly double my sentence, continue on as I've been, serving you at the crossroads, if you would grant me a reprieve."

"A reprieve?" He grinned. "Sounds like you want to make a deal."

"Yes." *Please work,* he mentally begged. All he needed was a little grace so he could become the very monster Rue needed to survive all that plagued her. "I need to go to war."

His chin was forcefully gripped, face jerked up to look into the white voids of Eshu's gaze. Pain shot through his jaw. Eshu's grip was strong enough to grind his bones into dust as he stared at him with a mischievous grin. "And what kind of war would call for a fallen harbinger of misery?"

Harbinger of misery. That was what he was, underneath this demon flesh he wore like a prison uniform. A being meant to spread misery like a plague. Feed off it where Fate and Karma deemed fit. And yet... his greed had angered them both. Misery was a funny thing. Contrary to Jinx's words, it *did* enjoy company. It was like fire, forever catching. Pressing it into the wrong chest was like placing a bomb he knew would destroy everything around them.

That destruction was addictive, and all too quickly, Killian had spread more than he should have. The mayhem that came on the cusp of all that misery dug in, sprouting roots deep enough for him to be shackled. Imprisoned.

After all the war he'd caused as he walked through worlds, it was due time for him to fight his own.

Killian ignored the agony in his jaw as he let his darkness push through, lifting his lips into a slow smile. "The kind that would likely have me right back here, kneeling before you."

Eshu sat back on his heels, considering. "Are you sure this is what you want? The kind of marks a soul acquires fighting for love are the kind that don't so easily wipe away... not even with penance."

He levelled his gaze. "I'm sure."

"You've planted enough seeds of doom in your lifetime to warrant being on your knees before me for the rest of your eternal life... and now you wish to plant even more. In the name of love?" His chuckle was the crackling of wood in the hottest of fires. "How interesting. I'm curious to see just what sins will grow from the seeds you plant this time."

It was a question he wasn't given the chance to answer.

Eshu slammed his fiery palm against Killian's chest. The flames devoured him. His chin was released, and Killian threw his head up, screaming up to a god who would never hear him as he was engulfed in a thousand miseries. His flesh burnt away, then muscle. It ate him down to the bone, his flesh falling off in burning chunks before the smoke blew it, dousing it and wrapping him in a chilled cocoon.

The agony was all-consuming. He couldn't think through it, let alone breathe. The scream that had made his throat feel raw dissipated to a weak, pitiful gasp. The sensation of himself coming together was almost as painful as falling apart. His muscles quivered as he fell forward, his chest — now fully formed — slamming against the dirt. He choked on the taste of blood and bile, dirt coating his nostrils with each ragged inhale.

He felt the first bit of his magic slip out of the cage Eshu opened. Twigs pushed out of the mortal flesh of his back, sprouting black, wilted leaves.

"I'm excited to see what you'll look like when you taste the bitterness of a war that ruins you. A war Fate herself crafted..." Eshu chuckled, the sound as dark as the smoke that slowly released Killian, leaving him a sweating mess on the dirt road. "Either way, you'll return to me on your knees."

18

RUE

THE SUFFERING SHE KNEW so well, had draped around her like an expensive throw she couldn't shrug off, ebbed away. Fatigue was phantom hands slowly surrendering their hold on her as she peeled her eyes open and looked around her bedroom.

It was dim; only a few of her candles flickered with her presence.

Warmth covered her, a belt securing her to the bed. Frowning, she tried to sit up but was met with resistance.

Her palms rested on unbridled warmth, a steady rhythm under her hand. Eyes widened, she lifted her head to look up at the man who had been assigned to her by Fate. His eyes were closed, dark lashes resting against his cheek, thicker than should ever be allowed. His brown skin was both deep and warm but just shy of dark. His curls piled atop his head in a bun that allowed too many curls to fall from its pile like decorative ribbons, curled to perfection. Ivory horns protruded from his brow, the skin around them raised and cracked, meeting his flesh with charred veins. They reached up like a stag, branching off to climb up before they turned into spirals at their tips. They were pretty in an odd way. Their tips were pointed with scraps of something dark and macabre hanging from them.

"You're staring," he growled. Voice gruff and heavy with sleep.

"Just wondering what the hell you're doing in my bed." It was true. The last thing she thought she'd wake to after the hybrid took yet another bite out of her was Killian in her bed.

"I couldn't heal you from downstairs," he muttered, voice low as he adjusted his hold, getting more comfortable.

His words turned over in her mind, and she lifted her arm. Her skin was dark around the wound — or where the wound used to be. The same black veins that worked over Killian's brow sprouted from the closed wound. Little black branches with dainty leaves, dark and wilted, climbed up from her skin.

She touched a leaf against her will, confusion moving through her as she watched the small branches grow from her wound like it was split soil.

"Don't worry. They'll fall off once you're fully healed."

This kind of healing was one she'd never seen before. She'd thought he was merely a crossroad demon and that her healing would come with brimstone and fire, not whatever this was.

"Stay still," he groaned as she tried to push away from him to get a better look. "You'll break free before you're ready."

"What the hell does that mean?" She kicked the blankets off. Whatever she had been expecting, it wasn't this. A cage of branches surrounded her, the same little branches reaching into her wounds and sprouting dead leaves. It was jarring looking at herself trapped, even for healing. Her hand shook as she reached down, touching her finger to the wound in her side. There was no pain, just the odd sensation of something moving under her skin.

Killian offered no explanation.

"I don't..." Panic made her heart thud in her chest. "What are you doing to me?" He'd told her he was healing her, but this felt invasive. Like he was planting something within her skin, letting it roam through her veins. Crawl through her. "Stop. Stop it!"

"Just a little while longer, you're nearly healed enough for the pain to pass."

"I would rather pain than this."

"Confusion?" He chuckled low, releasing a slow sigh. "Welcome to my life. I've been nothing but confused since the two of you summoned me to the crossroads."

She felt imprisoned. Everything in her wanted to swipe the branches away. Free herself. As though reading her thoughts, his hands covered hers, his thumbs rubbing slow circles on her wrists. The press of his rings against her skin made the memory of him kneeling before her flash through her mind.

She swallowed hard, heart suddenly racing for another reason entirely.

"If it bothers you so much, go back to sleep. I'll be gone when you wake up."

Something had changed.

She didn't know Killian well, but there was a confidence in him he lacked before. He held onto her without permission, comfortable in bed behind her. His touch was sure. Strong.

Who the hell was he?

That question ricocheted through her mind, building her nerves. Sleep was something that wouldn't come, not when she was so unsure. Instead, she let her eyes look everywhere but at the sinister-looking branches.

"Where's Jinx?" It annoyed her that Jinx was the first thing that came to mind. That she even cared where she was while still healing from the consequences Rue took on her behalf.

The chuckle that left him was softer than the ones she'd heard before. It comforted her against her will. "She's pouting in the hall."

Her eyes narrowed at the door. She could see where the light stopped halfway, obstructed by something on the other side. "You made her stay out there? While you're in here?"

"Not me. You."

Her brow cocked. "Jinx doesn't make a habit of listening to me."

"For some reason, she does when your bedroom is concerned. She worried you would wake, see her in here and throw a fit. Apparently, she's not allowed in this room."

She wasn't. It was a rule Rue had drilled into her through violence, and she was relieved now, as she lay there vulnerable and confused, that it had stuck. Sometimes Jinx's very presence was enough to make her feel completely irritated. Rubbed raw mentally and emotionally.

Though she was still tense, Rue adjusted deeper into his hold.

The relief he brought her couldn't be denied. The hollow of her chest wasn't filled with desolation anymore, the pain lighting it on fire as she rejoiced in the burn. Her flesh slowly knit back together, assisted by the weird foliage that was somehow both alive and dead.

Poe's words about not being broken played over in her mind. Maybe it was the vulnerability of being cradled against Killian's chest that made her want that to be true. To give herself a chance to love the person she was, even if it was just pieces of who she'd once been.

"Your mind is loud," Killian muttered. His very voice had changed. It deepened into something that bellowed from the centre of his chest. A boom in the void of darkness.

"It often is."

He groaned low, the sound an engine in his chest that wouldn't catch. "From what Jinx has told me, that makes sense. Goblins, witches, and all sorts of things."

A slow sigh left her. "Jinx has a way of getting into trouble."

"Did you have a way of getting into trouble before you were untethered?"

Rue thought about it. Before she had come across Duke DuTerre, who used her blood to kill those who stood in his way and damned her in the eyes of her coven, she had been reserved. She listened to the teachings of her grandmother and the chastising of her mother and priestess, afraid that if she didn't, the prophecy that was a cinderblock attached to her ankle would drag her down. Trouble was something she carefully avoided.

"No." There wasn't much more she could say. She wasn't sure if she was ready for Killian to know about the past she was constantly running from. The one she was still paying for. She wasn't sure if she'd ever tell him. Everything with Killian felt temporary.

"It's interesting," he hummed at her answer.

"What is?"

He was quiet, as though sorting through his thoughts before he answered. "To think that the only thing that kept your soul from getting into trouble before you were untethered was the skin that housed it."

That thought made her frown.

"It's not as though your soul could have been so different without you knowing. Without you fighting against the constant whisper of chaos in your ear."

Did she hear a whisper? Those days had been so full of worry, she wasn't sure if she could remember. But, there must have been a part of her that had been foolish, or else she wouldn't be there, untethered from her soul.

"It feels like you and Jinx are two sides of the same coin. It makes me wonder if Fate hadn't planned your untethering, just as she plans everything else."

Bitterness sat like bile at the back of her throat. "Lucky me. Fate seems to have interjected in every aspect of my life, and never for the better."

His hold tightened ever so slightly. "Or maybe, you've yet to let yourself see the benefits of her intervention."

Rue rolled her eyes. "Oh, all these benefits. How will I sort through them?" Sarcasm dripped from every word.

"Well," Killian started with authority. "Your coven doesn't seem to be the kind you would have wanted to be a part of. Had you not been exiled, you would be under the thumb of witches you seem to hate."

A knot creased the space between her brow. That much was true.

"And had you not been untethered from Jinx, once banished, you would have been completely alone."

Alone sounded nice after all these years of torment.

"You might not always get along—"

"Pretty much never," she interrupted.

"But loneliness... true loneliness, eats away at you."

Rue sighed again. She wasn't sure she liked how much sense he was making. Poe's words rang through her head again. Because if Killian was right and Fate had done all this for her own good, and Poe was right, and she wasn't broken, then she had a lot to sit with.

She had to sit with the possibility that all her misery was moulded by her own hands.

She adjusted, suddenly uncomfortable with having to confront herself while in the arms of someone she barely knew.

"This changes nothing between us," she said, forcing her eyes closed.

Killian hummed against her, a silent understanding moving between them.

And despite all she swore to herself, she fell asleep.

She dreamed.

Of her grandmother singing an ancient song in a voice that echoed through her being. Her hand reached out, and darkness enveloped them. It was soothing, despite the macabre setting. A chill moved through her, blowing against her bare shoulders, and she was grown. Her grandmother still stood there, ushering her forward. To where? She didn't get to see.

Her teeth chattered as she stretched out, her hands brushing against the cooled sheets beside her. She continued to stretch, basking in the way sleep still rolled over her, soothing all the parts of her that constantly called for rest, before she sat up.

Her eyes were wide, looking over her room.

Braids curtained her face, her bantu bumps taken out. She touched a hand to her head, frowning.

Killlian taking down her hair while she slept felt... intimate.

Her room was empty, nothing but piles of wax where her candles had burned out and a chill in the air as her company. Rue wrapped her arms around herself. It was the cold that made her feel out of place and not his absence.

So what if he snuck out of her room while she slept? That was what she told him to do.

Still, she felt uneasy.

It was silly, she told herself as she pushed her blankets off and ran her hands down the smooth skin of her side. It was flawless. Skin that hadn't met a volatile monster the likes of Poe and suffered the consequences. Her eyes dropped, inspecting.

Her thumb traced a ghost of the wound, the place where she knew it should be.

Just what was Killian? she thought again.

On her feet, she slowly walked to the mirror in the corner. It had a cathedral window frame in gold. She leaned in, tilting her head to inspect her neck.

The skin was smooth there, too.

Rue frowned, looking herself over.

He'd kept his word. Healed her and disappeared, leaving her alone. Bottom lip pushed out, she turned and looked around her room. There were no signs of the weird little branches that were planted in her flesh. No sign of the cage that held them together. It was like a dream, gone the moment she woke up.

She scratched at her brow, thick in her thoughts.

Her knowledge of demons was limited. She was much like Poe in that sense. She only paid attention to the ones who would benefit her. The Dark Realm was vast. The beings who called it home, countless. Aside from the ones she dealt with at the apothecaries for trading, she had no reason to seek them out. It wasn't like she was a mortal who would do something foolish, like try to summon one. In all honesty, there were so many other beings in the Dark Realm she would deal with before a demon. Their darkness was as unpredictable as some witch's magic.

Rue stared at her reflection. At the smooth plains of brown skin on her soft, round belly.

He'd helped her, and that didn't sit right with her. Worse than that, he'd made her think about who she was and the misery she'd been wearing like a cloak since she was cast out of her coven.

A gift from Fate, perhaps, if she let Killian's words plant in her mind like a seed.

There had been truth to his words. She *had* practically been a prisoner in her coven. Leaving them was as much a gift as it was a curse. She got to be free from their oppressive hands, even though they tore her in two.

Oppressive hands were reaching for her again. Her hands viciously rubbed the sleep from her eyes, also ridding her mind of all thoughts of Poe, Killian, and their words. Before she confronted all the baggage she carried around, she had to get rid of the coven that haunted her.

Leaning toward the mirror, she breathed on the glass, fogging it with her breath. Her finger slowly dragged through the moisture, creating the Lumena's seal before she swiped the script for Fortuna sloppily in the middle. Her reflection wavered. Shimmering like rippled water from the symbols before it showed Fortuna.

If Poe had visited her, she wore no signs of it. She looked just as she had in the woods. Determined. Cold. Calculating. Rue watched with a brow cocked, needing to focus on something she understood. There was no way for her to make sense of Killian and his actions because she didn't know him, and she had very little intention of changing that. But Fortuna? She was a villain she knew well. One she could understand because she had the same poisonous rage in her own blood, urging her efforts.

The bedroom was in disarray. Sheets hanging from the bed, pillows on the floor, books askew on their dark shelves. Fortuna hissed, swiping an angry arm over the table, making everything topple. Her long nails were practically claws, her hands contorted as she bent at the waist and shrieked.

Her anger was potent. Feral. The parts of Rue that wanted to destroy her coven — one built on the backs of her mother and her mother's mother — revelled in the sight.

"What a tantrum. So juvenile for the woman who wants to become the priestess of Lumena." Rue clicked her tongue in mock disapproval. As much as she hated Ferula for all she'd done to her family, there was a regal air to her. She had an authority that commanded even her mother. Fortuna was a child playing make-believe. So out of touch. So... *new.*

Chest heaving, Fortuna shoved her fingers through her hair, brushing it back from her face. It took her a moment to gather herself. Each huff cut shorter and shorter until she finally sucked in a breath, held it, and released it with a malicious grin.

"Just what are you planning, Fortuna?" Rue whispered.

The unmistakable sound of a match being struck filled the silence of Rue's room as Fortuna lit a thick black candle. The green flame danced too high as she leaned down and whispered into the fire. "Show me Ruin Crowe."

A slight breath doused the flame, and green smoke billowed up from the wick, climbing like a phantom vine into a twisted frame. The space between flickered, static as it tried to hone in on the sight of Rue standing in her room, looking at Fortuna in turn. The smoke fell, weighed down by something unseen until it dissipated to nothing.

Fortuna hissed.

Rue smiled. It seemed the heir of her coven wasn't strong enough to get past her wards. Not even as weak as Rue was.

"What a sorry thing my coven has become," she whispered lightly, as she watched Fortuna rage. If this was a show of their power, maybe she had nothing to worry about.

19

JiNX

THERE WAS A CHURNING in the pit of her belly. A roll of hunger that made her throat tight and her saliva thin.

"My kitty is hungry!" she whined, throwing her head back. Her arm rested on her brow as she dramatically draped herself across her bed. Her body pillow of a giant bear was wedged under her back, as her toes brushed against the floor.

Unlike Rue's bedroom, hers was beautiful. Everything was in different shades of pink and purple. Her walls were covered in different portraits of Black men and women in bronze frames. She just couldn't see one sitting on a shelf and not buy it. It drove Rue crazy, but she loved how it made her feel connected to a world that wasn't hers. There was something about seeing people — mortals — that looked like her. It soothed the frantic parts of her mind. Twinkle lights covered her ceiling, casting a glow through her room. Piles of books she would likely never read were stacked randomly. She felt like she would love fantasy books... if she ever sat down long enough to read one. The covers were so pretty, and the tease of different worlds called to her.

Her belly tightened.

"Down, kitty."

Everything clenched.

This was so very annoying. Since she saw Killian at those crossroads, she was an addict. Her body needed a fix. STAT!

If only Rue weren't being such a buzzkill.

Jinx rolled her eyes, blowing air through her lips until they vibrated together. She blew harder, enjoying the way the sound sharpened before she dropped it low and rose it high again. Giggling, she rolled onto her side. Her legs tangled in the fabric of her skirt.

Thud!

She hit the floor with a groan.

Scrambling to sit, she huffed a breath.

That tightness in her lower belly intensified with each passing minute.

"How the hell is Rue so unbothered?" she whined. "There is no way her cat isn't meowing like mine, and she's just... not doing anything about it. It's going to hiss any second now. Turn on me!" On her feet, she planted her hands on her hips.

It's not like she didn't know where Killian was.

"I'll feed my kitty a little treat." She dropped her hands to her crotch, cupping herself through her skirt. "Hush now... treats are coming!"

Determined, she slipped out into the hall. Her bedroom was on the second floor, alongside a full bath and the guest room. Rue's room was the only room on the third floor — once the attic. Jinx closed the door quietly behind her, tiptoeing toward the guest room.

She'd heard Killian moving around in there. He'd been in Rue's room for a while before he slunk out like some trespasser.

Everyone was a trespasser to Rue, so that wasn't exactly an exaggeration.

Jinx rolled her eyes. "Rue can be such a meanie."

Maybe if she rode that stick up her butt instead of just leaving it wedged in there, she would be more fun.

Depending on how big the stick was.

Or the texture.

And maybe...

She shook her head before she spiralled. Her thoughts had this way of running away all on their own if she didn't remember to focus. She had a kitty to calm, after all. She couldn't forget that. Not when it was already so angry.

Her hand wrapped around the doorknob. "Time for a little snacky snack."

Without another thought, she pushed the door open.

This room was the barest in the house. It had a simple white dresser they'd gotten during a forced trip to IKEA. She liked going there; usually it ended with Rue buying her an ice cream to shut her up. The only other piece of furniture was a silver, metal-framed king bed. A rug had been in here once... though she had no idea what happened to it.

Killian stood with his back to her, muscles rippling under his dark, taut skin as he fussed with papers on the bed. His tattooed flesh was breathtaking. His long fingers sparkled with rings. His sweats sat low on his waist — black instead of grey, but she wouldn't fuss over something so small. And the horns! Whew, the horns really did something for her. He should keep them out all the time.

He looked over his shoulder, a smirk dimpling his cheek. "Jinx."

She ran across the room. Her feet left the floor and wrapped around his waist as she clung to his back. His warmth soothed that hunger a bit, her hands rubbing over his pecs, her hips rolling as she humped him.

"To what do I owe the pleasure?" The confusion he normally wore when she appeared practically out of thin air was absent. She wanted to question it, but she couldn't. Not now while her belly ached and her kitty threatened to show its angry claws.

She giggled at the thought. A pussy with claws would be absolutely terrifying... but also oddly hilarious.

"What is so funny?"

"Shh... kitty is hungry."

"You have a cat?"

"Mmm, a demanding one." She rolled her hips harder, annoyed about all the clothes.

"Jinx." Killian reached around, his hand wrapped around her thigh to tug her from his back.

She let him move her, if for no other reason than he was moving her toward what she really wanted. The beast hiding inside the sweatpants. The treat she came for.

His hands wrapped around her waist when she finally settled with her hands around his neck, her legs around his waist, and her hips moving against his lower belly. He may be lithe, but he was pure muscle in his slim build. She appreciated the hardness of him as she gyrated. She wanted something hard between her legs.

He chuckled, the low revving sound making her groan. "Can I help you?" It wasn't really a question. It was a tease. A playful invitation he waited for her to accept.

And damn, would she. "Oh, I think you can help me very well."

"Is that right?"

She reached between them, her frantic hands trying to push down the waistband of his sweats. "Yes. Just take these off and we can..." Hands fisted in the fabric of her skirt, she pulled it up. The feeling of her flesh hitting his was enough to make her eyes roll back.

This was a type of magic she'd never felt before.

Which was saying something.

Having Rue at her side, capable of magic that often made others envious, she'd thought she'd experienced it all, either as a witness or a victim, but this? This was a different beast. This was being wrapped up in something so intense, it breathed into her, filling her. It clouded her mind, weighed down her thoughts, and stole them. It held her heart in a grip, daring her to try and make it beat on its own.

Everything about her felt like it belonged to Killian, and she needed to have him.

Now!

He caught her wrist right as her fingers slipped under his waistband. "Jinx, this isn't the time for this."

Why was everyone being so difficult?

"There's *always* time for this!" she argued.

His dark eyes searched hers, but she could see in the depths of them that he felt the same way. He was in the same thick smoke of magic she was. The kind of magic only Fate herself could conjure.

"Always." She slipped her hand lower as he loosened his grip. His thickness throbbed in her hand as she held onto it, squeezing gently.

"Fuck," he groaned.

"Now... let's stop being so silly and feed this kitty."

His brow cocked. "Ah. The kitty..."

Jinx nodded slowly. "She's hungry."

Killian shook his head, light laughter slipping from him as he walked to the bed and dropped them onto it. His hand swiped the papers away, the sound of them fluttering through the air loud in the quiet.

Her back hit the mattress, knocking relief into her. She breathed it in, filling her lungs. It felt almost as good as he did.

Frantic, they didn't waste time. The head of his dick pressed up against her before he guided it through her slick folds. Every stroke wound her up, making her lift her hips and try to meet him.

Her body was being a needy bitch. It wasn't her in control, not anymore. It was her kitty, and it was tired of waiting.

She shimmied.

If only he would stop toying with her.

But she liked it as much as she didn't. Something about being teased while drunk on whatever magic surged through her made her buzz.

"Killian," she moaned. "Quit playing with me."

"Jinx, Jinx, Jinx." He pressed into her, just enough that the head of him slipped in before he pulled out again. He held himself above her, dark eyes staring like she was something to be read so he could learn all he could about her. He breathed across her cheek until his lips brushed against her ear, making her shudder. "Quit acting like you don't like being played with. Like you haven't been asking the universe to deliver you someone who will play with you right."

Well... *gods be damned.*

She had to offer her thanks to Fate, because she got this so right, Jinx wasn't sure if she'd ever be able to tell that goddess she was wrong. Ever. Again.

He pressed into her, making her toes curl. Just a tease. Just the tip.

"Killian," she groaned again.

"I wonder," he whispered, the sound of his voice strained. "If this is how you make Rue feel. Frustrated beyond reason, knowing she won't get her way... not without..." He pressed into her again, pausing barely inside her. "You toying with her first."

"A lesson?" Her eyes widened, lips pressed thin. "How very dare you!"

"You'll see I dare to do a lot of things, Jinx." He pushed in a little more, blissfully stretching her. "I think it's time you had someone push you back. Someone to teach you *hard* lessons."

She whined low in her throat as he slipped in further. "I don't..." she panted. "I don't like lessons."

This man. Maybe it was the demon in him that made her feel like he was touching every one of her sinful pleasures.

"Well, that's too bad." He thrusted, the heat of him hitting a button inside her that made her eyes fog over before they rolled back, her bottom lip clasped tightly in her teeth to keep from screaming. "Since I plan to teach you all the ones you've been skipping."

Fuck that.

No one was the boss of her.

Not even this fine, perfect, fat dicked, god... no, demon. Not even him. She was in charge. She was *always* in charge, even when she wasn't. She was Jinx. She was the boss!

Legs wrapped around him, she threw her weight, rolling on top.

Mischief curled her lips at the edges as she stared down at him. The horns on his head made him look like something forbidden. That thought only made her want him more.

Knees planted at his sides, she rolled her hips, gliding him back in.

His smile broadened, arms folding with his hands behind his head as he watched her move.

"Lessons are boring." She rode him with a hard, relentless pace, eyes locked on his. "No matter who is teaching them."

Killian said nothing, but that smile said it all. It was cocky. Confident. The kind of smile someone wore when they were about to prove her wrong.

That both irritated and excited her.

Her nails dug into his chest, holding him steady as her thrusts became fierce things that made the bedframe squeak.

Black ash rose from his brow around his horns, floating in the air like morbid fireflies.

"Look at me," he demanded.

Jinx hadn't realized she hadn't been. Her eyes rolled closed, her bottom lip caught in her teeth.

"No." Her chin was caught between his thumb and finger as he forced her face toward his.

Her hands braced on his chest, eyes snapping open as she whined low in her throat.

"Let me see you."

It was a simple sentence. It shouldn't have meant as much as it did as he held her chin, looking into her eyes. He held her there, allowing her no escape as he stared past her wicked grin to the Jinx she was too afraid to be. The one that was more than a mere curse. The one with a yearning she sometimes thought would completely fracture her until she shattered into irreparable pieces. Her heart stuttered as her hips slowed.

Killian leaned up, his eyes shifting back and forth between hers. A wicked smile stretched his lips, and she knew he was about to do something or say something she would never recover from. "There you are."

Her eyes blurred with tears, and her throat tightened. She did her best to swallow down the emotions she wasn't ready to feel, clearing her throat.

"There's my girl."

Well, fuck. She blinked hard, trapping the tears behind her lids. This man was more than she would have ever dared dream of. During the nights when sleep was something she didn't need, and she wandered around the dark alone, she would spare a wish for something, but nothing as grand as him.

He was *everything.*

She hated to admit it, but she would likely get on her knees and beg him for whatever lessons he would teach her. This was more than sex. This was something in the centre of her chest, finally being soothed by something that lived in his.

Ugh! Maybe she would let him be the boss... sometimes.

Her smile wobbled as she resumed her brutal pace. "Sometimes would be okay," she hissed the words as her stomach tightened and she started to pulse around him. "Sometimes..."

"Sometimes what?" Killian gasped. His fingers pressed into her hips. They felt like claws as they dug in, nails sharp enough to cut. The pain pushed her toward the edge.

"I'm close," she huffed.

"Jinx."

"I'm close!"

"Jinx!"

Pain shot through the back of her head, and everything went black.

20

KILLIAN

JINX SLUMPED ONTO HIS chest.

Eyes wide, his hand wrapped around her. Relief poured into him when he felt the gentle rise and fall of her breath, but it was short-lived as he looked up at Rue.

She was wrath personified as she stood, a cast-iron pan still held over her head. Her dark eyes looked like voids of pitch, the flesh around them just as dark. Her lips were brushed over with darkness as her chest huffed in angry breaths of air like she was trying to contain something vicious inside her.

Rue looked… *beautiful.*

There was such a macabre beauty to her barely constrained darkness. Wisps of true madness hidden behind the mask of her rage made her something he couldn't take his eyes off of—even with himself firmly planted inside Jinx.

Her eyes pinched closed, nostrils flared. "The thing about a person and their soul is, even with it free and walking around making my life nothing but one challenge after the next, I can still feel my soul. I can feel her pain, her fear, her…" Her nose curled. "Pleasure."

Killian gently set Jinx on the bed beside him. He tucked her in, brushing her hair from her face, but all the while, he couldn't take his eyes off Rue.

It was like seeing a monster lurking in the dark. Barely more than a silhouette, but he wanted to keep it in his sights because he wasn't entirely sure what would happen if he looked away.

Intrigue pulled at the centre of his chest, but that darkness… it called to him. Beckoned him like a lost child with its hands out, searching for someone to hold its hand.

Her words finally registered, and he pulled his eyes away to look at Jinx. The sheets were only pulled over one of her breasts; the other hung to the side, her mouth gaping, locs, braids, and tangles pouring off the pillow.

"Her… pleasure."

Rue pinched the bridge of her nose, squeezing her eyes closed. "Yes."

"So every time Jinx and I—"

"Yes."

His lips pursed. He didn't know how to feel about all that. He wanted to tease her, but something told him Rue wouldn't be as receptive to pestering — even if painted over with seduction — as Jinx was.

She huffed a breath, deep enough to deflate her. The darkness receded from around her eyes, leaving hollows behind. She looked worn. Weary. He had healed her, but there were parts of her that were so broken, he may never be able to reach them.

"I..." He let the words trail off because, honestly, he wasn't sure what to say. "We..."

"You both do as you want because none of what I'm dealing with affects you." She turned on her heel, leaving the room and taking her pan with her.

Killian stood there at a loss.

It made him ache knowing he'd upset her, especially because he knew it would erect another wall he wasn't sure he'd be able to knock down.

"Fuck."

He sighed, throwing his head back and linking his hands behind his head. Fate might have gotten it right with Jinx, but he was seriously starting to doubt if he was meant for Rue. Despite the pull in his chest, making him long for something as simple as her smile, he couldn't convince himself he had anything to offer her.

Another sigh left him.

Killian walked over to the bed, pressing a gentle kiss to Jinx's brow before he moved to follow Rue. All he could do now was try to smooth whatever new wrinkles he made in the relationship he barely had with her.

His footsteps felt weighted as he made his way downstairs. He followed the sound of gentle clinking to the living room, where Rue stood next to the bar cart, pouring herself a drink.

She didn't turn when he entered, leaning on the doorway. The living room looked like new. Any signs of the hybrid and the havoc she brought with her were gone. He saw her tense the longer he stood there, trying to keep hold of the annoyance thickening the air.

Navigating relationships wasn't his thing. Before all this — before the crossroads — he was a lone beast. Something people saw and ran from. An apparition that sent a chill up one's spine and made them pray for deliverance to whoever would listen.

"Will... Jinx be okay?" It probably wasn't the best place to start.

"Yup." The word was clipped. "Unlike me, my magic still protects her. She'll be good as new as soon as she wakes up... likely sooner."

"Good..." His eyes squeezed closed, lips pressed thin. "Good for her, anyway."

She said nothing. He felt like he was stumbling around in the dark. Everything he said was a misstep, and no matter how hard he tried, he couldn't catch his damn footing. It was frustrating beyond reason.

Killian had to navigate two of the most important relationships he would have in his life. Mates. And he felt like he was failing miserably.

"I don't hate her," Rue said finally, breaking the silence. "It may seem like that from the outside. I can see that. I *know* how it looks. We are opposites in a way... forever clashing." She lifted her glass, throwing the entire contents back before she picked up another decanter to refill it. She paused, staring into the glass as though her next words drowned in the dark amber, before she took a sip. She held it in her cheeks before she slowly swallowed. "I envy her freedom. Her ability to be whole without constantly being reminded something is missing... an emptiness that someone has made sure can't be filled. I envy not being consumed with a longing. Feeling like I spend every waking hour of my life chasing after it, knowing I'll never catch it."

Her words made him reach up and touch his fingers to his chest. It was only recently that he became whole, but he could still feel that phantom emptiness.

"She is entirely Jinx... and me? I'm barely Rue." She threw the drink back, tossing the glass on the cart, making everything rattle. "And knowing that makes me constantly annoyed with her... because it reminds me that I don't hate her. I hate myself." She swayed on her feet, slumping forward.

Killian rushed across the room, his arms wrapping around her stomach. She slumped back against him, her head rolling on her neck. "And here I thought witches would be able to hold their liquor."

"It's not the liquor," she moaned. She pushed at him, trying to free herself from his hold, but lacking the strength.

Panic made his heart jump into the base of his throat. With an arm behind her legs, he scooped her up in his arms and carried her to the couch. She lost some of her fight, resigning herself to staying in his arms as he sat, cradling her. His hands smoothed over the sides of her face, trying to force her to look at him.

She resisted, pinching her eyes closed.

"What's wrong?" His knuckle bent under her chin, forcing her face toward his. "What happened?"

"I swung a pan," she groaned, swallowing hard.

"What?"

She opened her eyes, but it was slow, and they were unfocused. "I swung a pan," she repeated.

His eyes searched hers before they lifted to look at the pan sitting on the coffee table. "Her pleasure is yours... and her pain." Eyes wide, he looked down at her. "Why the hell would you hit her?"

"Because she annoys me." She sucked in a sharp breath, her eyes closing again. "*You* annoy me."

"Me?"

"Mmm," she hummed, letting her head fall against his arm. "Before you, I could at least pretend there was a solution to all of this. That I could be whole. Then you slept with her."

He said nothing. He wasn't entirely sure if there was something he *could* say.

"And you fell in love with her... like so many people easily do." She huffed in a breath. "And now you're hers... more than you'll ever be mine."

His brows dropped. If he didn't know any better, he would think that was a confession of some kind. A whisper in the dark, when her eyes were closed, and she was likely concussed.

A single tear broke free from her closed lids, leaving a slow trail down the bridge of her nose. "Nothing is ever mine anymore," she whispered. "Because I'm not Rue... not anymore."

His heart — or whatever dried and dark thing pumped in his chest — shattered.

The squabbling between Rue and Jinx suddenly felt like a war, but only Jinx was armed. Rue had to feel it all. Even if she won, she lost.

This curse was a kind that was meant to break someone down and then grind them to dust. It was evil in a way he would celebrate if it wasn't directed at the woman in his arms.

She's been pulled into their pleasure, a pleasure she herself had never gotten, and so she gave them both pain.

Killian's hand shook as he gently brushed his fingertips along the scar on her cheek. He followed it up to her ear, tracing the edges where a piece had been carved off. This scar was so much like Rue's curse. It was something she had to carry. Something that stole a piece of her.

Jinx's skin was smooth. Flawless. Like she'd never had to carry anything for too long before her slate was wiped clean. It made her reckless. Nothing but her moods and wants drove her.

How many of these scars belonged to Jinx? he wondered.

Fate had a cruel way of doing things.

She bound him so completely to two women who were supposed to be one, and made him fall for one while he stumbled behind another. And now, looking down at the woman in his arms, he found himself lost.

There was a part of him that wanted to give this woman whatever she wanted, to see if he could soften the crease between her brows, or soothe the scowl that turned down the corner of her lips. He wanted to see if she could smile.

Something told him it would be a vicious sight.

He sighed, adjusting where he sat so he could pull her tightly into his chest.

He may not be able to give her everything she wanted, but it was entirely possible that he could do what he did best and bring a misery to her coven the likes of which would make them beg for death.

21

RUE

SOMETHING SMELLED DELICIOUS.

The smell made the ache in her head feel like she could push it to the back of her mind and still function around it. She ran a sluggish hand over her face, pausing to rub the sleep from the corner of her eyes before she forced herself to sit. Her hand ran along the couch.

Rue sat up, the abrupt motion making her head spin when she realized she wasn't in her room.

The crease between her brows deepened as she ran her palms over her thighs and looked toward the kitchen.

Killian had his back to her as he stood over the stove. A stove she used for potions. Instead of the herb-rich smell that usually swirled around the house when she was brewing in the kitchen, the smell was rich and enticing.

The quiet unnerved her. Usually, when she and Jinx broke out into blows, chaos followed. Jinx may always lose when fists flew between them, but she rarely wore that loss quietly. She needed to remind Rue afterwards that she could still win at something, even if it was merely annoying her.

Her footsteps were quiet as she walked to the kitchen island, leaning on it with weird caution. The space didn't feel like hers, and standing there, she had this odd thought that she was somehow invading somewhere she shouldn't.

"Where's Jinx?" Her voice was too loud in the quiet, and she squeezed her eyes closed for a split second when she heard it.

The wooden spoon Killian held clattered against the pot before he whirled, looking at her. He cleared his throat, the smile he donned tight as he looked her over. "She's sulking."

Rue figured as much. "Where?"

He tilted his head slightly back, the wooden spoon he awkwardly picked up dripping red sauce onto the front of his shirt. "The yard. I asked her not to go far, and she basically told me to go fuck myself."

Her nod was slow, but even that gentle motion rocked her mind. "Checks out." She slid onto the barstool, elbows on the counter as she rested her brow on the tops of her fists.

Her head was pounding.

Tears pooled on her bottom lid as she tried to suppress the bulk of her pain.

The pan had been a bad idea. She knew that. As soon as she swung it, her brain tried to tell her it was one of those things she would regret in the morning. But she'd just been so... *mad.*

And tired.

She was tired of feeling like she was screaming at the top of her lungs and still not being heard. All while being stared at and wondering how the hell they couldn't hear her. Jinx had a way of looking at her as though she was the only thing she could see sometimes, all her attention captivated by Rue in her fury, and still she heard nothing.

Forcing herself to swallow the bile at the back of her throat, she lifted her head and looked at him. Her hand lazily pointed to the sauce on his shirt. "What are you making?"

"Bolognese. Jinx said it was the only way she'd forgive me." He set the spoon down, collecting the sauce with his thumb and pushing it past his lips.

"Gods forbid she doesn't get her way," she muttered, dropping her head into her hands again.

It felt like the whole world revolved around Jinx. Her's certainly did.

Calmness made her inflate. She sucked in a deep breath, shuddering as her headache waned. Warmth cupped her chin, lifting her face. Marmalade eyes stared into hers, soft and sticky enough to get stuck in. His smirk could almost be delicious, if she didn't know he wasn't truly hers and likely never would be.

Suddenly beside her, Killian's thumb held her chin, pulling it slightly to make her lips part.

Her heart fluttered, and she tried to tug her face free. She shouldn't give him these little moments that made her stagger. She'd lose her step, and before she knew it, she would be walking down a path she couldn't find her way back from. One she thought would lead to him.

Gods, she was needy these days.

She blamed it on centuries of being alone with no one but her soul to torment her.

"Just a few moments." His grip wasn't tight enough to actually keep her trapped, but she relented. "Just until you stop looking like you'll collapse from your bad decisions."

Brow creased, she looked down to see the same little vines over her arms, embedded in her skin.

He was *healing* her.

Again.

"I don't need—"

"Rue." His eyes danced between hers. "When will you stop pretending you don't crave what this could be?"

The fluttering halted in her chest, leaving a depressed chill behind. She couldn't fall for this man. There was no point. She would die before the curse was lifted — likely soon if Killian and Jinx kept at it the way they were, sending ripples of magic into the world to stir their coven. Her soul would never be hers. Killian wouldn't be either. "When you make a deal."

She wasn't a fool. It wasn't like she could pretend at this point, even for a second, that a deal could solve anything. Still, it was drawing a line in the sand. Letting Killian know, no matter how close they got, nothing would happen between them.

"A deal could cost me everything." He was so close, practically breathing the words onto her lips.

"It could cost me everything if I stop pretending." The truth of those words made her ache.

His lips brushed against hers, and those blasted tears returned, burning her eyes as she tried with everything she was to hold them back.

Pull away, Rue. Don't be ridiculous. This will bring you nothing but misery.

Their noses bumped gently, skin brushing against skin, before Killian tilted his head and captured her lips with his.

Pure bliss.

It stole her breath. Her body leaned into his, something in her very core craving him. A whimper bubbled up from the depths of her belly, turning into a sob that lodged in her throat.

A taste was fine. A single taste of all the things she knew she couldn't have.

Something in her chest shattered as she pressed a hand to his chest, slowly pushing him away.

A taste was all she could afford.

Killian exhaled a shaky breath, resting his brow against hers. "You're meant to be mine."

"No." It was barely a protest. She felt like she didn't have the energy to truly deny what he was saying. "Maybe once. Maybe when I had a soul to bind to someone else's. Now, Jinx is meant to be yours. And me..." She wasn't sure where that left her yet. Abandoned by the one thing meant to follow her wherever she went and destined to a life of being haunted by the love she couldn't have. Feeling it without ever experiencing it herself.

"A black soul like mine never imagined Fate would be able to see me, consumed by a darkness that made me invisible. Yet, here you are." He exhaled again. "I wonder if you're meant to be my true punishment, since my time at the crossroads didn't break me down enough to absolve me of my sins."

"I'm not yours." Saying it out loud was like hammering the final nail in the coffin of this mating.

"Fate herself has decided this. Must you be so difficult?"

The feeling of his branches leaving her skin as she stood and stepped away from him was disconcerting. It was like peeling off skin that was flaking; it didn't hurt, but the sensation was odd. "Yes. Being difficult is my only freedom these days. Fighting against the bars of the cage so many have told me would be easier to merely learn to live inside. Fate and my coven may have made decisions about me. How I'll live... how I'll die... but they'll forever be haunted by how difficult I was through it all."

The little thorns and vines turned to black smoke, disappearing from her skin as though they were merely an apparition. A side effect of the concussion she undoubtedly gave herself.

His eyes darkened, lips set in a thin line as he rested his hands on the stool she'd abandoned, staring at her. His nostrils flared, barely restrained anger flexing the muscles in his jaw.

"Hmm..." he hummed low. She could practically see the cogs moving in his mind as he tried to decide just how he'd change her mind. "The kind of deal I'd make with you is likely one you wouldn't accept."

Her brow cocked as she moved to sit on the back of the couch, wanting to put more space between them.

"Aren't you going to ask me what sort of deal I'd make?"

"You and Jinx are alike. Both of you like to be heard, so I doubt I have to ask. You'll tell me because you need to." They were like children with a secret.

Killian sighed, sitting on the stool she'd abandoned. "I could make you feel whole."

Her chuckle was the sad kind that made her body feel heavy. "It's a bit funny, isn't it? That you'll make me feel whole at the cost of my soul?"

He leaned his elbows back against the counter, staring at her with hungry eyes. "I already have your soul."

Lips pursed, she gave him a single nod, happy it didn't make her feel like she would throw up now that the pain had subsided. "True enough." But it wouldn't be real. It would be an illusion of something she would never truly have. A deal to remain untethered but trick her mind into believing the hole in her chest wasn't there.

"It's your dissecting of things that makes you unhappy."

Rue rolled her eyes. "And you know this after knowing me for what, less than a week?"

"Happiness is an absurd thing to imagine monsters can grab hold of, don't you think? The best we can do is feel the rush of depravity. To relish in the blissful burn of sin... happiness isn't for the damned, my pretty little dark cloud. We're too hungry to be satisfied by something so trivial."

"Hungry doesn't even begin to cover it."

Killian's head tilted, his eyes deep. "No. I don't imagine it does. But your hunger is one I have no doubt I could satisfy."

Tension built between them. Unspoken words were a fog in the air she didn't know how to decipher.

On his feet, he took slow, calculated steps toward her. His hands were sunk into the pockets of his black slacks, belt at the waist. Her eyes were glued to the stain on his white shirt. Nerves kept her from looking at him when she knew he was about to do something she wasn't sure she could defend herself against.

He stopped in front of her, close enough that she could see the exact shape of that stain as it hovered before her nose. “Ask me.”

A huff trapped in her chest. “Something tells me you’re no longer a demon who makes deals, but even if you were, the deal you’re offering doesn’t entice me.”

He chuckled, and damn if it didn’t pull something in her chest. “I had a feeling it wouldn’t, but that’s not what I’m hoping you’ll ask me for.”

Don’t look at him, Rue. Never look at him again if it means guarding your heart.

“Ask me.”

“For what?” She stood her ground, nose practically bumping into his chest in her stubbornness.

“You know what, dark cloud. Ask me.”

The depressing nickname suited her and made something flutter in her belly. There was a nagging in the back of her mind. A voice that whispered the question she would never ask him, no matter how many times he demanded it.

His hand gripped the front of her throat. His long, slender fingers wrapped effortlessly around the back of her neck, nails digging rapturously. It teased something dark inside her that slammed against her ribs, begging to be free. “Ask me,” he demanded, tightening his hold.

Killian's thumb pressed against the front of her throat, forcing her to tilt her head back to look at him. His eyes had all but turned black, the honey a simple swirl that danced in the darkness. She swallowed hard, marvelling in the way his hand barely allowed her the space she needed to do it.

"Ask me," he demanded again. In all his authority, it unnerved her that she could only envision him on his knees.

Her eyes moved back and forth between his before they dropped down to his lips. "No."

"No?" He chuckled again, tightening his grip. "No, because you're too afraid to ask, or because you don't know the question?"

"I'm not afraid of anything." But that was a lie, because as she stared up at him, she realized she was afraid to ask for anything she would eventually lose.

Killian dipped his head so his lips pressed against her ear. "Liar."

Her heart leapt into her throat.

"You can't pretend to long for happiness if you're too afraid to ask for it." His lips captured her earlobe in a painful nip before he stood, staring down at her. "You'll ask me for it eventually, and when you do, I'll make it my mission to make you happy. Deal or not."

He released her, leaving nothing but the phantom memory of his hand behind. Rue ran her fingers along her throat, missing the threat and demand he put there only to remove.

She was getting sappy.

Perhaps it was because she was no longer fighting. Not really. She had surrendered, even if no one else could tell. She'd cast the dice and turned away, letting the universe make the call.

That surrender untied the emotions she kept bound so she could keep on fighting.

And she hated it.

Rue watched him walk away. He made his way back to the stove, slowly stirring the pot. She watched the way his back rippled beneath his shirt, wondering if happiness was something he could truly offer her. How could a woman without her soul ever truly be happy?

Her tongue ran slowly along her lips, suddenly too dry.

Swallowing again, Rue shook her head. "Don't make promises you can't keep." Turning on her heel, she made her way toward the hall.

"Rue," Killian called.

Even though she knew she shouldn't, she paused and looked over her shoulder.

"The promises I make, I destroy people to keep."

She turned without an answer because a part of her already knew that. Just as she knew the person he would destroy to keep that promise would likely be her.

22

JiNX

SADNESS WAS A WAVE that threatened to pull her under its depths. Drown her. Not that anyone would care. These people didn't care about her. They didn't care that she was funny, charismatic or had great boobs. She was absolutely wonderful, but Killian kept moving around the house, doing things he thought would make Rue happy. Like she wasn't even there.

Stupid demon. Rue was never happy.

This was all pointless.

They likely didn't even realize she was gone.

Bare toes in the wood chips, she sat on a swing, leaning her brow against the chains. She liked playgrounds at night. It was haunting to be somewhere that was supposed to be loud and crowded when it was quiet and empty.

Sucking in a desperate breath, she pushed back and started to swing. Rue was gone off somewhere. Jinx couldn't be bothered to wonder where, but Killian was likely following her around, begging to be seen.

She knew what that felt like, begging to be seen when someone refused to look at her.

"There you are." Killian settled on the swing beside her.

Her heart fluttered. "You were looking for me?"

Planting his feet in the wood chips, he made the swing gently sway side to side, hands wrapped around the chains and eyes glued to her. "I may have had to bribe your bat." He tilted his head toward the climbing structure.

Bram stood at the top of the slide, beady eyes watching. Jinx grinned. "What did you have to give him?"

"It took a while to figure him out. I wasn't sure what kind of bat he was. He looks... too big. I ended up having to give him a chocolate bar." Killian chuckled low.

"Mr. Big." Jinx nodded. "He loves those."

"I know. He made me give him two."

'I like what I like,' Bram squeaked.

Jinx chuckled. That was true. She knew, despite that, he would have brought Killian even if he had nothing to offer her little cutie patootie. "I know."

Killian looked at the bat. "He seems to always know where you are."

'It's only my job,' Bram opened his wings, stretching before he wrapped them around himself.

"He's linked to Rue's soul." Just like Killian was.

That thought soured her mood.

"Where did you go?" Killian had disappeared for a few hours last night. She felt his absence in the house. It returned to the stale nothingness it often was. Loneliness breathed into everything without the smell of heat that accompanied him and made their house almost feel like a home. She'd been too preoccupied with soothing her kitty to ask him before, but now she wanted answers.

He stilled, before he smiled at her, eyes deep. "Why? Did you miss me?" he teased.

She was mad at him. She had to keep repeating that in her mind so she wouldn't forget. Killian made it so easy for her to forget. She wasn't used to that, after a century of Rue making it so easy to remember.

Killian watched her with a slow smirk. "I had some business to take care of."

Jinx shifted, her swing close enough to him that she could almost bump into him. The warm smell of him was... different. The heat was covered with something. A thick layer of melancholy and despair. Wicked sheets of darkness covered the warmness she often wanted to curl into. Her heart stuttered, fear seeping in. "Is that why you smell different now?"

He closed the space between them with a gentle sway. "Do I?"

She nodded slowly, inhaling the air between them. "You smell darker than you did before. Heavier. Like dread. It's nice but... different from before."

Something had changed.

She didn't know how she felt about that. Killian had come into their lives, all because Rue was trying to get rid of her, but seeing his attachment to her almost made her hopeful that plan was something that would never be carried out. Now... he had changed.

Her eyes glassed over, nostrils quivering. "What did you do?"

Killian got to his feet. His hands grabbed hold of the chains of her swing as he leaned down, trying to unravel her thoughts.

"You did something," she sobbed. "I can tell."

He was flustered, eyes wide as he froze in place. "Hopefully nothing that warrants tears."

"But you did something!" A sob lodged in her throat, making her gasp around it. It made her ache that he did it, not because it was a change but because she knew why. "For Rue!"

His brows dropped. Killian grabbed her hands, lifting her from where she sat. He held her close to his chest, taking her place on the swing. Her back nestled into his chest, his face settled on her shoulder. One arm wrapped around her stomach, his thumb tracing slow circles. He dipped his thumb under her corset. His hands soothed her as soon as they touched her skin, like they were reaching past her flesh and to the parts that belonged to him.

How very annoying!

She didn't want to be soothed. She wanted to be angry. Why did no one ever let her be angry?

Bottom lip pushed out, she adjusted, so her ass was resting evenly on his thighs. "You'll get rid of me, won't you?" For the first time, the implications of that felt heavy. "Everyone always wants to get rid of me. Every day, Rue talks about plans to finally be rid of me, and now you're going to help her, aren't you? You're going to help her because you think that somehow, that will make her happy. You don't want me anymore." She sniffled, but it did nothing to keep the snot from running onto her lip.

This was no longer Rue shaking her fist at the sky to gods she didn't believe in. This wasn't veiled threats and boob punches. This wasn't some phantom in the corner, haunting her but unable to reach out and take hold of her — this was real. Killian may be able to do the thing Rue had been trying to accomplish for as long as Jinx could remember. Tears clouded her eyes as that knowledge hit her in the centre of her chest like a ton of bricks.

"No," he whispered against the top of her head.

"I don't believe you."

His chuckle was a vicious sound, like growls in the dark that had no right to comfort her the way it did. "For all your differences, you are both equally stubborn."

Jinx scowled, sniffling and making her snot rattle in her nose. "Nuh uh! I'm more stubborn than she is!"

"Sure you are," he cooed. He shoved the swing back, and she had to wrap her hands back around the chains. The wind blew gently past her, as if it were on his side and trying to wear her down.

"I am!" If there was one thing she had over Rue, it was that she was more stubborn. If she weren't, she would have rolled over after all these years and become the obedient little soul Rue wanted her to be.

But if she had, they wouldn't be in this mess.

Because Rue wouldn't have had to save Jinx again.

Jinx scoffed, rolling her eyes at that realization.

It wasn't her fault that Rue lived her life like she was living out some kind of sentence. So, the Lumena Coven were all spiteful bitches that had it out for the Crowe women. *What the hell did that have to do with her, anyway?* Really, Rue could have just ignored them until they pissed her off. Even with Jinx, she was stronger. But noooooo! She had to be all miserable for absolutely no reason.

Well... for some reasons, sure. But still...

"Jinx?" He pumped his legs, making them go higher. "Are you going to stop forcing yourself to be mad at me?"

She scoffed again, trying her best not to squeal as they went higher and higher.

Killian laughed, and what a dark and delicious thing that laugh was.

Against her will, she smiled back. "You're too handsome to stay mad at."

"What high praise."

She inhaled the new, heavy scent of him. It made her heart sink to sit above her stomach, the erratic beat waking her butterflies and making them flutter.

She wanted to keep him. Regardless of what that could mean for Rue, she wasn't ready to give Killian up, even if it could save them both.

The swing came to a sudden stop as Killian dove his feet into the ground. A yelp was caught in her throat as he picked her up, carrying her across the park before he set her feet down in the grass.

"Should we head back?" he asked.

That was the last thing she wanted. She lifted her shoulders, feeling completely resigned.

His eyes dipped to her bare feet, and he turned, offering her his back. "Come on, I'll carry you."

Jinx grinned, unable to resist the elation that went through her. The idea of a piggyback made excitement course through her. It was romantic in all the shows she watched. Being carried while pressed to someone's back, shoes in his hand as they whispered secrets to each other.

Giddiness filled her as she climbed on.

A hand clasped her wrist against his chest as the heat of his back melted the frigid parts of her. She sighed, settling her face against his shoulder. Going home was the last thing she wanted in the world right now, but it wouldn't be as bad with Killian carrying her when she was tired of it all.

Something lurked in the depths of her that was making her... not herself.

Jinx wanted to laugh off the changes in Killian. Tell herself this was just another fruitless mission for someone to get close to Rue, something she knew firsthand was impossible, but she couldn't. There was a wall there keeping her from throwing all her troubles off that cliff in her mind into the abyss below. The vast part of her brain where she tossed all her worries, hoping she wouldn't have to deal with them again until Rue discovered them.

And she always did.

Rue. On her endless quest for misery and troubles.

Frustration mounted as she paced the small front yard.

Killian was hers. She deserved him. After all these years, being cursed by Rue for merely existing, she deserved to have a hot demon burn sins into her that could never be scrubbed clean. And she wanted him to herself. A part of her life that wasn't Rue's to manage.

The crease between her brows was deep as that thought settled in her mind.

It wasn't like her not to want to share with Rue. Unlike Rue, who lived her life on an endless quest to be rid of Jinx, she *liked* the sullen witch's company. She liked Rue.

"We're all changing," she whispered.

No. Her head dipped back, her mess of hair trailing down her back as she stared at the sky. Rue felt like she would eternally be the same. Always barking. Always angry. Always... Rue.

"Why won't *she* change?" Jinx muttered, her voice a whine she knew would irritate Rue to no end. It was a good thing she wasn't there.

"Change is a funny thing..."

Jinx twirled, her eyes searching the darkness for the voice she knew.

A rock flew toward her as Poe stepped out of the shadows. She kicked another, a smirk on her face that made Jinx's shoulders shoot up beside her ears. Her reaction only broadened Poe's grin as her dark eyes looked Jinx over.

Poe was a different kind of darkness than Rue. Where Rue's oppressive hand wrapped around the back of Jinx's neck as she led her around, Poe's fist was wrapped in the front of her shirt. She was a predator that wanted to look Jinx in the eyes as she bit into her.

Somehow, Jinx couldn't figure out if that was worse.

"We really only like it if it goes exactly how we wanted it to." Poe cocked a brow, her smile showing her fangs. "Isn't that right?"

"What are you doing here?" Jinx took a step back.

Poe toyed with the small speaker attached to the loop of her denim shorts. They were black, the same colour as the plain T-shirt she was wearing. It felt odd looking at Poe in complete silence without whatever soundtrack she brought with her.

Jinx frowned, missing the music.

"Well." Poe inspected her nails, picking something from under the scarlet points and flicking it away. "Giving you a chance to control the change."

Her stomach dropped at the glint in Poe's eyes and the shine of her fangs. "You're trying to trick me, but... you can't." Jinx pushed her fists into her waist and widened her stance. Sucking in a deep breath, she puffed out her chest.

"What is this?" Poe chuckled lightly. "Trying to assert some kind of dominance?"

Jinx sputtered, faltering for a second before she took a bold step forward. "I *am* dominant."

Poe grinned. "Monsters usually are."

A pout turned down her lips, and she instantly deflated. "I'm not a monster."

Head slightly tilted, Poe inhaled the air. "Aren't you?"

She could take a lot of things. Being called a pain in the ass, a headache, a curse, but she was no monster. “No! I’m a delight. A princess. I’m not a monster.”

“Could have fooled me.”

“I’m *not* a monster!” Tears pooled in her eyes as she looked at Poe, trying to swallow back the tightness in her throat. “I’m not a burden or a consequence of fate. I’m not something to be settled on!” Her voice rose, hoarse as the words pushed past the small space her emotions left her. “I’m... I’m Jinx. I’m my own person. I’m my own...” Her words were stolen by her sobs.

She hated this.

This wasn’t her.

She cried — a lot and often enough for Rue to threaten her with consequences if she didn’t stop — but she didn’t feel this destitution that came with it. This lost feeling of stumbling around all by herself. Holding out a hand that no one wanted to hold onto.

It... hurt.

“When it comes to love, don’t we all become monsters?”

Snot left a hot path from Jinx’s nostril, pooling on the line of her upper lip as her bottom quivered. Her chest ached as her heart thrummed against it, an angry fist pounding in protest from the cage of her ribs. “Love?” She sniffled.

“Hmm.” Poe hummed as she sauntered toward her, eyes dark and full of something terrifying.

Jinx's shoulders shook as a shiver moved through her, but she didn't step away.

"I find I'm at my most... *vicious* when Dex is at risk. How the dark parts of me that usually seem playful become malevolent." Her lips pursed, thoughts darkening her eyes as she smiled too wide, her fangs glinting in the dark. "Even now, the thought of devouring your soul makes me shake with anticipation."

"Dex?"

Her smile faltered.

Jinx's weight fell back before she was lifted, weightlessness making her heart leap to sit in her chest as she stared down at Poe. Pain pinched at her throat, making her wince as Poe wrapped a hand around her neck and held her effortlessly.

"You don't get to say his name."

Teeth bared, Jinx swallowed hard. "Why?"

"Because you've basically stolen him from me. You and that stupid beast."

"Rue?" She forced the name out, but it still sounded hoarse.

Hot breath blew against her face. It smelled oddly sweet as Poe pulled her in and stared into her eyes. "But you'll know how that feels soon enough, won't you? Once Rue gets what she wants. Because she *will* get what she wants, won't she? Something tells me she always does. And you? You'll be the thing she sacrifices to make that happen. And your love... that will be what *he* sacrifices." Her smile turned wretched. "Doesn't that make you mad, little princess?"

Everything in her bristled. Bile turned over in her stomach, making her ache as she tried to keep it down. "He?"

Poe waved her other hand, dismissing it as though her question was foolish.

She hated that! Rue did that to her all the time. Gave mere crumbs of information that always left her starving, and she was tired of being hungry.

"He?" Jinx forced out, anger fuelling her words and making them rattle through her pinched throat.

"The one masquerading as a demon."

That crease of confusion wrinkled the space between her brows as Jinx tried to figure it all out. The only demon Rue and Jinx knew was Killian, and he...

Her gaze snapped to Poe, eyes bouncing back and forth between Poe's as the cogs in her mind ticked slowly. "Killian."

"Mmm," Poe hummed.

"But he's—"

"The perfect thing to use to break you."

Her lip wobbled. "Why do you want to break us?

Black eyes stared into hers. "Because I quite like true monsters. Dark things that gnash their teeth and swipe their claws. Beasts that feed on mortals without guilt. Hunters merely hunting their prey. And once Rue is broken, truly broken, not this pity party broken she keeps harping about, the true monster beneath her skin can be unleashed."

Jinx frowned. Nothing she was saying made any sense. Killian *wasn't* a demon, and Rue wasn't a monster. "Why?" She needed to know why Poe wanted to do all this. She may not love Rue all the time, but she was hers alone to torment.

"Because once Rue becomes the monster she was always meant to be, she can finally put my Dexy back together." Her smile broadened, making Jinx shrink back in fear. "But first, we need to get her attention."

Poe's hand shot forward, sharp claws glinting in the dark.

Jinx screamed.

23

RUE

"This is impressive." Killian walked behind Rue, his eyes taking in her most sacred of places. He dragged a hand against the damp stone.

After he succeeded in his quest to find the ever-cumbersome Jinx and bring her back, Killian let her march dramatically out into the front yard. Apparently, Jinx thought she was owed an apology, and she would sooner end up sleeping in the yard than get one from Rue.

She should pity Killian coming in and trying to play referee, but she didn't have the patience or the brain space. The best he could accomplish was deciding to give Jinx time to sort through her big emotions before following Rue down to her altar.

"Don't touch anything."

He flashed her a smile, curling his fingers into a fist. "Always so sharp. I like that."

Rue rolled her eyes.

"So." He came up behind her, his chest bumping into her back as he looked over her shoulder onto her altar. "What is it you're looking for?"

"If Poe actually does what she says and gets rid of my coven, I'll have to keep my word and curse the Duke. Again." She opened her grimoire, whispers of her ancestors swirling around her when she did.

Heat bore into her back, making her stiffen as he leaned further in. He smelled like thick smoke meant to take every last bit of her breath. "Is this not a curse you know?"

Curses were a hard thing to explain, especially when she could practically feel his heart beating against her back. She swallowed hard, flipping the page. "The kind of curse I wrapped around the Duke was one of pure rage. It's the kind that doesn't come easy." And if she didn't do it exactly right, she would have hell to pay. Poe didn't seem like the forgiving kind.

"Are you not still full of rage?"

She flipped another page. "Yes, but this is a different flavour."

Killian chuckled. "And the book will tell you how to capture that rage again?"

No, it wouldn't. That was the problem. "I hope that when my coven is gone, I can pull my magic back. Once I have all my magic, the answers will come. If not..." She set palms on the open pages. "I'll need something else."

"A backup plan," Killian confirmed.

Once she had all her magic back, she hoped she wouldn't need a backup plan. Her magic was deep-rooted. The kind she felt in every breath she took. If she needed a curse, her magic would give her one.

So long as Poe got rid of her coven, she had nothing to worry about. If she failed, she would be dead...

A dead reaper.

Fat chance.

Rue flipped another page.

Killian reached over her, his pointed finger skimming the page. "You can read this?"

"Can't you?" she teased, though she already knew the answer. The language was one only those in her family knew.

His face dipped beside hers, cheeks brushing. She shuddered, eyes wide. "No," he hummed.

"W-what are you doing?" Killian invaded her space as if she were something he was trying to conquer. She wasn't used to *feeling* so much. Irritation was the only thing she felt for so long. Irritation and despair. Maybe topped with a light dusting of hopelessness. This... churning unsettled her.

"Me?" She felt his smile. "Nothing."

Rue rolled her eyes, but it took effort. She was trying to force herself not to feel things that made her uncomfortable. And she was failing. "Want to take a step back?"

"Not really."

She huffed a breath. "Look, you don't have to do this." She dipped under his arm and stepped away from the altar. She needed to busy herself. Put space between them. For lack of anything else to do, she picked up a jar and inspected the ingredients inside.

Killlian planted his hands on the altar, his lips curling up ever so slightly at the edges. His brow quirked, the honey in his eyes shining. "Do what, dark cloud?"

That freaking nickname. She grabbed another jar, cupping them both to her chest. The scarabs in one vibrated against the glass. "Be so close to me. Get close to me, or whatever. You don't need to."

"Don't I?"

Her cheeks puffed with air. These conversations unnerved her, not that she had many. Maybe that was why she felt so out of place. Because she had no experience. "Look, Fate dealt us a hand, I get it. But you don't have to make this a thing. You don't feel anything for me, I don't feel anything for you. Let's just leave it at that."

Killian leaned onto his elbow, propping his chin on his hand as he stared. He didn't just look at her. Those eyes stripped her and forced her to stand completely bare before him. "I don't think I can. You see, I *do* feel something for you. And, I'm quite certain you feel something for me."

Panic squeezed her heart in its unrelenting grip. She didn't. She couldn't. But that was a lie, and she knew it. At some point between waking up in his arms, caged in the unknown, and now, he'd wormed his way beneath her armour. Maybe not into the depths of her heart — she wasn't sure anyone could accomplish that — but he was beneath her skin.

He came around the altar, steps slow and eyes honed. They shone in the dim light, little beacons that demanded all her attention. One hand in his pocket, he moved like he had his eyes set on his prey. His hand slid down her arm, eyes locked so forcefully onto hers, she tilted her head to look at him against her will.

"We have a real problem here, dark cloud." His hand closed around a jar, setting it back where she had taken it from, emptying her hands. Warmth brushed against her fingers as he covered her hands with his, linking their fingers together.

Her heart thrummed an angry rhythm that pushed all her thoughts somewhere she couldn't hear them. It was just so loud.

His hand rested above her head, his body boxing her in. "It seems you've lived in a delusion where you believe I would be doing this for some reason other than my satisfaction. Like I am not drawn to you, starving for any crumbs of attention you'll offer me."

"Killian," she tried to swallow his name, but it came out on a whisper.

A hand snaked around her neck, fingers pressing into her flesh. Killian's thumb pressed in the sensitive space under her chin, gleaming eyes staring into hers with challenge. His breath stuttered in him, like it was something he could barely contain. Eyes closed, his nostrils flared as he pressed his chin against her brow. "I've spread a misery that could destroy worlds ten times over, and none of that destruction will ever compare to this. You crumble the parts of me I thought would always stand."

"Romantic words whispered in the dark," she hissed, but they burrowed under her skin against her will. "They might as well be dreams with how quickly they disappear and are forgotten."

"Dreams." A groan sounded low in his throat as he spun her around. Her cheek pressed into the damp wall, a hand braced beside her face while the other still tangled with his. "If this is all dreams that are going to be forgotten, then I might as well do what I please. I might as well do the very things you won't admit to me you want."

His hand dragged down from her chest to her waist. The slow path heated her blood, making her hold her breath so she didn't pant against the sensation. His jaw pressed into her temple, forcing her head to the side.

Any words she wanted to say disappeared when his lips touched her neck. Her stomach clenched, eyes falling closed.

He held her sealed to his chest, her ass fitting perfectly against his legs as his grip on her hand tightened. Each pull of his lips made her chest heave, her breath rough huffs of air that barely filled her.

Rue's teeth broke skin as she tried to keep the moans from escaping. She fell into him, surrendering in the dark where she couldn't before in the light.

"Tell me, Rue," he murmured against her skin. "If this were a dream, just what wicked things would that mind of yours conjure?" His hand dropped lower, toying with the front of her pants. "Just what relief would you take in your dreams without permission, in a place that's only yours, not fearing the consequences?"

She throbbed with a need she told herself she didn't feel. Empty as she was, she denied any possibility of ties to the man behind her. But there was a yearning in the pit of her stomach that her pleasure wouldn't let her ignore.

His fingers pushed into her pants, beneath the fabric to her waiting flesh.

"Tell me no," he whispered. "Wake up from this dream."

Rue said nothing because, in that moment, there was nothing she wanted more than to live in a dream.

Killian dove his fingers into her, his thumb pressed against her clit.

Her mouth opened, a silent sigh inflating her throat as her head fell back against his chest. There was something so much like relief dancing with her pleasure. His fingers pumped into her, thumb pressing just shy of painfully against her as his hand tightened, making the knuckles of her clasped fingers ache.

Lifted on her toes, she turned her face to look at him.

His eyes were dark. Hungry. *Hers.*

Killian took her lips. Something ravenous poured into her. Something that took and took, never satisfied. His lips devoured hers, tongue tasting every inch of her mouth, sucking every breath from her lungs until she swayed on her feet, and only his fingers inside her kept her standing.

He broke the kiss on a gasp, a drowning man with no choice but to come up for air. A growl ripped through him as she tightened around his fingers, her nails pressing into the back of his hand as she held onto him, needing an anchor through her pleasure.

Everything inside her exploded, the release shaking her very foundations. Stars lit behind her eyes before they welled with tears.

This was a dream, she reminded herself. *Just a dream.* And in this dream, he was hers.

Rue panted. She still felt so full; his fingers sank inside her as they leaned on one another. She opened her hand, trying to pull hers free from his.

"No." He rested his brow on the top of her head. "Don't wake up yet. Stay with me."

Tears blurred her vision as she wrestled her hand free. He held on a moment before he relented.

A chill moved through her as she stepped away from him. No heat at her back, no hand pressed in her pants, no hand holding hers. It felt very much like pulling the covers off and waking up.

Rue swallowed her sigh, pushing a braid back behind her scarred ear.

Killian turned, a sigh floating through the space between them. "Don't you think the dream was better?" His voice was light, but she could hear the desperation there.

"I don't think—"

Pain lanced through her, stealing her words.

Jars shattered against the stone at her feet as Rue staggered, her arm draping over her altar and sending her grimoire to the ground. The book moaned, a protest from her ancestors for allowing their hard work to end up on the cold floor. Ingredients blended, creating mists and ghosts in the air. Bugs scattering into the shadows. A wail echoed through the stone walls, shaking everything.

Everything inside her felt wrapped in a cocoon, the threads slowly tightening to hold her against her will.

Killian was beside her, his hands holding her arms as he tried to turn her. Inspect her. "What's happening? Rue! What's wrong?"

"J-Jinx," she sputtered.

The room around her careened. It swayed and bobbed, doubling as saliva thinned in her mouth and bile sat at the back of her throat. Her fingers dug into the cold stone, nails threatening to break as they scraped.

Something was wrong.

"Rue!" Killian tried to grab hold of her, but she shook him off.

She closed her eyes, holding them pinched before she sucked in a shaky breath and staggered to the steps. Visions of her grandmother played behind her eyes as she stumbled, her palms pressed against the wall in an attempt to guide her.

'You must protect your soul, Rue. It holds more power than you'll ever truly know.' Warm eyes bore into hers, her palm dusting against her cheek, containing all the warmth Rue had been constantly chasing since.

"No!" Her knees ached as she dropped to the hallway floor, the frame shimmering behind her. "No. No. No!"

Bram appeared, fluttering overhead. He flew around her, an anxious blur that moved in and out of her focus.

Tears burned hot paths down her cheeks. She did her best to force herself to her feet, looking up at the familiar that was hers as much as he wasn't. He squeaked, the sound grating.

The chubby bat dipped, his little claws wrapping around her shoulder to pull her to her feet.

"Jinx!"

Dark forests whirred past, blurring with shadows and threats.

Something unseen tried to pull her back and keep her in her cave, where she would be safe from whatever waited for her, using Jinx as bait.

Was it Killian? She honestly didn't know.

"Rue?" She turned, looking for the voice.

The image of the man standing in the hall blurred. A mirage that came in and out of existence as the pinch in her chest intensified, stealing her breath. Her fist clasped at the fabric of her shirt, trying to reach past her skin to the space where she felt the link between her and Jinx pulled too tight.

"What's wrong?" The words didn't quite reach her. Gargled and pushed underwater, they were further away than they should have been as she staggered, her palm pressed against the wall.

"J-Jinx..."

Bram's foot touched the top of her head, and she reached up, wrapping her hand around it.

"Take me to her."

24

RUE

RUE GASPED AS SHE burst up out of the water. Her hands whipped out, desperate for purchase as she tried to grab hold of anything. Water sputtered out of her mouth with each cough, her fingers finally wrapping around the dark lip of the pool.

She blinked hard, rubbing a hand over her eyes to rid her lashes of the beads of water still left behind. Each laboured breath felt like a gift that burned her lungs. Summoning strength she wasn't sure she had, she pulled herself out of the frigid water.

Her back slammed hard against the floor as she slid slightly against it. Her hands were out at her side, eyes closed as she let each breath come. Choked by every shaky inhale, her stomach bottomed out when she opened her eyes and looked around.

No.

If Jinx was there, it was worse than she thought. Nothing good could come from returning to the place of her nightmares.

The covenstead resembled a gothic church with its stained glass arched windows, vaulted ceiling painted in a grotesque mural, and its dark marble floors. All it lacked were the pews. It was so different from the woods. Once in the town, the rustic feel of the woods melted away and was replaced with quiet opulence.

Raised on a dais was what her coven would argue wasn't a throne. The seat of the priestess. The dim ritual room looked haunted. Endless silhouettes surrounded the dark edges, the candelabra above flickering.

Rolling over, she got to her hands and knees before she forced herself to her feet.

"You're so fascinating." A familiar voice echoed around her. It was humorous through the darkness. Playful, even though Rue could feel the barbs in her words. Darkness poured into her mind, smothering all her thoughts.

For once, she wasn't the problem solver. Wasn't the rescuer waiting to swoop in and save Jinx from whatever turmoil she threw them into. She wasn't the cautious witch afraid of the consequences thrust at her by her coven, consequences she often didn't feel she deserved. It was all so unfair. And as she waded through the waters of that contempt for the life she never wanted to live but had to survive, she felt rage swim up and grab her. It weighed her down at the ankles.

Hands linked behind her back, Poe stepped out of the shadows. Her smile was sinister, stretched too wide. "How does it feel to be home, Rue?"

Despite herself, Rue couldn't help snarling. "This was never my home."

Lips pursed, Poe nodded slowly. "No. I suppose it wasn't. There is a special kind of loneliness that comes from not belonging anywhere, isn't there?"

As a hybrid, Poe likely knew that loneliness well.

"Still, we do what we can to keep from feeling it, don't we. Me? Well, I fuck as many mortals as I can, feeding on them. Daring the reapers to confront me for all the souls I steal... hoping one of them will be dear old dad. There are other ways, though. Perhaps a story or two to comfort us on the darkest of nights."

Stories? "What are you getting at, Poe?"

That smile would have made Rue shudder if she weren't already intimate with evil. She bent at the waist, leaning in slightly. "Tell me one of your stories, *witch.*"

It annoyed Rue the way she said witch. Like she was whispering the name of something she didn't believe in. Something that wasn't real.

Rue said nothing.

"Oh, come now. Tell me a story. I love stories."

"I don't know any." She had no time for stories.

Poe's brow quirked. "Don't you?"

Her question was weighted, and it bothered Rue that she didn't understand why.

"Let's see if I can help you remember it." Poe stepped back into the darkness. Rue narrowed her eyes, but before they could adjust, the darkness was pulled away in twists and turns of black. It swirled and whispered as they settled back into the darkness.

Wraiths.

With the blanket of shadows lifted, Rue gasped.

Jinx sat at Poe's feet, her whimpers echoing through the covenstead. A symbol was carved in the stone beneath her knees. Black smoke lifted from the carvings, wrapped around Jinx's wrists like shackles, binding her in place.

Her chest bowed out, wraiths flying through her. She screamed before she dropped down onto her hands, barely able to support her weight. This was a kind of torment only a reaper could deal, and death had a way of pushing through all kinds of magic — even Rue's.

Poe had been toying with them all this time. Pulling her punches. What Rue didn't understand was why.

"Tell me a story," Poe urged. "One from your pretty little book."

Her grimoire?

Rue swayed on her feet, her breath caught in her throat as Jinx's chest bowed again. The bitter taste of copper pooled in her mouth.

Clicking her tongue in disapproval, Poe turned away from them. She ignored Jinx's screams as she moved in and out of the shadows. "I always found it humorous that so many houses of worship look the same. They're all just churches, aren't they? Weird buildings that tower in prosperity, even when they sit surrounded by poverty. Places like this never know hunger, do they? They seem to feed on everything around them. Tell me, *witch*, does this place feed on you?"

"What?" She swayed, falling to a knee as the room careened.

"They all feed on power," Her eyes narrowed, smile turning malevolent. "In one way or another."

Rue's eyes rolled back in her head as she sucked in a hopeless breath. Her skin pebbled. A shiver moved through her as her damp, frigid clothes clung to her.

"Once upon a time," Poe sang.

Jinx screamed.

Rue gagged as bile climbed up from her belly to sit in the back of her throat.

"Stop," she almost begged. She didn't have the strength to beg. All she could muster was a mere whisper.

"Just what did your dear old grandmama whisper to you in the dark when sleep evaded you?" Poe asked. "What stories of witches did she tell? Of the shadows that ruled them?"

"This," she forced the word out on a weak, bated breath. "This wasn't part of the deal."

"Deal? I wasn't aware we made one. You said some things..." Poe walked back, resting a hand on Jinx's head as she heaved, struggling to catch her breath. "I said some things."

"The Lumena—"

"Isn't really my problem," Poe interrupted. How she managed to keep her voice playful as she tormented them was a skill Rue promised herself she would learn. Even if only to show Poe what it felt like. "I mean... it is, in a way. I get that. But my real problem is your cage."

"I already told you—" Rue winced, dropping to her hands as Jinx screamed again.

"Shh." Poe pressed a finger to Jinx's lips as she smiled. "They'll hear you before we're ready."

"Stop it." Rue's hand shot out. Magic zipped through the air, hitting Poe square in the chest.

Poe jolted, taking a single step back before she laughed. It was a manic sound that droned on and on, too high and grating. "Yes! Finally... some fun."

"You're crazy." Bile sat at the back of her throat as Jinx slumped to the ground. Her cries quieted, nothing but the sound of her panted breathing closing the space between them as wraiths circled like storm clouds overhead.

"I know, right?" She smiled proudly.

Rue struggled to summon her strength. Whispers sounded, flowing in and out of her ears, swirling around her. They were the same ones she had heard so many times when her anger got the best of her, but this time, they came with clarity. Words cut through the hiss of wind and whimpers.

Get her!

Kill!

Destroy!

Poe's head tilted slightly. "Just what have they told you, I wonder, to make you smell that way?" Throwing her head back, Poe inhaled the air between them. "You reek of self-pity... it's hiding that blissful smell of darkness."

Jinx sobbed, the quiet sound filled with anguish.

Her heart hammered in her chest at the sight. When she propositioned the hybrid, she should have considered that she would double-cross them. She should have expected it, but she had hoped Poe's obsession with Dex would have been enough to keep Jinx safe until the coven was handled.

Pain made her thoughts hazy. She swallowed the bile sitting at the back of her throat and mustered all the strength she had left to get to her feet.

"What's the plan here, Poe?" There was no way to know just what this twisted monster had planned. The thing about monsters was that they were often unpredictable. Living without her soul may have forced Rue into a tiring routine, but true monsters, the likes of which stood before her now with a malicious smile and a glint in her eye, there was no rhyme or reason to them.

"Plan?" Poe laughed, the cackle as unhinged as she was. "How very boring. You see, I have this problem with obsession. Right now, I'm obsessed with the idea of you telling me a story."

Her brows dropped low. She kept asking for a story, just what story did she want? What tale could she tell Poe to make all this end?

Familiarity hit her in the centre of the chest like a punch from her past. It was brutal, making her force harsh breaths around it. Lumena magic was rife in the air. Smoke that stuck to the flesh inside her lungs.

Poe's hand wrapped in the back of Jinx's shirt, pulling her back when she tried to crawl forward. She didn't spare Jinx a single glance as she fell on her ass, skirt pooled around her waist and her bare feet.

"Why here?" Rue asked.

"Do you know what I love the most?" Poe's eyes glinted in the dark.

A slow sigh slipped from Rue's lips as she forced words up her throat. "I don't know? If I were to guess, probably the orgasms? A good orgasm can really change a girl."

Poe laughed. It was a brutal sound, high and melodic. "You know what... I like you."

"So you've said."

"That being said, this whole coven thing is quite the headache, isn't it?" She licked her lips, fangs on display. "Having looked into each and every witch in your measly little coven, it looks like there aren't many who have the kind of power that can give me what I want. You'd think curses were like... introductory for witches. What the hell else are you guys doing that no one else in your coven could curse a man the way you do?"

Rue said nothing.

"So, the way I see it, it would benefit me to free you not only from your coven but also this delusion."

"Delusion?" Rue asked.

Her eyes lit red, the hunger in her dark and monstrous. "Can you not feel it? The power that keeps whispering in your ear, demanding you do something treacherous. *Eat, eat, eat,* it must say." She giggled. "Aren't you listening?"

Rue's brows dropped. "Listening."

She pressed her finger to her lips, long nail gleaming even in the dark. "Shhh. Pretty dark thing, why don't you quiet all those nagging thoughts and just listen?"

This hybrid was starting to work on Rue's last nerve. They were standing in Lumena's covenstead, in the very centre of the town that housed almost every Lumena witch. She didn't have the time to sit with herself and try to hear some inner voice. Some voice that would tell her something about herself, as though she hadn't spent enough time alone to know every nook and cranny of her bogged-down mind.

"Shhh..." Poe shushed.

Her skin felt uncomfortable as signs of her forgotten coven pushed in at her from all sides.

"Listen," she sang.

"Listen," Jinx sobbed.

Rue grunted under her breath. "Would you shut up? This isn't really the time to do a deep dive into the voices in my head."

Poe tilted her head. She looked so like a feral animal trying to make sense of something. "Isn't it?" Her lips pursed, curls falling over her eyes. "And here I thought it would be the perfect time." Snatching Jinx up, Poe pulled her back against her chest. The phantom binds disappeared to nothing, as the wraiths circled them until there was nothing but a cocoon of darkness. "Listen or don't... but you can't fight them as is."

The cocoon burst, and Poe, Jinx, and the symbol that bound her were all gone.

"Fight them?" The pain ebbed away, giving way to her thoughts.

Before she had time to sort through them, the doors to the covenstead slammed open. Light poured into the room, casting long and distorted silhouettes of Fortuna and the other witches at her back onto the floor.

"And look what we have here," Fortuna sang.

Fuck.

Her stomach sank.

"I thought I would have to hunt you to the ends of the earth, bringing you back here, to coven soil, so I could reclaim all the magic that is meant to be ours."

Tell me a story.

Trapped magic.

What your grandmama whispered to you in the dark...

All clues, if only she could figure out how they fit together. Poe was turning out to be more calculating than Rue initially thought the hybrid was.

"Do you feel it?" Fortuna held her arms out, taking slow steps into the covenstead. "Mother is gone."

Rue had been too busy dealing with Poe to feel the ripples of Ferula's death. If she felt anything at all, it was under the storm of other emotions blowing through her.

Listen.

To what?

Ugh, why did her life have to be so gods damn frustrating?

At least Poe and Jinx were out of the way.

She adjusted her stance, turning just in time to watch more witches step out of the shadows.

"With my mother's strength, I think it's finally time I cut you down, Ruin Crowe. But first, there is enough magic in you to fill the wells of Lumena until my dying day."

This was it. Sink or swim. There was no time to wonder about anything; the day of her reckoning had finally come. Her nod was slow as she felt magic coat her hands. “Come take it... if you can.”

25

KILLIAN

PAST THE WOODS THAT felt as though they stretched on for miles was a town. Not a small, quaint town with wooden houses and cobblestone walkways. This town was so much more than he would have imagined.

The streets were perfectly paved. Intersections had streetlights and signs. Cars lined the street, the storefronts dimly lit with signs overhead.

Apothecary.

Brews and Books.

Curses and Candles.

Everything from bookstores to sandwich shops, even banks. This was a fully functioning town, no different from so many other mortal towns he'd come across while striking deals or spreading misery.

Killian made his way through the barren streets with his hackles raised.

"Where the hell is everyone?"

He walked down the street without running into a single soul. It made the place feel haunted. To have enough witches in a coven to fill a town and not come across one made him feel anxious. From the number of cars alone, there should be hundreds of witches here. Thousands.

At the centre of the town was a fountain, with a statue of a woman standing in the middle, water pouring from her hands into the pool below. Killian stood there, staring at it. She was oddly familiar.

"It's gloomy, isn't it?"

He walked around the fountain to see Poe sitting on its edge. Her eyes were closed as she turned her face up to the moon, legs outstretched before her.

"A whole town of witches and not a soul around. I wonder just what they could be up to..." She grinned. "There isn't even a mosquito flying through this place. How very depressing... and that's coming from a reaper. Well... sort of."

Her black tights were covered in holes and rips, baring her warm brown skin from beneath them. They were pulled up over her belly button, her cropped black tank that read *Fuck for a buck,* leaving a slice of skin around her ribs. Her short curls were wild. Her red lips parted, showing her fangs.

"You." Anger boiled in his belly, clashing with his panic.

Arms wide, she stood and bowed dramatically. "Me."

Killian snarled.

Poe's head tilted, nose turned up as she inhaled deeply. "Well, look who finally smells like he can play with the big boys." Her grin broadened, half mad. "Just what did you get up to since I saw you last?" She inhaled again. "No way." She clapped her hands together, jumping in place.

Her reaction to him made him pause. If she knew what he was, she should be afraid. Not this. She looked almost *giddy*.

This monster was out of her mind.

She strutted toward him, her wide hips shaking as she closed the space without the smallest measure of fear. Her hand whipped out, circling his throat before he could react, and she lifted onto her toes. "Sweet, treacherous misery. I wonder just what you taste like."

The bitter scent of blood filled the air as branches protruded from his skin. They twisted, covering his arms as he shed his mortal wrappings. Freedom came with a single exhale as he towered above her, her suddenly small form dangling as she refused to surrender her grip.

"Too bad you'll never get your chance to find out."

"Hmm." She pursed her lips, dark eyes turning scarlet as she looked up at him. "I have a way of getting what I want."

His hand wrapped around her wrist, where she held his throat. His fingers were longer now, twisted branches that ended in talons. She winced as he tightened his hold, but her smile only spread with the pain. "This time you'll be disappointed."

This woman had come into Rue and Jinx's house and harmed them. He didn't care that she was part reaper. He wasn't going to let that stand.

Rage filled him, but just as quickly as it came, he felt it slipping away.

"Lust is such an interesting thing, isn't it? It clouds the minds of mortals and monsters alike." Her voice was humorous.

She was... *beautiful.*

No. No, that wasn't right. She was...

Her lips were so very red and deep. That smile called to him, telling him just how sweet they would taste if he only leaned down and took a—

No!

His hand whipped out, and he tossed her.

Poe's small frame flew across the square. Glass shattered as she flew through a window under the signage *Britches and Broomsticks.* Mannequin pieces fell out onto the street, clothes and their matching broomsticks hanging from the window.

Killian's hands clasped the sides of his head. These were not his thoughts. He pressed at his temples. There was pressure in his mind. His head felt fuller than it should be, his skull trying to house thoughts that weren't his. Feelings that didn't belong to him.

"How interesting." Poe climbed through the window, stepping onto the sidewalk. She brushed her hands over her thighs, wiping away some debris before she pulled something out of a hidden pocket against her thigh. Her phone illuminated her face through the dark as she ignored him, her thumb moving against the screen. "I have the perfect thing," she muttered.

Slow music started playing, and Poe returned her phone to her pocket.

Was she serious? Was she going to start a playlist while they fought in this witchy little town?

Killian stood confused.

Poe tilted her head, taking in the form he had yet to reveal to his mates. Her gaze hovered at his hoofed feet, climbing up legs of vines and branches, his thatch of shadows that parted to an almost human chest. Flaps of flesh hung loosely at the edges before the vines and branches started up again. His face was the one she'd seen before, only harder. Darker, framed in the same vines and branches as the rest of him, before his antlers cut out of his temples to climb half a metre above him.

"I smell... misery." Her grin broadened, suddenly inhuman.

He adjusted his stance.

"Exciting." Dark shadows lifted from her skin, before howling skulls draped in darkness billowed around her.

Wraiths.

She ran toward him.

They clashed together with more force than he thought possible. She was a small thing compared to his towering form, and yet, his hooves pushed back, carving at the street. Her fingers dove between his vines and branches, trying to push through them to something vulnerable beneath.

His arm slashed down, slamming hard against her forearm with a sickening crack.

She... *laughed!*

Eyes hard, Poe looked at him as she held her broken arm in her grasp, that manic smile still in place as she hummed along to the song that played through her cellphone speaker. "Wonderful. Much more fun than your little beast and her soul."

The mention of Jinx and Rue stirred something in him. "Leave them out of this." The growl of his voice was so different than the one his contract had made him grow used to.

"What's up, treeman? Have I struck a nerve?"

She had. The grinding of his teeth told him as much. "I'm not a tree."

"No." She chuckled with a light shake of her head, red eyes honing in on him. "A tree is about life and all that, and you're so much darker than that. Aren't you? Something so many don't think has a physical form, but the reaper in me sees you... harbinger. Sowing seeds of misery from rotten intentions."

He stalled. It had been so long since anyone called him anything other than a demon. To finally hear the word uttered was a release he didn't realize he needed.

"A harbinger of doom and misery. In the flesh... sort of. This is going to be a problem for me." She nodded down toward her broken arm. "Luckily for you, a taste of your witch won't fix this."

White poked from her brown flesh. Bone.

Poe grinned as though she didn't know pain. Worse. As though she knew it well enough to become intimate with it. Enjoy it. "And lucky for me, this forsaken town still has enough souls hiding in its shadows to feed even something as hungry as me."

Before he could say anything, Poe was enveloped in wraiths, a mere blur shifting through the dark. She floated up and into a building before she returned before him, clutching a woman to her chest. She hissed, teeth bared, as she kicked out, trying to free herself from her grip. Her chestnut hair was straw-straight, her olive skin dulled in the dark.

"You have no idea what you're doing. What we will do to you," the witch spat, venom in her words.

Poe grinned, running her tongue along her lips before she said, "I do love when there is some fight in them. It adds a spice to their soul."

He could smell the stench of dark magic on the witch and wasn't about to intervene.

The witch's eyes fogged over, anger melting off her face. "Fuck me," she whispered.

A click of her tongue and a hungry grin before Poe said, "If only I had the time."

"Please," she begged.

Poe's lips twisted. She lifted the woman until their lips met. The woman's worry melted from her face, ecstasy making her features look heavy. Her hands reached up into Poe's hair, disappearing in her curls as she clasped her head, trying to hold onto her. A moan echoed through the air as Poe pressed her palm between the witch's legs.

It was an odd sight when he had thoughts of battle in his mind.

They moved together, tantric and overtly sexual. It stalled him even as anger burned through him, and his need to find Rue and Jinx strangled him.

The witch writhed, head falling back as she gasped, trying to suck in more air than her lungs could take. Her whine was high, eyes closed as she clung to Poe. Poe's palm became more vicious, teasing her through her clothes until the witch cried out, and Poe sank her teeth into her throat.

The concoction of lust, blood, and death was intoxicating.

Poe let the witch fall into a lifeless pile at her feet, her arm snapping back into place, the flesh becoming whole and new.

"I do hate to rush, but something told me you wouldn't stand there and let me give her the type of orgasm I'd be famous for if I let anyone live." She flexed her fingers with a grin. "Good as new. Care to try again?"

"I don't have time for this."

"No..." She laced her fingers together behind her back, slowly pacing. "I bet you don't, but right now that little *witch* of yours needs to follow in your footsteps. There is so much darkness in her that needs to be released. I'm only hoping I pushed her enough to release it."

"What are you talking about? Where is she?"

"Sometimes, in order to go forward, we have to remember the way back to the beginning. She needs to do that on her own." Poe looked him over. "The relief you feel in letting what you truly are out of the packaging they trapped you up in, she needs that too. Do make sure you give her the chance to break out... and let the monster she really is free."

Without another word, Poe stepped back into the whir of wraiths, disappearing. Her laughter echoed through the town as haunting as visions of Death himself would be.

Killian stood there like a dark vision. Something haunted. A vicious blend of life, death, and misery.

There was an urging in the centre of his chest to tear through this place. To rip all the doors off the hinges until he opened one that revealed Rue and Jinx behind it. Dark magic was a fog in the air that poured into his nose and teased his lungs with each breath.

He would get nowhere chasing his tail. That was what he would have done if he were still a demon. Still limited in his power. Now he was a harbinger of doom and misery.

Whispers were vicious whips of wind blowing around him.

Eyes glowed green from the shadows as witches stepped out from where they were hiding, stalking into the square.

It seemed they were watching. Waiting.

A hoof stretched behind him as he dropped to a knee. His hand rested on the ground before his fingers sprouted, releasing vicious black roots that dove through the concrete. He felt the battle of magic, the stench of lies and deceit like fertilizer mixed in with the soil. Eyes closed, he released the seeds that would quickly spread and bloom. Satisfaction planted heavily in his chest, the kind that only came when he knew he'd released something dark and unforgiving into the world.

The water in the fountain paused, the sound of it rushing replaced with eerie silence. The holes in the statue's hands sputtered before black water poured out. Thick. Heavy. Reeking of sulphur.

Glances were exchanged as Killian got to his feet. He squared his shoulders, revelling at the way fresh vines sprouted, adding to the width of them before he set his hooves.

He was ready. Holding out a hand, he ushered them forward.

"As you reap, so shall you sow."

26

RUE

MEMBERS OF LUMENA FLOWED in and out of focus. They surrounded the pool with their arms clasped, swaying from side to side as their chanting blended into a ceaseless hum. Voices droned on and on as the scent of burnt magic was like incense in the air.

Blood smeared each face. Symbols marked each brow as the whites of their eyes fluttered behind their lids. Storm clouds covered the ceiling, booming. Torches lit behind each witch, the flames dancing too high, the orange flickering in and out, turning green at their burning tips before they broke off into embers that flitted like haunted fireflies in the air.

The voices were nails on a chalkboard in her mind, making all of Rue's muscles contract and the pain in her arms burn. Suspended over the pool, her blood dripped down into the dark water she emerged from.

Drip, drip, drip.

Each drop of her blood illuminated the water below, making it pulse. Beat with her magic.

How did she get there? What was happening?

Her vision wavered, mind muddled.

She smiled through the pain she knew well, welcoming it. Pain was something that was entirely hers. It wasn't something that could be divided. Shared. Stolen. It had her name carved into it, and it loved to stare her in the face. Blood poured from deep cuts in her arms.

The world kept lifting at the edges. Dropping back into its place, then suddenly sinking like a seesaw that turned her stomach and spun her mind.

Crying.

Rue blinked, trying to chase away some of the darkness edging her vision.

Someone was crying.

Who?

Her saliva was both too thin and too thick in her mouth. It slid down her throat, a slow trickle of bitterness that stirred the bile in her belly even though she felt like she couldn't swallow it down.

"So this is the power of an infamous Crowe." Fortuna appeared before her. Bare feet stood on the edge of the pool as she walked along the rim. Arms out at her side for balance, she spared Rue mere glances as though she had so much more to do than drain her of magic.

The droning continued, slipping into the background. Muffled behind something unseen as Fortuna's voice slipped through. Boomed.

"I worried my blessing wouldn't compare, and yet you stumbled around looking for a solution to the impossible." Fortuna threw back her head and laughed before she spun on the tips of her toes, eyes sinister and shining.

Thoughts slipped through her fingers.

Find it, Rue. Remember...

Remember what?

Whose voice was that? It sounded like Poe, but it changed toward the end, becoming warm and familiar.

Grandma...

Drip. Drip. Drip.

"Draining power takes so long, doesn't it? However will we pass the time?" Fortuna clapped her hands together, her grin showing too many teeth. "I know, how about a story?"

A story...

"There was a tale once... one all witches knew. The folklore of our people, passed down from mother to daughter over and over again. A tale whispered to us in the dark when we were babes, and our minds were nothing more than clay to be moulded."

'Tell me a story.' Was this the story Poe wanted?

"A story etched on our bones, whispered to our hearts, and inked onto the pages of every grimoire. It told us of the beginning of witches. A time when the ground cracked open, and magic poured out into those with souls strong enough to keep it. But that magic that burst free was planted by someone once. The source of all witches' magic."

"Rue..." someone called.

Fortuna stepped out, her foot hovering atop the water. "You see, this witch who planted the source of our magic didn't even plant all her magic. She would travel the worlds, collecting magic and planting it. Shaping worlds while hollowing herself out to make room for more. The empty witch."

A manic chuckle was the backdrop for Fortuna's words.

Who was it again? Poe. Poe was here...

"Tell me a story. T-tell me a s-story. Tell me a story-y." The words repeated in a loop. Glitching to repeat itself over and over and over.

"Magic is funny sometimes, isn't it?" Fortuna painfully gripped Rue's face, jerking it toward her. "A person can only hold so much... something about the soul. It takes up so much space."

Rue's brows dropped.

"And so... the empty witch pulled her soul out of her chest and made it walk beside her." Fortuna's eyes flashed, her head tilting as she stared into Rue's eyes, waiting.

"What?" A blur of harsh whispers moved around her. They cut through the droning of the ritual. Vicious words that sliced at her mind.

"Do you feel it?" Pain radiated through Rue's neck as her head snapped back. A pinhole of her vision honed onto the face of the witch about to become the priestess of the Lumena coven. Her lips brushed against Rue's cheek, breath hot and muggy. "All that power your grandmother worked so hard for... the power she kept caged in her chest and passed through blood... it's all about to be mine. Just as I always planned."

Rue's head lobbed as her stomach dropped, eyes rolling in her head. She felt like she held all the puzzle pieces in her hands and knew where they all went, but she stood frozen, her hands unable to pick them up and put them where they belonged.

Drip. Drip. Drip.

"Nothing to say, Rue? How out of character for you."

A powerful witch without her soul. An empty witch. Pieces. All pieces she was meant to put together.

"The empty witch became my mother's obsession," Fortuna continued. "She was so sure that if she found one, she could welcome them into our coven with open arms, and it would forever change our path. We were just another drop in the water. Just another coven vying for a place. And then came Cineraria Crowe. An empty witch. In the flesh."

Rue's eyes widened. Her mouth gaped, but it felt like it was full of cotton balls she couldn't speak around. Was it the blood dripping from her wounds, or was it the endless chanting that rendered her completely useless?

"It should have been impossible. What use did an empty witch have for a coven, but it would seem she was with a small child, a child who didn't share her power. Luckily for my mother, all she had to do was offer her a safe place for her daughter, and Cineraria was all too willing to bury some of that magic right here... beneath this pool." She released Rue's face, taking a step back and spreading her arms as she hovered over the pool.

If her grandmother's magic was there, she didn't feel it.

"My mother was a fool. Starstruck over Cineraria and all her power. She thought she was some kind of goddess that would carry all of witchcraft on her back toward something wonderful." She dramatically rolled her eyes, her body hitching unnaturally to the side as strands of her hair wildly curtained her face.

What? No... it couldn't be true.

'Tell me a story...'

Something pinched in the centre of Rue's chest. All the hate she had harboured, planted like a vicious seed to spread roots through her, turning what she was into something dark and unforgiving. It stole her breath, making her heart boom in her ears. Her hands fisted, freezing against her clammy palms. Her nails felt too tight as her back hunched. Fortuna's voice droned on.

"Even as a child, watching her look up to Cineraria and then Jessamine," Fortuna practically hissed their names. "Revered beyond reason, made me seethe. And the thought that my mother, if given the opportunity, would leave all this to them. To the empty witch and her ordinary daughter." She laughed, the sound a vicious bark. "Could you imagine? This coven was mine. It was my right by birth. And she was just going to give it all away? To some beast she found lurking in the dark? No."

The blur of witches quickened, their words nothing more than a high-pitched screaming in her ears.

"I wasn't worthy of taking her place, in her eyes, and yet my blessing was enough to fracture all she'd built." She laughed again, chest heaving and shoulders shaking. Her wide eyes were bloodshot, grin tight. She bent at the waist, dropping her voice to a whisper. "My mere blessing of corruption planted worms in the minds of every witch in this coven, including my mother... and yours."

She tried not to flinch at the mention of her mother and all the foul memories that knocked on the door of her mind whenever she was brought up.

The scent of their magic intensified. Ferula's magic was slowly being passed to Fortuna, spreading through the coven in turn. Intensifying the ritual that would pour more of the empty witch's magic into the pool. The well that fed magic into every witch in their coven.

"My mother was superstitious; it made her mind so easy to enter. To corrupt with ideals that weren't hers, fears that didn't belong to her. And so a prophecy was born. Just like that. Isn't that hilarious? The very woman who made the empty witch her whole purpose suddenly feared the magic she thought would save us. And your mother was so weak, barely stronger than I was. All I had to do was rewrite the tale, change what it meant, and suddenly what they once believed to be their salvation became their damnation."

Rue's eyes squeezed closed. She swallowed hard, ignoring the way her throat scratched. "My grandmother."

Fortuna snapped her fingers. "Ah. Yes. Your grandmother. She was a lot more tricky. Blessings like my corruption obviously weren't strong enough to affect the mind of the empty witch, but she'd foolishly delivered her weakness right to us. And that weakness birthed the very weapon we could use against her. It made setting you up so easy."

There was no space in Rue's chest for disbelief. It was already too full of something else. Of dark sludge that seeped from her dark roots, pouring into her until her skin felt too tight and she couldn't breathe around it. Her breath was ragged as her vision shook, the blackness that devoured the world around her slowly chased away.

"She would rather you be exiled. Removed from the coven so she could stay and keep an eye on poor and helpless Jessamine." Fortuna cackled. "How very ridiculous! With the fabricated prophecy already moving through the coven and even being whispered about by rival covens, it was only a matter of time before my mother told Cineraria to choose. Sacrifice the child who could bring about our end, or pour her magic into Lumena so they would continue to protect Jessamine and prevent the prophecy from ever coming to pass. And choose she did."

Fortuna's words weren't doing whatever she wanted them to do. Rue knew she wanted these words to be vicious cuts aimed at her. Strikes that would rip away her skin and tear at the vulnerability underneath, but she had been hardened. Weathered. She had lived her life as a cursed witch. Banished. Any part of her that would have been torn apart by this predictable monologue was as dead as the woman Fortuna tried to taunt her with.

All she heard now were the playful words of a hybrid whispering in her ear. Telling her to listen.

Pain splintered her. It cracked at the centre of her chest, turning everything under her skin into jagged pieces.

"The best part of all this? You've been searching to the ends of this world and many others for centuries for a way to undo a curse that doesn't exist. We never untethered you from your soul. I merely made you forget that she never lived inside you.

And that obsession with a curse that never existed blackened your mind. Such power, it fuelled my corruption so beautifully. Your misery..." she grinned. "Is all of your own making, Ruin Crowe."

"Blah, blah, blah," Poe's bored voice broke through the monotony of Fortuna's words and the endless chanting. "How boring."

Fortuna snarled, flicking her hands. Water rose from the pool, slithering through the air like a snake that slammed into Poe. Her feet lifted from the floor, her back slamming into a marble pillar until it cracked. The water wrapped around Poe's wrists, pulling them up above her head and binding her against the pillar. She didn't fight against their hold, all too content as blood dripped from her temple into her face.

"Oh no!" Sarcasm dripped from Poe's words. "I'm trapped. Whatever will I do?"

If she was trapped, it was because she wanted to be. That thought should terrify Fortuna, but she was too worked up to take a moment and assess who she was dealing with.

Poe's hand waved, directing an orchestra only she could see and hear. "*Woe is me, I am a weak little witch who didn't get mommy's attention, so I was forced to ruin everything*. Pah-lease. Spare us the whole *pity party* section of this. We're monsters. I fuck people until their minds are mush and get them to beg me to bite them because I like being begged to take their very souls. I like taking with permission. It's wicked, and it's me. You don't see me blaming my whore of a mother for fucking a reaper and screwing me with a poor hand... well, at least not today." Poe giggled, the sound too light for the dark moment. "You're a monster, Fortuna. We don't care about your reasons."

The tension in the air thickened as Fortuna took a dangerous step toward Poe.

"Careful now." Poe grinned, her eyes dark. "I have been known to bite at the best of times." Her tongue dragged a slow, threatening path over her top lip, eyes ringed in red. "These aren't the best of times."

"Come on now, reaper. You must sense the shift in the air. The power that will soon be mine."

Poe grinned. "I've lived a long time, witch. Power doesn't really make much difference. My bite takes weak and powerful souls just the same."

Fortuna's gaze hardened. "We'll see."

Manic laughter vibrated from Poe, making Fortuna take a cautious step back. "That we will. You know... I have the perfect playlist for when we find out." She bit the air before her, snapping her teeth.

The circle closed in, the witches of the Lumena letting their heads fall back as they looked up at the clouds moving over the ceiling. Green mists surrounded them, coiling around their arms like ropes that bound them all together. An incantation was chanted, creating a dull humming that made the air moan.

Rue's eyes squeezed shut, her back bowed.

Something was happening to her.

Tears forced their way past her tight lids as she gasped. The need to curl up in a ball battled against her need to stand against them, and she was stuck in the middle, with her hands stretched out, the pool of water bubbling below her.

You are not weak, a voice in her mind droned.

You are not meant to be chained to your soul... you need to be empty. Empty enough to permit yourself to be monstrous. In a body that will not stop when you do vicious things...

Whatever she harboured in the cage of her chest quieted for a split second. It made her shudder in its absence before she was thrown back. Her chest arched up, her mouth gaped as everything inside her exploded.

Rage bubbled through her veins as visions played behind her eyes. Releasing a slow breath, she let herself fall back into complete darkness.

27

RUE

EMPTY YOURSELF OF YOUR burdens so that you can house true power.

Empty yourself of your burdens so that you can house true power.

Empty yourself.

Empty yourself.

Protect your soul.

Empty yourself.

Fingers ripped out from the centre of her chest. She could feel the flesh move. Stretch. Pointed nails stabbed at her from the inside, trying to escape. It wasn't quite pain. It was pressure. A threat of bursting.

Her flesh split, and whatever was inside her broke free.

There was no blood. Black sludge leaked as long, dark fingers clawed their way out. Rue arched back, a scream trapped in her throat. Her feet lifted off the surface of the pool, and she floated, black sludge dripping down her like tar that erased any sign of the old Rue. The corrupted Rue. Absorbed her. A single black eye stared out from the gaping hole in her chest. It blinked slowly before it forced the rest of its face out.

It was Rue, only it wasn't.

It was an apparition of darkness. It breathed smoke before it climbed out of her open flesh. Tattered skin became a train at the ends of her shadows, trailing behind her. The version of Rue that was afraid of her coven and the curse she thought they shackled her with was inhaled by the shadows. Her skin was endless obsidian. Darker than dark. It was the absence of all light as her bare feet were set back on the pool. Tar dropped down onto the water, sizzling. She stood in endless pitch, limbs stretching slightly as she straightened.

Yellow eyes snapped open.

She was a malicious thing. The breath of nightmares breathed from under a bed while someone shuddered beneath the blankets above. The purple smoke that always wisped with her power danced in and out of the darkness. This new, darker version barely let the Rue she thought she was all this time breathe.

The arrogance Fortuna wore like the magic she wished she had slowly ebbed away, and fear worked its way over her features. She swallowed hard, scrambling back until she fell over the rim of the pool and hit the dark marble floor. A hush fell over the witches gathered there, their arms still bound as they looked on with wide eyes.

Shadows danced over Rue where her clothes used to be, shielding her. It was wicked armour.

Poe's laughter rang through the air. "I have the perfect song for this. How glorious."

Scrambling to her feet, Fortuna swallowed her fear and summoned strength. "Well, would you look at this. It seems you've finally become the very thing Cineraria always hoped you would become." She clicked her tongue, her tone heavy with disapproval. "How unfortunate."

A snort of disbelief came from Poe. "Aw, don't tell me you're going to try to keep up this facade. How stupid. Dumb, dumb, dumb."

The watery chains tightened, pulling Poe's arms higher.

She winced for a split second, her lips curving into a smile. "I can smell your fear, witch. It's as potent as the smell of death that dances around you... waiting to be fed."

Fortuna laughed, but the sound was jolted and unsure. Barks of laughter that were too loud and short. "Death will not have me."

"Oh?" Poe pursed her lips, tilting her head as she looked Fortuna over. "I doubt that, but you may be right. If I get my fangs in you, the only end your soul will see is my appetite."

Rue looked at the hybrid chained to the pillar. She glowed red; everything around her tinged in darkness. Lifting her eyes, she looked at Fortuna, who was dimly lit green. Her glow was wavering. Weak.

Everything in her exhaled, and for the first time in as long as she remembered, she felt like she could breathe. She stretched her fingers, knuckles cracking.

'One day,' Cineraria began as she pulled Rue onto her lap, 'You will finally become everything you've been forced to keep hidden. When that day comes, surrender to your darkness.'

She let her head fall back, listening to the words from her grandmother. The voices that forever whispered in the back of her mind became shouts.

Eat!

Break!

Destroy!

Devour!

That was exactly what she was going to do.

Her hand flicked, and a whip of shadows shot out. It wrapped around Fortuna's neck, lifting her into the air. The barrier set around the Lumena's land quivered and shook. It made the ground groan. Remnants of the power her grandmother gifted the coven bowed in recognition. It surrendered, running to find home in the shadows.

Witches cried out, falling to their hands and knees.

The silence that surrounded the Lumena town was sliced through. The bubble the coven existed in up until now popped and let the rest of the world in.

Fortuna's eyes widened, her feet kicking out as she tried to claw herself free. "You are... nothing... without... the coven." She forced the words out, teeth bared.

"No..." Rue stepped forward. Her steps were light, cushioned by clouds of shadow beneath her feet. "I think there will be nothing left of the coven when I'm through."

A witch got to her feet, her arms lit with the same green magic as Fortuna's. She twisted, cupping her hands together until an orb of green static vibrated between them. Her blonde hair was pulled back from her face, dark eyes glowing. Another woman stood beside her, taking the same stance.

Their mouths moved, muttering incantations.

A vine shot from a crack in the marble, black and twisted. It grew behind the blonde witch, slowly growing taller and sprouting wilted leaves before it shot forward. The sickening sound of pierced flesh was deafening as she screamed. Her chest burst open, and the vine appeared in a dark point. The magic on her hands flickered before she slumped, the vine the only thing holding her up.

"Finally!" Poe yelled. "This is the misery I was waiting for!"

The witch beside her turned to run. The vine pointed toward her before it shot through the air, spearing her.

Screams sounded through the covenstead as panic rose.

Poe's shrill laughter droned.

Rue outstretched her palms, setting her shadows free.

Ropes of darkness shot out. They wrapped around Fortuna's legs, pulling them apart. Stretching. She screamed, pain pulsing through her. Those screams dwindled, sputtering as she struggled to breathe.

"Wait," she rasped. "You need to plant your magic somewhere anyway. You can't house it all... why not plant it where your grandmother deemed fit?"

"You must be joking," Poe scoffed.

There was nothing she could say now that would undo the damage they'd done to not only her but to her family.

"Get her! Get her! Get her!" Poe chanted. Her voice was humorous. Hungry. Wicked.

"It would seem the person most affected by your corruption was you, Fortuna." Rue's voice was haunted, dark, and vicious.

"Wait!"

She would wait for nothing. Exhaling a deep breath, shadows burst from Rue's chest. It was phantom hands, vicious claws, and sharp beaks. They moved quickly, separating to burst through the room. More screams sounded. Whatever witches were foolish enough to stay and try to complete the ritual didn't have the opportunity to beg. To plead for their lives and for salvation.

Rue had none to offer.

Fortuna's eyes widened as her skin turned red.

Cold eyes watched the heir to the Lumena coven. If she went by the screams that suddenly went silent, Rue would guess she was the only one left alive. Her shadows returned, creating a thick fog on the ground that climbed up around her knees. She felt their grasp. Felt the arms that hugged her legs with each step. She paused, staring up at Fortuna as Poe's chanting continued.

Their eyes locked, and Rue stared at the woman who had been foolish enough to try to destroy a monster. She had lied, corrupted minds, and created a prophecy that made their coven afraid, while simultaneously feeding off Crowe magic.

"What a fool you are... to think you have what it takes to house this kind of power."

She didn't give Fortuna a chance to say anything else. Instead, her shadows pulled down. The sound of flesh being pulled apart was sickening. A scream bubbled up Fortuna's throat, making it bulge as she was ripped apart. Joints popped, flesh snapped, and blood splattered on Rue's face. Her shadows lifted, surrounding Fortuna as cries and bellows echoed through the town outside.

The hunger that had plagued her every waking moment of her life, the craving she thought she'd carry to her grave, subsided.

Inhaling sharply, all her shadows returned. She felt them sink into her skin, settling against her bones. The fog lifted, and

Rue looked at the space where Fortuna had stared down at her. There was nothing but a pile of wreckage pooled on the ground. All that was left of the witch she'd spent so much time hiding from.

Rue's hand smeared the blood over her face. She rubbed her finger against her thumb, letting the scarlet coat both. "Well, Poe," she said with a sigh as the beast she was settled against the Rue she believed herself to be. "It seems you have somewhat kept your end of the bargain... in your own twisted way."

As angry as she'd been with Poe when she'd stolen Jinx, she finally understood what she was trying to do. The reaper in her could sense her soul and see her monster. Knew she was way more than a mere exiled witch.

The hybrid who barged into her life with plans to kill her had set her free.

How ridiculous.

Rue turned, eyes narrowing as she looked at a barren pillar. Turning on her heel, she looked around the covenstead and found herself completely alone.

"Poe," she called.

Nothing but silence was her answer.

Sucking in a deep breath, Rue lifted her weight onto her toes, clasping her hands behind her back. "I wonder just what kind of trouble she's gone to get up to without getting her curse."

28

KILLIAN

BLOOD COATED THE VINES that wrapped through his arms and legs. An eerie whistle sliced through the air as Killian followed the seeds he had planted.

Inhaling sharply, he closed his eyes and shuddered.

There was something so wonderful about the scent of true misery. The kind that came on the cusp of a hope they'd cut down. Sorrow found in the sifted ash of burnt dreams... it was absolutely delicious.

He shuddered, bliss pouring into him.

It carried through the town, broken bodies strewn on the street. Grotesque strips of flesh decorated a street lamp as he walked by, blackened leaves floating around like haunted snow. Holding out a hand, he caught a dark petal. Pausing his whistling, he blew it away, watching it flutter.

Destruction paved the way toward what he hoped would be his mates.

His heart hammered. Jinx was the kind of chaos that survived storms because she was always at the centre, but Rue... he worried that she would fracture under the constant pressure.

Sure, being mated with Rue and Jinx had freed him from his sentence at the crossroads for a time, but he was starting to believe these two women might just be the death of him.

Birds chirped, critters scurried. The sounds came so suddenly that they made him flinch. The eerie silence that blanketed the town disappeared. He had to hope that was a good sign.

With Rue, he was sure it was. She had the kind of fight in her he hadn't seen before.

Little talons sunk into the branches of his shoulder, and he looked over to see beady black eyes staring at him.

"Bram." The bat was growing on him. He ran his hand gently against the bat's head. "Can you take me to them?"

'Rue is just ahead... in the covenstead.' He stretched his wings and flew out in front of him.

"What the hell is a covenhead?" Killian muttered.

'A covenstead... it's the witch's place of worship. A church." Bram flew up slightly, turning to look at him. *'You can hear me?'*

Killian's eyes widened. He looked up at the bat staring down at him. "I can... what does this mean?"

Bram resumed leading the way, the gentle flapping of his wings oddly comforting. The quiet went on, and Killian began to wonder if he'd heard him at all. So much was changing. Evolving. Perhaps his imagination had evolved alongside everything else.

'I think it means Rue has finally pushed free from the cracked box she's been keeping herself in.'

Brows dropped, Killian frowned.

Despite the desperation in his chest, his pace was slow. It felt like it took mere moments and also an eternity to get to the large doors that stood before what Bram had rightfully referred to as a church.

It stood looming over the town square. The light from the rising sun cut through the windows and streamed colour onto the sidewalk where he stood.

"So this is a covenstead..." It didn't look impressive enough. Knowing the pain the curse had caused Rue, likely cast within this place the Lumena found sacred, he expected it to be a dominating force. It was a mere building.

Bram flew ahead, disappearing in a puff of black smoke before he reached the doors.

It seemed he had to do the next part alone.

The door whined when it was open. The sound was a wail that split through the muffled quiet. His hooves echoed off the marble floor as he looked around and took in the haunting sight. Chunks of flesh littered the ground and stuck to the walls, puddles of blood shining against the black of the floors.

In the middle of the gruesome scene, at the edge of a black pool, stood Rue.

Darkness swirled around her as she stood with her back to him, face lifted to something unseen. The air vibrated, leaves that sprouted from his seeds of misery raining through the air.

"Rue."

She said nothing.

He carefully took in the scene. The hybrid and Jinx were absent from it.

Rue turned, looking at him. Purple smoke lifted from her flesh, blending with the darkness around her. The woman who practically smelled mortal the whole time he had known her suddenly smelled like misery, pain, and power. Blood darkened the tips of her fingers, and she brushed them against her lips, painting them in the macabre colour.

This was what Poe meant when she spoke about the beast Rue really was.

She was nightmares barely contained by the shadows in a dark room. She was... wondrous.

The dark thing he called his soul whined for her, desperate. Where Jinx satisfied his lack of inhibitions, this darkness fed the sinful thing he was. His heart fluttered just looking at her, something deep in his belly aching.

She stalked toward him, blood and flesh squelching under her bare feet, before she stood toe to toe with him. Her eyes took him in, seeing him for what he truly was.

"So this is the real you?" There was something vicious in her voice now.

He'd almost forgotten he hadn't fully shown her who he was. Anxious energy filled him. "Yes," he forced out, throat tight.

Her fingers danced up his vines.

Something in the centre of his chest tightened. A dark chain that bound them together, locking around his heart to control and own its beating. It stole his breath, making his flesh pebble and his teeth grind together.

She *owned* him, he realized. In the beginning, staring at her standing there at the crossroads with a chip on her shoulder and a ditch dug between her brows, there was a whisper of knowing that Fate had paved the paths of their destiny. Now? Now it felt like he had been harpooned by it. Impaled. Struck down.

Carve away the flesh of his chest and break off his bones to see the heart caged within, and he knew it would be branded: *Ruin Crowe.*

Fuuuuuuck.

She lifted on her toes, black smoke billowing from her eyes, making her lids look painted obsidian. "It seems we have a lot to discuss."

He inhaled the thick scent of blood. "Mmm. It looks like you've cleared our schedules by getting rid of your coven."

Rue's breaths were heavy. Sultry, even. Her eyes narrowed on the vines surrounding his face. "Something tells me you took your pound of flesh."

"Nothing could have stopped me."

Her nod was slow as she continued to trace the foliage that made up his form. "This coven was never truly mine... or my mother's..." She sucked in another breath. "Or my grandmother's. And the curse? It turns out that was never mine either."

Killian didn't know what to say. Her entire air had shifted. Changed into something he wasn't entirely sure how to perceive. Something with a darkness he knew wouldn't match his — her kind of darkness would surpass his. It would feed him. He felt drunk off it even now.

"Ruin," he whispered. Long, slender fingers resembling small branches brushed against her face. "Just what is happening?" Her eyes flashed when he said her name, and it unravelled the parts of him that weren't already undone.

"Just what..." Her eyes dropped past his bare chest and lower still. "Is under there?"

His heart fluttered as a groan sat at the back of his throat. To have her so openly look at him, eyes heavy with lust, made him feel like he was finally whole. "Care to find out?"

"Yes." Confidence swelled around her.

It had been so long since he was free from his cage. Since his original form was hidden beneath flesh, with the sole purpose of being palatable to mortal minds. He felt the thatch of branches over his crotch part, and his dick slipped through. It was fleshy, like his chest. The underside was textured, a row of planted seeds sat just under the skin all the way up until under the head. The tip was the large and bulbous head of a mushroom. The veins were thick and pronounced along his length.

"Tell me, dark cloud, are you ready? Are you finally ready to ask me?"

Rue wrapped a hand around him. "I would... but misery fits me so well, and something tells me it's a flavour you enjoy."

"Something tells me..." He wrapped a hand around her neck, thumb brushing against her jaw. "I'd quite like the taste of your happiness."

"Happiness... is that something either of us will even be able to swallow?"

Killian's grip tightened, jerking her face toward his. "Anything that offers a taste of you is something I would happily swallow."

Rue's eyes dropped, and her lips curved into a mischievous smile. Rue took his hand, dragging his palm against her naked flesh. She kept her eyes locked on his, the threat of his claw dangerous.

Killian wasn't sure what excited him more, the heavy look in her eyes as she took him in or the way she took charge. She was treacherous. Something he should fear, as he enjoyed the pleasurable sting.

She didn't wait. Arm wrapped around his neck, she pressed one knee into his side and grabbed the length of him. She lined them up, her eyes locked on his.

"No going back now." His voice was slightly nervous. He wasn't sure if this was a warning or something else.

"Don't worry. I can take care of myself." She rolled her hips and sank onto him. A low moan was trapped in her throat, vibrating through her as she rested her brow on his chest.

"Ruin..."

"Remember that name, because that's exactly what I plan to do to you." She lifted herself, sinking onto him again.

Killian groaned.

Rue took control. She held onto his neck, nails pressed into the branches of his nape as she wrapped her legs around him and used him. She rolled her hips, taking the full length of him in until he bumped against something inside her that made him suck in a sharp breath. She clasped around him with each thrust, holding him as she slowly pulled away. How was it possible she was making *him* feel every inch?

Sweet Lilith, he mentally cursed.

"Ruin," he moaned.

Her throaty laugh was her reply. "I'm not someone who likes my name uttered during sex unless it's a beg. Beg for me, Killian. Pray to whatever dark power you serve for me." Her grip changed, a hand moving to the front of his throat, nails scraping against his branches.

The pressure burned, the feel of her magic radiating from her palm.

"Beg, Killian," she demanded.

His arm snaked under her ass, and he carried her through the wreckage at their feet. The brutality in him demanded to be used as he slammed her back against a pillar. A hand slapped the stone above her head, fingertips cracked through the marble as he growled.

There was nothing he wouldn't swallow down, nothing he wouldn't utter that she demanded from him.

"Ruin me," he begged.

And he would beg every chance he got, because this kind of rapturous bliss wasn't the kind dark creatures like him often got to touch. And here it was... practically fucking him out of his senses.

29

Jinx

On her knees, Jinx leaned forward, pressing her palms into the soil as though she could plant herself there. She was desperate with a need to feel rooted. To steady herself after being hit with a contentment that felt abnormal. Her back arched, her breath trapped in her chest.

She felt ripped open. Exposed.

All the parts of her she kept carefully hidden — parts of her she thought if she ever dared show, she would be stealing just another thing from Rue — were suddenly uncovered. Unleashed. Set free.

A thousand thoughts went through her mind, memories that were as much hers as Rue's. *Her grandmother whispered into her ear, foretelling this exact moment as her soul, Sybil, wastched on. Telling them both this was exactly what was meant to happen. Telling them a story as they both clung together in bed, giggling because they thought that alone would keep sleep from claiming them.*

Rue and Jinx. Jinx and Rue.

An empty witch needed to set her soul free to allow space for all the magic they collected.

A darkness... one that held both Rue and Jinx in tight arms, cradling them the way their coven — and mother — never would.

Grandma touched both of their heads in turn, her smile as bright as it was dark. Together... they were always together.

"W-what?" Her back bowed.

Heat brushed against her ear, making her shudder. "Feel it? All that power you've so foolishly believed they could take or control?" Poe's voice was dark relief. "Isn't it wonderful? Falling into your monstrous skin and realizing it feels like home?"

Jinx whipped her head up. Wide eyes looked around, but Poe was already gone. She was an apparition at times, haunting them. Stumbling to her feet, Jinx ran through the woods.

She needed to get to Killian — to Rue.

There was always a rope wrapped around her. As much as she liked to pretend there wasn't, that there was nothing that chained her down or worried her, she always felt leashed. Maybe that was why she constantly acted out. She wanted to feel free, even if just for a moment.

That rope was gone now, and true freedom made her feel like she couldn't breathe around it.

Her feet were desperate as she stumbled into the town. It felt like a mirage. Something her mind conjured up that wasn't real. She had been there before, lived there, but it looked so different now. Felt so different. She ran past the rubble strewn through the square, the broken fountain and the bodies of dozens of witches.

The scent of something dark and depraved was in the air. A hunger that should never be fed, suddenly fully satisfied. The town was a blur as she followed the scent, bursting through the doors.

Moaning met her before she saw them.

Killian's back was to her; nothing seen of Rue but her hands around his neck and her legs around his waist. He was massive in this form. Constantly moving vines and branches that fit perfectly together, but when they shifted, they showed a chasm of shadows between each one. The antlers she had quickly fallen in love with on his head.

The sound of flesh slapping against flesh echoed through the covenstead, making her throb with need. What an odd sound, knowing he looked like very few parts of him were flesh.

Her feet were slow, something in her chest making her cling to the shadows as she watched them. The selfish parts of her that would have leapt at Killian's back, urging to be accepted and take part, had fallen to the floor. Ill-fitted clothes she stepped out of somewhere back in the woods. Now, her heart beat a steady rhythm, merely watching.

Bliss moved through her as she clung to a pillar, eyes wide.

She watched the way they moved, the synced roll of hips, the lock of eyes that held a quiet conversation Jinx heard, even from where she stood.

Pleasure vibrated under her skin. Borrowed, not stolen.

It felt different. A surrendered sharing instead of the taking she had grown so used to.

She was mesmerized by the vision of them. The dark acceptance that swirled around them like smoke and magic. Rue's hand carved over Killian's vines, moving around his neck to clasp the front of his thick throat. He dropped his head, lifting her higher, pressing them together, chest against chest.

The intimacy there made Jinx's eyes glass over.

"There you are, dark cloud," Killain whispered. "My ruinous promise."

Rue's smile wobbled.

His sweet words somehow fit the brutality of their movements so perfectly. Jinx's breath stuttered, her hand clasped over her mouth as she caught her blissful exhale. Her toes curled, her pussy throbbing. This was a pleasure she wanted to share.

Instead, she held the pillar tighter, refraining from reaching between her legs and satisfying her own hunger. This pleasure was theirs, and for the first time in a long time, Jinx was going to let something be completely Rue's.

Killian's hand fisted in Rue's braids, tilting her face to claim her lips. Their kiss was endless wanting finally satisfied. A desperate clash of hunger.

The kiss broke on a wretched groan. "Come for me," Killian demanded. "Let me claim the pleasure I've promised myself I would give you. Let me feel it."

Rue moaned.

His hip jutted forward. "Fuck."

He lifted Rue higher, Killian's dick covered in her cream. Just seeing how aroused Rue was made Jinx's pussy flutter. She felt the muscles tense and release, desperate to be filled.

"Come for me, please," he begged.

Rue's whine turned desperate. Inhales that inflated her chest, but never left it before she called out and gave Killlian exactly what he asked her for. They came together, covered in smoke, while ash snowed down from nowhere. Their panted breaths kept time, as they clung to one another, life rafts that had saved them both in one way or another.

Rue's quiet laughter came first, her hands cupping the side of Killian's face as she looked up at him with eyes that shimmered with mischief and longing. "You kept your promise," she whispered.

Killian's laughter danced with hers, dark sounds haunting the dark. "My first of many. Tell me what you want, and I promise to give it to you."

"I think saving me from myself was a good start."

"No, dark cloud... it was always you. You were the one meant to save yourself."

Jinx smiled.

For the first time, in as long as she could remember, she felt like she'd been saved, too.

30

RUE

THE EMPTINESS SHE FELT in her chest as she clung to Killian was a different beast. It wasn't a hollow she wished to fill, but an emptying of all the things that weighed her down. Of the burdens that shackled her, holding her hostage. A slow smile touched her lips as she continued to throb around Killian. She didn't want to climb off him just yet, not when she finally surrendered to him.

Nothing but their breathing could be heard through the quiet of the place that had all but birthed the power of the Lumena. Held it. Contained in a mere pool they needed to soak in. Absorb. The stench of blood was still heavy in the air, now made all the more sweet by the unmistakable smell of sex.

"What is that? Don't tell me it's... happiness." He all but chuckled the words.

"Are you mocking me?" Rue cocked a brow. It was odd looking at him now. She saw him with new eyes. Before now, under the thick haze of Fortuna's corruption, it was like looking at him with blurry vision. It was clear now, and he suddenly looked like everything she ever wanted.

He shook his head, but his smile was playful. "No. I'm not brave enough to mock you, pretty darkness."

She laughed, rolling her eyes.

The rough bark-like flesh of his thumb traced the scar along her cheek up to the missing part of her ear. "I've wondered about this."

She laughed, clarity giving her answers where corruption and anger once lived. "A gift from Jinx, that part was true. A soul is very important to an empty witch. As much as we make one another stronger, we can also cause each other great pain… lasting pain."

He frowned, but she chased it away with a smile.

"We became exactly what Fortuna wanted us to be. Adversaries who refused to work together because we were enemies. Some swipes we took at each other carved out larger chunks than others." She shook her head, annoyed at all the time they'd wasted and how cruel they'd been to one another in their own way. "Deservedly so."

"And now? Now that all that is done, will this heal?"

A deep breath filled her. "No. Consider it a reminder of just how important she is to me… even when she's being a pain in my ass."

His nod was slow.

"Speaking of pains in the ass… just how long are you going to lurk in the shadows? Enjoy the show, Jinx?"

Jinx sulked out from behind the pillar, looking... almost bashful. "I thought, in honour of our freedom, I should remind you there was a time when I didn't just take." Her eyes whipped over to Killian, shame darkening them.

"You look different," Killian noted lightly, tightening his hold on Rue's ass when she tried to climb down.

"Don't let her fool you. Even before all this, she was the chaotic little shit she was when you met her... she just wasn't as selfish."

Jinx lifted a shoulder, closing the space between them. "What monster isn't a little selfish?" She held her finger and thumb together, peeking through the small space between them.

Rue laughed. "True enough."

Killian looked down at her, eyes deep. "It would seem..." he whispered words just for her. "That you found happiness all on your own, dark cloud."

"Happiness," she scoffed. "Let's not get ahead of ourselves."

A slow clap pulled their attention. All three turned their heads at once to watch Poe step out of the shadows. She looked positively satisfied. Her brow arched, hands clasping together with her tongue out. Hand above her head, she dropped into a squat, throwing her ass around. "I had the perfect playlist for this, but unfortunately, I shoved my speaker inside one of these witches... and I can't remember which one." She pouted.

Despite her urge to keep Killian inside her, Rue climbed off him. She made no attempt to shield herself. It had been a long time since she was comfortable in her own skin, she wasn't about to shy away from it now. Instead, she crossed her arms under her breasts and looked Poe over.

"You're still here?" Rue asked.

Jinx moved to stand next to Killian, throwing her arm through his as she leaned into him.

Poe approached, inhaling deeply. "Lust like that... ugh. It's so very filling." She dragged her tongue over her lips. "It complements the souls I devoured quite nicely."

Rue snapped her fingers, impatient. "Why are you still here?"

"Isn't it obvious? We still have unfinished business."

Killlian's branches sprouted new ones, his size growing.

Rue stepped forward; she didn't need anyone to protect her. "Oh?"

"The way I see it," Poe began, fingers interlocked behind her back as she kicked her feet out in front of her, pacing. She paused to pull a strip of fabric covered in gore from the wall, dropping it to the floor. "You would still be cowering in your house, hiding from these *almost* witches, if it weren't for me. Living in the very delusion they created. A thank you is in order, but I have no use for those. Instead, I would like a curse."

Rue rolled her eyes. "The curse I cast all those years ago? On the Duke?"

"On my Dexy," Poe clarified.

"Right." Rue sighed. The last thing she thought would ever happen would be that she would have to look at the man she once believed was responsible for her banishment. Now, with her newfound clarity, she realized he was merely an excuse used for her to be pushed out. To be controlled by a fear she didn't understand. "Dex DuTerre."

"Dex DuTerre," Jinx repeated. "The naughty man."

Rue released a slow breath. "I suppose I could get a good curse going. You know, considering I was never cursed and all that."

Poe danced on her feet. "It would be easy work for you now, wouldn't it? All that power finally uncaged. You're welcome, by the way. You all made it so difficult to get things going."

"Mhmm..." Rue hummed her agreement. "Plus, not being constantly stalked by you would be a plus."

"I'm an amazing stalker," Poe all but beamed.

"What an absurd thing to be proud of." Killian shook his head.

"Why wouldn't I be proud of my many skills?" She shrugged, not understanding why Killian would think that was weird. "Anyway, the sooner the better. Let's go."

"Now?" Jinx's mouth dropped open. "But, we were just... I mean, we didn't really get a good chance to..." She stomped her feet, the beginning of a tantrum coming on.

Rue stepped into her, throwing her arm around her shoulder and pulling her in tight. Her thumb traced a slow circle on Jinx's shoulder, hoping to cool her rising temper.

Jinx's eyes widened, their eyes locking. "Hi."

A silent conversation moved between them, the corner of Rue's mouth quirking. "Hi." Comfort moved through Rue as Jinx settled, clearing her throat. The normalcy in the embrace felt odd but right.

"More?" Poe grinned, showing her fangs. "I mean, I could always go for more."

Bram appeared in a puff of smoke.

"Bram!" Jinx beamed.

"There you are... right when everything is over. How very useful," Rue grumbled.

'Well, excuse me if I had more important things to do. Being a familiar doesn't mean I have to be at your beck and call.' Bram's recovered attitude was another sign things were returning back to normal. She forgot what a sassy flying rat he often was.

"Doesn't it, though?" Killian's brows dropped in confusion.

'There is a lot I do that goes unseen.'

"Yeah?" Rue scoffed. "Like what?"

Everything in her tensed, eyes wide as she looked from Bram to Killian. "You can..." She frowned, confused.

'Yeah, yeah, yeah. He can hear me now.'

"Why is that a big deal? The bat speaks. Don't all familiars?" Poe rolled her eyes, agitation contorting her features. "It's not exactly like he has anything important to say. *Over here. Jinx is this way. We'll let Rue handle her. Blah, blah, blah.*"

"*You* can hear him?" Killian asked.

Poe shrugged. "I can hear every soul. So... the curse?"

Rue sighed as Poe winked at her. "Alright. One curse." The last thing she wanted was to have this hybrid following them around, especially now, when she felt at home in her own skin and was tempted to ride Killian until she snapped a few of his branches. Shadows danced around her, dressing her in denim shorts and a casual tee.

"One curse!" Poe clapped again. "One curse! One curse! One curse!" she chanted.

Jinx's eyes widened as she hopped out from under Rue's arm. "One curse! One curse!" she joined the chant.

Killian's lips pursed as he slowly threw up a hand. "One curse?"

"One curse," Rue agreed, surrounding them all in dark shadows.

31

RUE

SHE WAS AN EMPTY witch. A witch who was always meant to be separate from her soul. In the end, Ferula's superstitions and the whispering in her ear of banishment instead of death by her grandmother was more blessing than curse. And the real downfall of Lumena, a coven her grandmother had poured into trying to find a place where Jessamine could belong, was Fortuna's greed.

What a wicked twist of Fate.

Thanks, Grandma.

Now, all she needed to truly start over was a curse.

Killian's arm snaked around her waist as they walked into the foyer of Poe's house. It was... gothic. Endless framed black and white photos littered the walls, all with the same man in each. Jinx barrelled in, making Rue and Killian stumble as she pushed past them.

"Wow..." She pointed to one of the pictures, eyes on Poe, who stood a step ahead of them. "You really like this guy."

"I do, don't I?" She skipped in. "Alexa, play something dramatic."

"Playing something dramatic."

Music started to play all around the house.

"What is this all about?" Dex appeared in the entryway, dish towel rubbing at his hands as he looked past Poe to Rue.

Poe leapt into his arms, forcing him to catch her. Her legs wrapped around his waist, face sinking into his neck as she inhaled him. A groan bubbled through her as her frustration mounted.

As deadly as Poe's bite was, Dex didn't shy away. He was what many people would call tall, dark, and handsome. He was slightly shorter than Killian, but broad. His muscles strained against the taut fabric of his black casual shirt. His brown skin was warm and deep, but lighter than Rue's or Jinx's. A shade darker than Poe's. His square jaw was strong and serious. It was covered in a thick beard that looked as though it took a lot of care to keep it looking so thoroughly groomed. His black hair was set in waves and lined sharply.

He looked so much more modern than Rue remembered him. Elegant in a different way from how he'd been in the past.

He held Poe pressed against him, eyes still locked on Rue.

"You."

A deep breath inflated Rue's chest as she nodded. "Me."

Dex's eyes dropped to Poe. He pushed some of her curls out of her eyes as he stared down at her with more love than Rue would have ever believed was possible before she found it for herself. "Treacherous little monster, did you find what you were looking for?"

Poe shimmied, shaking her ass as she all but humped him in the foyer. "Don't I always?"

He clutched her closer. "Took you long enough."

She giggled, the sound breathless as he squeezed her. "And here I thought you were a patient beast."

"That was before I knew there existed something in this world to be so desperate for. To wait for you, my dark wonder, is to be damned every second."

Rue rolled her eyes. "Yes, yes. You're so in love. Great. Can we get this over with?"

"Over with. Over with," Jinx sang. She clutched the hem of her skirt in her hands as she twirled around where Dex stood, holding Poe.

Poe hopped down. She skipped over, grabbing Rue by the wrist and yanking her toward her. She was strong, and as powerful as Rue was now that she'd finally remembered what she was, her strength didn't quite rival that of a reaper — not even half of one. Killian released her, catching Jinx as she twirled into him.

Jinx wrapped her arms around his head, hopping onto him as Poe had done to Dex.

Killian sputtered, trying to free his face from her arms. "Jinx..."

"Love. Everyone is so in love! Did you see, Killie?" She said the words with longing.

"Yes, but I can't breathe when you cover my face like—" He grunted as her grip tightened.

"Come, come, come," Poe urged, shoving Rue toward Dex. "Curse him."

His dark eyes took Rue in. It felt surreal standing together again. The last time she had seen him, she had so much hate in her heart and blamed him for her untethering. Back then, she wanted nothing but heartache for him. To think the curse she put on him would have brought him to Poe was insane.

She chuckled under her breath, shaking her head. It made her wonder now, if Fate had a hand in all this. If by cursing Dex as she had, Fate had made sure he met his pair, just as she found hers when she was under the guise of a curse all her own.

The Dex of the past fluttered into her mind's eye, settling atop the modern man in front of her now. They were so similar and yet completely different.

The same could likely be said of her. Time had a way of changing everything, whether they wanted it to or not.

"Come on!" Poe urged.

"Ruin Crowe." Dex dipped his head. "To think I would be happy to see you."

She laughed again at the ridiculousness of their situations. "I'm just as baffled as you."

"Jinx," Killian moaned low. "Off my face. Please!"

Dex watched the scene behind her. "It looks like we've both found what we've been looking for. No, that's wrong, isn't it? I would dare to say neither one of us was looking."

"And yet, here we are." Rue nodded slowly.

His words pulled at her chest, making her feel more than she thought she was capable of. Especially after all this time, being nothing but a block of ice, afraid feeling too much would bring her coven to her doorstep.

Poe wrapped her arms around Dex's stomach, her face pressed into his back. "Isn't he just yummy?"

His hands smoothed over hers, his weight leaning back against her.

"Who would have thought being a zombie would have let you become the lover of a reaper/succubus hybrid. Fate has quite the sense of humour, doesn't she?" Rue's mouth quirked. "I'm finding that out for myself."

Dex chuckled low. "I hear you're an empty witch."

"So it would seem." When Poe had the time to tell him, Rue honestly didn't know.

"So really, all my misdeeds back then weren't the thing that damned you."

It was Rue's turn to chuckle. "As I said, Fate has a sense of humour."

He nodded. "I'd say I'm sorry for all of it, but knowing everything I did, every wicked sin that blackened my soul, were stones that lined the path leading me to her, I have no regrets."

Killian stepped into her back, Jinx bumping her as she struggled to stay on his chest. "I'd have tried to kill you for saying those words to me before all this." She tilted her head slightly, gesturing to Killian and Jinx behind her. "But I get it now."

Poe peered out from behind him. "What's the holdup? Do you know how long it's been since he's been in my guts? Since I've been in his? Get the cursing, woman!"

"Chop, chop!" Jinx clapped, slipping from Killian's waist to wrap around his thighs. "Get the cursing, woman!"

"Jinx, don't call Rue *woman*," Killian scolded lightly. "She's going to make us both pay for it."

She looked up at him, that wild smile of hers giving them no clue of whether or not she heard what he was saying.

"Here goes nothing," Rue whispered under her breath.

There was a tiny moment where she wondered if being freed from Fortuna's delusion would be enough. If inhaling all the magic left in Lumena's town and housing it in the hollows of her chest would feed the parts of her that used to be fuelled by her rage alone.

You know what to do, a voice whispered in the back of her mind.

Hand held up, Rue raised her palm until her magic coated it. It had changed. There was a darkness to it now. A smoke that danced with the purple. She let it build, glowing and glowing, until it went up her arm. Her hand whipped out. Her magic burned over him like a hungry flame. It devoured his flesh, making it glow. Dex dropped to his knees. His teeth gritted as he doubled over, Poe still clinging to him as she pulled him into her lap.

"What are you doing?" she hissed.

"What? Did you think a curse would tickle?"

"No... but..." Poe's lips thinned, chin quivering.

"Give it time." The magic intensified in a stream that made his flesh bubble and sear. "The pain will become something he enjoys... just like old times."

He shook in her arms until the flames doused and left him panting. He shuddered as the magic returned to the place she'd stolen it from under his skin, settling against his bones and marking them.

The power that moved through her made her shudder. This kind of magic was the kind she'd never been able to use before. The kind that had to be poured into the well of Lumena, so they could bathe in it while she stood on the outside, longing. Now, it was all hers. Every last drop of it.

Dex's chest bowed up, a drastic inhale echoing through the foyer as he sucked in breath like he'd been denied it. He coughed, lungs burning when he took in too much.

"Dexy!" Poe splattered his brow with kisses. "You're okay, aren't you?"

He grunted, but his hand reached out and took hers.

"Awww, aren't they cute?" Jinx whined. "Adorable little monsters."

"Yes, love. Adorable." Killian sounded like he didn't fully agree. It probably had something to do with Poe tormenting them all this time.

Jinx slid onto the floor. Her pout stretched down her lips before she hopped to her feet, dancing around.

Poe pressed her nose into Dex, inhaling him. "He smells..."

Dex's eyes fluttered open.

"He smells... like *mine!*" Glee transformed the face of the hybrid who had caused more trouble than Rue would have thought possible. Her smile looked almost pretty as she clutched the sides of Dex's face, barely giving him time to catch his breath before she forced him to sit, pressing her lips to his. "You're cursed, my dark prince."

He chuckled low, hand holding her back. "It sure feels that way..."

Poe straddled him, her claws ripping off his shirt.

Rue stiffened. "Oh. Well... yeah. Right to it then, I guess."

Poe rolled her hips, ripping at whatever fabric she could, fangs long.

Jinx stopped dancing, eyes alight with mischief as she looked on in fascination. “And there goes Poe’s top.”

Rue grabbed hold of Jinx’s wrist, pulling her away. “It would seem we’ve done all we need to do here. Restored the curse and all that.” She cleared her throat as the sound of flesh against flesh sounded, Poe’s throaty moans loud. They really didn’t waste any time. “Let’s go.”

“But I want to watch!” Jinx whined.

Rue pressed her palm against Killian’s face, shoving his head back as he gawked. “You too! Get moving.”

“I wasn’t—”

“Yeah, yeah. I bet you weren’t.”

Magic clouded around them, the mist chilling as it enveloped them and took them home.

32

JINX

HAPPINESS WAS NEVER SOMETHING she struggled to feel. She'd always told herself the light feeling that filled her chest, making her heart beat this easy rhythm, was joy. She wasn't entirely sure what else it could be.

Now, she knew.

Happiness was a naked Killian.

It was a Rue that let Jinx into her bedroom. Into her bed.

Cheeks puffed with air, Jinx sat on the floor beside the bed. Candlelight lit the room in warm tones, making the space that had always seemed dark and ominous warm and welcoming.

The room smelled like sex. Like sweat and regret... slightly metallic and bitter. It smelled like accepted shame, and that was the kind of thing that fed the depraved dark parts of all three of them.

Killian snored.

Rue talked in her sleep.

Grinning so wide it made her cheeks ache, Jinx danced her fingers along Rue's naked thigh. She walked her fingers along the smooth skin, over the rise and fall of her hip and over to where Killian's legs tangled with hers.

Peace was... quiet.

She tilted her head as she thought about it.

Everything was always so loud. Her thoughts shouted and whined, and discontent made her stomach growl. Rue was always shouting, cursing... but this... this was bliss.

Her smile broadened.

"He's mine," she whispered, crawling around the bottom of the bed to let her hands explore him. "And... she's mine too." *Finally.*

She was a loose soul. Set free from its cage to make space for... whatever seemed to fill Rue up when she was staring down the very coven who had haunted them both for so long. It was odd to exist knowing she was Rue's, but Rue was doing everything in her power to make sure she was never Jinx's.

But that all changed. Now... she was the companion she always longed to be.

"Was it him?" she muttered low. "Was it this demon who was actually so much more who bound us all together?"

Surely, it couldn't have been the hybrid that could smell exactly what they truly were. Who plotted and planned to have centuries of trickery undone.

It couldn't have been.

Still... she was thankful to her. Even if she did take as many bites out of Rue as she could along the way. And toss poor little Bram. Nothing came for free and all that. Costs paid in full, it was all worth it.

Every drop of blood, every shred of flesh brought them there. To the place Jinx felt they were always supposed to be.

Together.

Rue groaned as Jinx's hand moved over her ribcage, making her flesh tighten. "What 're you doin'?" she mumbled.

"Just looking at my things." Jinx giggled. "Mine." She poked Rue in the ribs. "And mine." She poked Killian's thigh.

"Mmphf." Killian's hand whipped out, grabbing her wrist and pulling her up. He turned, wiggling his back up against Rue's chest and making room for Jinx on the bed.

The warmth of his strong hold embraced her, pulling her tightly against him and sealing them together. He held her like something important. Not just a soul blowing in the wind, but like letting go and holding her any less would cost him something he simply couldn't afford.

Her smile stretched her face as her hands rubbed against his forearm. "Mine."

"Mhmm..." He adjusted so his chin rested on her shoulder. "Mine."

"Yeah, yeah. He's yours, you're his, you're both mine. You know what would be the best, though, if everyone, regardless of who they belonged to, were *quiet,*" Rue hissed.

"Ugh, can you not be cranky for one minute?" Jinx complained.

"If I weren't cranky, the two of you would run rampant. Kidnapped by hybrids and sentenced to crossroads..."

"Both of those things happened while you were being cranky," Jinx pointed out.

Killian chuckled low but knew better than to agree.

"Shut up, will you? I'm too tired to argue with you." Her words were clipped as she yawned.

"That's only because you're losing." Knowing she was winning an argument with Rue made her smile. "But since all that happened while you were being miserable, you'd think you'd just switch up and do whatever you want. Bad things are going to happen anyway. Might as well enjoy the ride."

"The ride?" Killian muttered against her skin, alighting a slew of butterflies in her stomach and making her pussy flutter. "I have a ride that will make you quiet."

"We all know Jinx is anything but quiet on *that* ride," Rue muttered.

His knee pressed between her legs, parting them slightly as he poked at her entrance. The heat of him made her eyes roll closed, and Jinx held her breath as he slowly pushed into her.

Her breath hitched, bottom lip clasped in her teeth as she tried with everything she was to make Rue a liar.

His hands kneaded the flesh of her chest, his pumps painfully slow. "You'll be quiet, won't you, little soul?" Killian's voice was barely restrained roughness.

Fuck, she wanted to be. Her gasp carried a slight whine that sounded so very loud in the expected quiet.

"Jinx," he warned. "Quiet."

Her eyes rolled back, pleasure pulsing through her.

Rue's exasperated sigh echoed around them. "You're both determined to make sure I don't get any sleep, aren't you?"

"Well... since you're up now anyway..." Killian pulled out of her, the absence of him making her whine as he got to his feet. His hands wrapped around Rue's knees, pulling her to the end of the bed, her ass hanging off the side. She was forced to plant her toes on the floor, eyes wide.

"Hey..."

Killian's arm snaked around Jinx's stomach. He lifted her, making her straddle Rue as he sank back into her. He pumped into her, Jinx's knees boxing in Rue's hips.

Jinx's eyes fluttered open. Sleepy, dark eyes looked up at her, the annoyance there playful. "Care for another round?" She grinned.

"I'm beginning to lose count." Rue smirked.

Killian pulled the pillow out from behind Rue's head, shoving it under the small of her back and lifting her hips. "What is the point of having two dicks if I have to take you both one at a time?"

That had been the most exciting revelation. Jinx held herself up, hands planted on both sides of Rue's head as she looked between them, back at Killian. She watched his dick slowly enter her, thick and fleshy, though the veins were thick and pronounced like the vines of his true form. Beneath his shaft was ribbed, seeds evenly spaced under taut skin. She felt every notch as he pulled out of her, slowly driving back in. Right below was another, equally impressive dick.

Fate really knew her shit.

Killian's dark hand wrapped around himself, smacking the head off Rue's pussy before he pulled completely out of Jinx and ran his second dick through her cream. He collected it, pushing into her before he pulled out, slicked in her juices.

Jinx gasped. "Killian."

"Patience," he chastised, cracking his palm against her ass before he drove into her, forcing her forward. Jinx's chest collided with Rue's as he filled her. His hand pushed on her lower back, pressing her against Rue before he scooped Rue's legs up on each side of Jinx, arms hooked behind her knees, lifting them both slightly and sealing them together.

Their eyes locked, Jinx's mouth open on a gasp as he drove into Rue. She saw the exact moment she was filled. Saw the way her eyes fluttered as he filled them both to the base, close enough Jinx could feel her heat.

Killian's pace was brutal; all that tiredness he claimed to feel was gone.

Her arms shook, any hope of holding herself up completely gone.

Each slam of Killian into them made her clit brush against Rue's, alighting her with pleasure.

"Fucking hell," Rue moaned before her fingers dove into Jinx's hair, wrapping around the back of her neck and pulling her face toward hers. Their lips sealed, and everything she was shattered. Each exhale was a moan Rue swallowed, as close as Jinx would ever get to being home inside Rue's skin.

Killian pressed a light kiss to Jinx's shoulder before his teeth dragged, nipping. Pressure built, toes curling as the heat from Rue's pussy and the fullness of Killian's dick made her feel like she was crafted to be used by both of them. To belong to them. To ache for them.

Her chest hitched, tears pushing past her lids as Rue broke the kiss on a desperate gasp. She held Jinx's face above hers as her thighs squeezed Jinx's hips. "Look at me," she demanded.

Jinx's eyes snapped open. They locked with Rue's, and all the pleasure she thought she could continue to ride threatened to make her explode.

"Are you going to come, my little soul?"

"You both are," Killian groaned.

"Are you ready... dark cloud?" Jinx borrowed the nickname Killian used for her. Borrowed, because everything passed between them moving forward would be borrowed and shared, not stolen.

Rue's eyes pinched closed, breath hitching before she forced them open. "Together."

Killian's pace quickened, erratic. "Now!"

Eyes locked, Rue and Jinx exploded. Smoke danced from Rue's eyes, surrounding them in heat as Jinx's toes curled and her pussy clenched, pulsing around him. Milking him. Her lips brushed against Rue's, the barest touches of flesh, before she slumped forward, her face in her neck.

They exploded together, Killian falling forward to sandwich them together. Heat filled her to bursting, pouring out of her to seep in the barest of spaces between her and Rue. Feeling Killian fill them made the depraved parts of her giddy.

Blissful pants was a song Jinx wished she would hear forever, marking the passage of time in a moment that felt frozen. Eventually, Rue groaned.

"You guys are heavy."

The last thing she wanted to do was move. "I'm just a wee thing," Jinx joked, remembering the way they argued on the beach what felt like a lifetime ago.

"Wee thing my ass."

Killian hooked his arm back around Jinx, lifted her off Rue and collapsed on the bed beside her. He curled into Jinx, pressing his face into her hair, inhaling her. Rue stayed where she was, making no move to climb further onto the bed, legs dangling.

"Come," Jinx urged, the familiar whine in her voice.

"Shh." Rue barely waved her off, eyes already closed.

"Come cuddle. I know how much you enjoy it, even though you pretend not to," Jinx teased.

Killian sat up, dragging Rue up the bed before he settled in the space between them. Rue nestled into him, getting comfortable.

Jinx reached over them, playfully pinching her underboob. "See. You enjoy it."

"Right now, I'm trying to enjoy sleep." Her voice was still tired as she threw her arm over Killian and slapped the side of Jinx's boob.

"Hey!"

"Shh," Killian hushed them both. "I'll have no energy to give you what I have planned later if you both don't let me get some rest."

Jinx's grin broadened. Those butterflies that had taken up permanent residence in her belly fluttered around, her heart following suit. "And just what do you have planned?"

"Just you wait and see."

The End?

AND OF COURSE THERE'S ANOTHER MONSTER

The chapter after this page will be a prologue to the next book in this monster romance series. If you intend to read this book as a standalone and don't wish to continue diving into this world of monsters, I would stop the book here.

KILLIAN

A SNOW GLOBE

SEVERAL MONTHS LATER

THE WIND WAS THE blistering kind. It whipped against Killian's cheeks, forcing him to fall back into his true form so his hooves could root down into the deep snow. Annoyance ate away at him, and not for the first time, he wondered if keeping Jinx's antics from Rue had been the best call.

If he'd told her, he knew exactly what would have happened. She would have broken something, punched him in the chest, and told him to just leave the wandering soul for dead. All before she reluctantly went and handled this herself, uncaring of the brutal way she handled things. She may have softened in the past few months. May have more love for Jinx than annoyance, but Jinx was still Jinx. And she liked to chase trouble. And Rue was still Rue.

A sigh inflated his massive chest as the flurries parted just enough to show him the ominous castle perched between two snow-covered mountains.

He should have at least brought Bram. Something told him he would need all the help he could get to negotiate with Jinx. Once she had an idea, there was really no putting the brakes on it.

It would have been helpful to him if he knew just what idea brought her to this tundra.

"Fuck..."

The grey castle looked dreadful. The windows blacked out, and dangerously long icicles hung from under each ledge. The door was several stories high, large enough to dwarf him even in his true form.

Killian ran his hand over the back of his neck, branches rubbing together.

When he had met Jinx and Rue at the crossroads, he never would have imagined just how much his life would change. Not only had they given him the courage to confront the King of the Crossroads, but they surely must be descendants of chaos herself. Neither allowed him a dull moment. The last thing he expected when he was finally free from his servitude was to look back on his crossroad deals and find them boring.

Everything was bound to be boring in comparison to the constant havoc Jinx brought.

Time wasn't really on his side. If Jinx was in there, he should be too. There was no telling just what she could get up to left unattended.

Killian pulled open the door. It wailed, alerting anyone in the massive castle to his entrance.

Of course, it did. It wasn't exactly like he could sneak in and sneak out with the owner of the castle being none the wiser. That would be entirely too easy for the mate of Jinx Crowe.

He sighed, head dropping slightly as the wind blew and slammed the door at his back.

If they hadn't known he was there before, they definitely knew now.

Oh, well.

A part of him wished mating worked more like how he always heard. He wished there was a little string wrapped around one end of his heart that would tug and tell him just where she was. Instead, his heart thrummed. It quickened its beat slightly, letting him know she was close, but did nothing to narrow down where for him.

When he found her, he was going to throw her over his knee.

That thought made him grin before it dropped to a frown. That wouldn't really teach her a lesson. She enjoyed that almost as much as he did, and the last thing he wanted to do was reward her bad behaviour.

Another sigh inflated his chest as he walked through the entryway. It was a massive half circle, larger than Rue's house, with haunting paintings on the wall and a glass dome overhead. In the low light, shadows of the storm outside played against the floor that looked grey, but he couldn't entirely be sure. Two sets of stairs hugged the walls, a darkened hallway set between them that went back into the castle. There were no torches or candles to light the way, and even with his enhanced eyesight, the darkness was the oppressive kind that swallowed everything whole. All he could see was silhouettes of furniture as he stood, debating.

"Up or through?" he whispered.

Once again, he cursed his poor decision-making. Sure, if Rue were there, she would be harried about the task of searching for Jinx in this haunting castle, but she would know where to go. Her link to Jinx far surpassed his. She was her soul, afterall.

Once again, he kicked himself for not bringing Bram. The furry familiar would have been a big help.

Wind howled down the long hall, beckoning him.

"Through it is," he decided.

Every second in this place stretched too long. Each step felt like he had already taken a dozen. Even as he quickened his pace, the hallways were never-ending.

"Just what magic is at work here?"

It was hard to know. The air felt too thin, like it burned his lungs with each breath. It was like gasping in the harsh winds outside, even though the air was still and not overly cold.

Jinx, what the hell have you gotten yourself into?

When she stormed out of the house, claiming she was running away just because she woke to Rue and Killian cuddling without her on the couch, neither of them thought she would get very far. In reality, she couldn't have wandered much further, deciding on the realm of the South Pole.

The end of the hall finally came. It was a greenhouse with frost covering all the windows. Killian exhaled a chilled breath, looking at the shelves that lined the windows. Each shelf held five snow globes.

He did a slow turn, taking in the large chandelier that looked like a snowflake with no candles or bulbs to hint that it provided any light. There was a massive leather chair set in the middle of the room with an obnoxiously high back. It sat on a tuft of fur with a small round table beside it. Atop the table was a mug, still steaming.

Killian walked up to the table, lifting the mug. The smell of fresh coffee hit his nose and practically made his eyes roll back. He would kill for a cup.

He raised it to his mouth, hesitating.

No, he couldn't. Shouldn't, really.

Annoyed, he set it down. If Jinx had already done something to piss whoever lived there off, the last thing he wanted was to add to their ire. *He* would definitely kill over coffee, there was no telling that whoever called this haunting place home wouldn't feel the same.

"Jinx," he hissed.

Walking up to one of the shelves, he inspected the snow globe. Tiny figurines were frozen sculptures inside. Their hands were stretched out, as though shielding them from something. Brow furrowed, he looked at the neighbouring one. It was similar, with a sole frozen woman on her knees, hands clasped in prayer.

As far as snow globes went, these were boring. They sat on onyx bases with names carved on them. There was no picturesque backdrop or fun scene inside. Everything was white. White snow, white figurine.

Henry Attwood.

Bethany Woods.

Travante Brown.

Abigail, Joseph, and Thomas Briggs.

He moved on to another shelf, a snow globe catching his eye.

Jinx Crowe.

He turned the snow globe over, watching the white flakes fall over the figurine who stood on one pointed toe, her skirts swishing around her, her hand stretched above as she twirled. Everything in him tensed, lips pressed thin. It looks just like her. Down to the playful grin.

The echoed sound of heeled feet rang out.

Killian turned, eyes on the darkened hall he'd come from.

Tall horns spiralled up above the face, cast in shadow, with yellow eyes beaming in the dark. His chest was bare, flesh dark. It was taut over muscle that ended at his lower belly, where thick, black fur covered his legs down to his hooves.

"Careful now." The voice that spoke was dark and twisted. "You break that, and the person inside loses all hope of ever returning."

"Returning?" Killian's grip on the snow globe tightened as he looked over the being who stood before him. "Where is she?"

"In a place where all the naughty beings go." His eyes disappeared as he blinked slowly before they flashed once more, vibrant and eerie. "Even wandering souls... and harbingers of doom and misery."

"Bring her back!" Killian demanded.

He stepped into the light pouring into the window, as dim as it was. White symbols lit all over his bare chest. The familiarity made Killian's heart pound as he realized just how much trouble they were in. Clutching the snow globe to his chest, he took in the mythological being in all his glory.

"You'll find I don't take demands... from anyone."

Snow flurried around his hand, the magic lighting his face and making his strong jaw seem dominating.

Killian held a hand out, hoping with all that he was, he would be able to get them both out of this. His fingers lengthened, black blooms sprouting.

The magic hit him quickly, and he felt himself slowly freezing. His eyes became heavy, closing as he fell to his knees. He clutched the snow globe to his chest, teeth chattering while he whispered through whatever bond bound Killian, Jinx, and Rue together.

She would find them. She would find them both and save them the way Killian wasn't able to.

Rue was made of more than he was.

Hear me, he pleaded. *Find us.*

"Don't worry... I'll place you both together. Jinx... and Killian Crowe."

Lips frozen, he forced out one final word. "K-Krampus."

To Be Continued...

Afterword

THIS ONE TOOK A long time to write.

I started this story right after A Bite Full of Death, knowing I wanted to jump back into the deep end with monsters. The problem? Rue is entirely too serious. Poe was fun to write because she was chaos incarnate, with a brutally dark sense of humour. As a character, she was easy. Words just flew, and she dragged me along, daring me to keep up. With Rue, her story had so many more layers.

Initially, when I jumped into this world, I was looking for something easy. Something where I could write all the nonsense with ease. What was supposed to be an exercise in getting back my love of writing became something the readers loved. (I honestly didn't think so many people would read the story of Dex and Poe) That being said, Rue arrived and threw a wrench into the whole operation. Why? Because she refused to be easy.

After talking it out with my characters, I realized not every story in this world has to feel the same. Not all monsters will be as carefree as Poe. Some will have baggage, and that's okay.

Monsters turned out to be a lot like people… who knew?

Anyway, even though this story was likely more serious than a lot of readers who loved A Bite Full of Death anticipated, I hope you'll still pick up the next book.

I mean… who wouldn't want to find out just what kind of beast could thaw the heart of Krampus himself?

xx

SJ

Acknowledgements

WHERE TO START?

This year has been the kind that whittled me away. It was the worst year of my life… but time stops for no one. So, I guess I'll start by thanking the people who stood by me when I nearly disappeared.

To my family, this year changed us. We buried more than any of us could bear, and were forced to keep moving. Keep living, even when that felt impossible. Thank you for taking it day by day… I know how hard that was.

To my husband, who will forever be the arms holding me up and holding me steady, this year really reshaped us. I can't imagine living through all this without you and will forever be grateful for your endless support.

LaTosha… I will always be so thankful that my stories brought us together. I would never dare to dream that I would gain a lifelong friend. The kind who listens to me rant, helps me carry my burdens, and shines light on my darker days. You're so amazing, and I will always be grateful for the friendship I know will last me a lifetime.

Jessica. Your chaos keeps you bogged down, but you always slice off a piece of time for me. Thank you.

To all my readers who supported me along the way, I will forever appreciate you.

To Zakai... thank you for all the days I got.

ALSO BY SJ STEWART

THE SEVEN REALMS BOOKS

Magic Stolen and Kept (A Villain's Prequel)

Bound Blossoms and Blades (A Prequel of Two Pixies)

Hidden In Darkness: Book One

Lost In Fire: Book Two

Bound By Fate: Book Three

THESE TWISTED BILLIONAIRES

Falling For Tormented Treasures

CHILDREN OF REFUGE

She Was No One

DARK MONSTER ROMANCES

A Bite Full Of Death

OTHER WORKS

A Summoned Husband

SHORT STORIES/NOVELLAS

The Impastusae Witch

Summer Island

The Seamstress

Winter's Spring

About Author

S.J. Stewart is a Bajan/Canadian author who lives in the bustling city of Toronto with her husband and little. She is a chaotic little word goblin, masquerading as an adult and falling to her knees before her characters and their endless demands. She wrote her first novel when she was sixteen and never stopped writing, though she didn't get around to publishing her first book until 2021. She is a genre jumper and dabbles in everything, but her published work is Romantasy, Billionaire Romance, Monster Romance and Dark Romance. Her goal is to get all the stories out of her head before they slowly drive her to madness.

sj@sjstewartbooks.ca

www.ingramcontent.com/pod-product-compliance
Lightning Source LLC
LaVergne TN
LVHW040825090826
845145LV00001BA/200

* 9 7 8 1 9 9 0 5 5 2 3 7 3 *